"AHHH!" I SCREAMED

Sam's face whipped in my direction, but he remained calm. "What's that all about?"

"It's to make you look at me! You swerve off the road, nearly throw me—and the groceries—out of the truck. Jump out and run through some strange pasture, refusing to speak to me. All to pick up some lousy hunk of metal? Are you crazy?"

Sam's mouth took on its stony look again as he started back the way he had come. When he spoke, he tossed his answer over his shoulder.

"I saw something red," he said.

This time I caught him. I grabbed his arm and hung on. "So what? You said that before. What is so important about something red?"

"I thought it might be Bill's pickup," he said quietly.

"Bill's dead."

Death DOWN HOME

EVE K. SANDSTROM

W🌐RLDWIDE®

TORONTO • NEW YORK • LONDON
AMSTERDAM • PARIS • SYDNEY • HAMBURG
STOCKHOLM • ATHENS • TOKYO • MILAN
MADRID • WARSAW • BUDAPEST • AUCKLAND

For Carolyn G. Hart

DEATH DOWN HOME

A Worldwide Mystery/August 1993

This edition is reprinted by arrangement with Charles Scribner's Sons; an imprint of Macmillan Publishing Company.

ISBN 0-373-26125-X

Printed in U.S.A.

ACKNOWLEDGMENTS

Many thanks go to the old and new friends who helped with research for this book. They include Joey Goodman, sports editor and rancher; Janet and Louis McGee, former presidents of the Oklahoma Ornithological Society; Dr. Charles Patton, petroleum engineer; Kay Brian, travel agent; Floyd Kennedy, Jr., banker and cattleman; Dr. Rosemary Bellino, who makes me healthy and my characters sick; Inspector Jim Avance of the Oklahoma State Bureau of Investigation, a professional with a sense of humor; Wanda Shaw Angotti, artist; Annette Briley, secretary of the Comanche County Election Board; Sue Brown, librarian and army wife; Jeff Dixon and Paul Bearce, photographers; and John Green, police reporter. These people were asked strange questions over cups of coffee or received strange phone calls and visits that interrupted their work or leisure. They responded with kindness, information and a certain narrowing of the eyes. Any inaccuracies are the result of my misunderstanding, not their misinformation.

ONE

THE PHONE RANG just as the walnut double dresser became securely jammed above the landing between the second and third floors.

Sam was pushing, and I was pulling, but the dresser wouldn't go up, and it didn't seem to want to go back down, either.

The telephone pealed again.

I kicked the back of the bureau. "Damn the idiots who design army quarters!"

Sam laughed. "Get the phone. I'll try to figure out how to do this without relying on brute force."

I let the dresser go—it was in no danger of sliding back down the stairs—and trotted up to our apartment. I kicked a packing box out of the way and found the telephone.

"Captain Titus's quarters." At least I'd remembered how to answer the phone properly. It was, after all, the first time I'd done that since our wedding.

"Is this Nicky?"

For a mad moment there I thought I was talking to Sam. The dry, flatland tone sounded exactly like my husband. I even whirled around and looked out the door to make sure Sam was still on the landing. He was.

I answered cautiously. "Yes."

"This is Bill. Bill Titus."

The light dawned. "Bill!" I held the receiver against my chest and yelled, "Sam! It's your brother!" Then I went back to the phone. "Bill, Sam's stuck on a narrow staircase behind a man-eating dresser. Hang on and I'll see if he can climb over and get here."

Sam edged past the dresser, his horn-rimmed glasses all askew. He squatted at the top end of the giant hunk of furniture and grasped it firmly, holding his back straight. He stood up slowly and got the dresser back to the landing, standing on end.

"How do you do that?" I asked. "You make lifting a ton of lumber look easy."

"It's all in the legs," Sam said. He turned around, straightened his glasses, and trotted up the stairs. "Learned it at my father's knee—or thigh. If Bill or I had hurt ourselves lifting, Big Sam would have taken the doctor's bill out of our calf money." He grazed my nose with a kiss as he went by, but his face was serious and his pace rapid.

He looked worried as he picked up the phone from the floor. "Hi. What's wrong?"

I studied him as he listened to the answer. He looked terrific, six feet two inches, sandy hair, nearsighted gaze, muscles—even the sweat rolling off the end of his nose. His serious expression didn't chance in response to Bill's news. He didn't say anything, just stood there, staring woodenly at the wall.

Then he gave a contemptuous "Huh!" before he spoke. "That's ridiculous. Big Sam would never have done that."

Big Sam. So the news was about Sam's father. I had met him just three weeks before, when he and Sam's mother came to Germany for our wedding. He was the western rancher personified—big hat, boots, dry humor, and all. He and my Sam—the family called him Young Sam—hadn't gotten along over the years, but they'd kept things cool for the wedding.

Most of the time.

I'd gotten along with Big Sam fine. He was one of those gruff men who are very open about their opinions. His face told you first; then he said it out loud. I like those guys. You know just where you stand with them.

Sam's mother, Marty, was the introspective member of the family. She'd been friendly and charming, but I'd felt there was an innate reticence in her personality, a natural wall between us.

They were quite different from each other. Strange how Sam took after both of them, usually open about his feelings but able to pull a blind down when he needed privacy.

He was speaking. "What do the doctors say?"

Sam's question indicated the situation wasn't good. Big Sam must be ill. What could have happened to him? He'd seemed to me to be blooming health personified.

Sam was silent for a long time while the telephone seemed to make little squawking noises. He frowned before he spoke again. "Of course I'll come," he said. "What else would I do?"

Sam was going to Oklahoma? The situation must be one of life and death. Only something momentous could send Sam to Oklahoma. I knew he hadn't been home, even for Christmas, for five years.

"How's Mom?" Sam listened, his lips tightening.

His voice was firm when he spoke again. "Don't act dumber than you have to, Bill. I'll call you there at the hospital as soon as I have a flight. What's the number?"

Sam snatched the pen I held out to him and wrote on top of a packing box.

He was still scowling as he read the number back into the phone. "Don't worry, Bill," he said coldly. "The Frankfurt CID department won't fall apart if I take another week of leave. And I promise not to hang around Holton long enough to threaten your status as heir to the Titus empire."

He dropped the receiver back in the cradle, then stood up and stared into space. His eyes had an expression I had never seen in them before.

I waited fearfully to hear the worst, but Sam didn't speak. Finally, I had to ask. "What's happened?"

Sam refocused his eyes on my face. "Somebody's tried to kill Big Sam."

I couldn't take it in. It didn't seem real. I might have married a policeman, but crime was simply beyond my ken. It was unrelated to my life. Meaningless.

Sam fished the telephone book out of the stuff on the couch, looked up an airline number, and began to dial.

Our first quarrel was about to begin. I hadn't realized you can fight with someone when you're both on the same side. Maybe we would have settled it if my father hadn't accidentally gotten into the act.

Sam was telling the airline he needed one ticket to Oklahoma City.

This caused me to shake my head. "Me," I mouthed. "I'm going, too."

Sam shook his head at me. "I'll hold," he said to the person on the phone. He covered the receiver and faced me. "There's no point in your coming along. This is just going to turn into a big Titus family mess."

"I'm part of the Titus family mess, remember?"

Sam shook his head again. "You'd better stay out of it as long as you can. I'm taking combat gear along."

"And just who do you intend to do battle with?"

"Probably Bill. He'll want to pull the plug on Big Sam if it means saving a buck."

"But what happened? Who tried to kill your dad?"

"We don't know yet."

"What do the police say?"

Sam curled his lip. "Tar-zan Thompson thinks it's an accident."

He'd stressed both syllables of the name equally. Tar. Zan. I repeated the pronunciation. "Tar-zan Thompson?"

"The sheriff. He's your typical small-town politician, even though he holds a county office. The rural areas always vote against him, but he keeps his job with the help of his cohorts in town. If you can call Holton a town.''

I was beginning to lose interest in going with Sam. I'd been on every continent but Australia and had lived on my own in Paris and in New York before I'd decided to play the traditional bride and get married from the parental home. And in all my roaming there was only one place I'd passionately disliked. That was my mother's hometown in Alabama.

I hated small towns. Especially small southern towns, and I was suspicious of small southwestern towns. At that moment Frankfurt began to look attractive.

But Sam was attractive, too. After all, we'd stood up in an army chapel in front of all the brass in central Germany and agreed to that ''for better or for worse'' stuff.

''Well...'' I looked at the floor. ''I don't want to be in your way. But I do feel I should go.''

Before Sam could answer, my father came through the door. He's a short guy with curly black hair. They say I look a lot like him. But my eyes couldn't have been as innocent as his looked at that moment.

My father is a brigadier general in the U.S. Army, assigned to Frankfurt. The dresser jammed in the stairwell came from my old room, a donation to a newly wed daughter, and my father was helping us move it and some other things into our new quarters on this Sunday, the final day of our honeymoon. My dad had been making another trip for my belongings when the call came.

He gestured back down the stairs. ''Dresser didn't behave?'' Then he saw that Sam was holding the phone. ''Oh! Sorry.''

''It's okay, sir. I'm on hold. But we got some bad news.'' He told us what Bill had reported.

It seemed Big Sam had been changing a tire on his pickup way out in a pasture someplace on the back side of the Titus Ranch. The truck had slipped off the jack, and Big Sam had been seriously hurt, a head injury. Sam wasn't quite clear on how long it had been until somebody found him. He was in an ICU in a hospital in Oklahoma City, 120 miles from his ranch. Unconscious.

"I'm calling the airline now, sir."

My dad nodded. "Yes, you need to go. How are you fixed for money? You two can't wait for cheap fares."

Silence. Finally, I spoke. "Sam doesn't— Well, maybe I should stay here, Daddy."

My dad frowned. "Oh, no, Nicky. When a family is in crisis, it's important for all its members to stick together. You're Sam's wife now, sugar. Your place is with him."

Sam made a funny sound. I couldn't tell if he was growling or grinding his teeth.

That, it seemed, was that. Captains don't argue with generals. Captains' wives don't, either. I was going. Sam reserved two tickets.

We divided up the chores. While Sam and my dad figured out a way to get that dresser on up the stairs, I got the laundry together. It was a job that allowed me to mull over what had just happened.

Why had Sam told two stories? He told me that his father had been attacked, that someone had tried to kill him. He hadn't mentioned that to my dad.

And why did Sheriff Thompson think it was an accident?

Well, I knew that Sam was wonderful in all things, which meant that he was a top-notch military detective. He was assigned to the army's Criminal Investigation Division in Frankfurt. He had extensive technical training, including a bachelor's degree in political science with a minor in criminal justice. I would back him against some small-town sheriff all the way.

But the sheriff was on the spot and had seen the evidence. He might be right.

Sam appeared in the doorway. "I'm going over to the officers' club to cash a check." Then he just stood there, staring at me.

"I hope I'm not letting you get into something dangerous."

TWO

SAM'S SENSE OF HUMOR was one of the three things that first attracted me to him. The second was a cool modesty that is based on total confidence, and the third one was his—well, I'll call it animal attraction. I'm not listing these in the actual order I noticed them, of course.

I don't know what he saw in me besides a temper.

When I graduated from college, my parents were stationed in Frankfurt. I first worked in New York, but when we learned that my mother had only a few months to live, I joined them in Germany. I stayed with my dad for a while after my mother died. I wanted a career in photography, artistic photography, and I was lucky enough to get a job in the studio of a highly respected man in Paris. My dad was nervous about turning me loose in what he regarded as the world's leading sin city, although I was nearly twenty-four. But after he figured out I was going anyway, he gave me his blessing and even some financial backing—artistic photography not being one of your high-paying fields.

My photographer-boss turned out to be a man of middle-class standards who hovered over what he naively saw as his innocent little American apprentice. I, of course, wanted to take pictures of hard cases in Montmartre and of Notre Dame reflected in a puddle and sit in sidewalk cafés drinking café au lait or *vin ordinaire,* discussing the meaning of life.

As part of my research into the meaning of life, I acquired a boyfriend. He was not like the guys I had dated in New York, who talked about Art with a capital A, or like the lieutenants and captains I had dated at army posts, who had approached the general's daughter with kid gloves. Jacques did not give a damn about art or Art, and he did not wear gloves, kid or otherwise. Jacques was almost an attorney, and he was a militant conservationist.

I wasn't going to do anything sneaky, but it still took me a couple of months to write my father telling him I was considering moving in with a new roommate of the opposite sex. And maybe I wrote home then because I wanted somebody to point out that I had intended to do more with photography than take pictures of beached whales and industrial waste—the subjects Jacques wanted me to tackle.

Still, I got a little angry, two days after the letter had been mailed, when the army's Criminal Investigation Division showed up on my doorstep and I found myself hustled onto a military flight to Frankfurt.

I felt that using an agency of the U.S. government to police my moral standards was a bit much, and I arrived in Frankfurt ready to commit patricide.

My dad didn't meet me at the airport. The CID picked me up at Rhein-Main Air Force Base, which made me even angrier. I had been too well brought up to yell at innocent military lawmen, but by the time we reached my father's quarters I had had enough.

The general's quarters are in a spacious post-World War II house. My mother, who had come a long way artistically from her small-town origins, had loved decorating it with the furniture and art objects she had collected on tours of duty all over the world. I looked around the entry hall at the gilt-framed mirror and the mahogany table littered with mail and magazines, the replica of an Etruscan bronze horse, the silver candelabra, and the print of a horse-drawn caisson crossing a creek, its frame labeled with a brass presentation plate. My father was not among the furnishings.

I crossed to the first room on the left, the living room. I shoved the door all the way open, stepped onto the carpet my parents had bought during their Mideastern tour of duty, and pivoted toward the alcove that held the inlaid desk Daddy had sent home from Hong Kong and the tall wing chair that sat before it, its back to the room.

Ah, there he was. A shoulder garbed in camouflage print extended from behind the flame-stitched wing of the chair.

"What do you mean hauling me back from Paris in this humiliating way!" I snapped. "Are you crazy! I knew you wouldn't like it, but I didn't expect you to go into a second childhood over that letter. I'm over twenty-one."

I stomped across the carpet and into the alcove.

"You'd better have a good explanation for this or—"

I swung around the end of the desk and turned to face my father. "—or I'm going straight back to Paris."

I was facing a perfectly strange man. A damn good-looking guy—blond, muscular, late twenties—sat in my father's chair. He was peering at me through a giant pair of horn-rimmed glasses. I could see a set of marvelous eyes back there, brown flecked with gold.

I stared. He stared back. Neither of us spoke.

Then he stood up. He was tall, too. His head was way up there, at least compared to mine. His face was expressionless.

"Oh, God!" I said.

"No. The general's out," he replied.

Then he grinned, a grin that would have won him the role of Huckleberry Finn's sexy big brother in any theater in America. He looked so friendly and so amused that I knew his little joke hadn't been an accident.

Then we both cracked up. Laughed like fools.

"I feel like a complete idiot."

"I'm just glad to know there's someone in the world General Carmichael can't intimidate," he said.

By the time we had our laughter under control I knew he was Capt. Sam Titus, a nice, easygoing soldier on a mission he didn't offer to explain. Sam built a fire in the living-room fireplace, and Jacques faded into a memory. I found the letter to my father, still unopened, in the pile of mail on the hall table and hid it in my purse on my way to the kitchen to make cocoa.

I saw the confident side of Sam's personality when my father came home. My dad had barely walked through the door and given me a hug when the doorbell rang.

He looked a bit annoyed. "I don't want company right now," he said curtly, moving toward the door.

"Hold it!"

The voice came from behind me, and it was so sharp and commanding I nearly came to attention myself.

It was Sam's voice. He strode down the hall, passing my dad the general and almost shoving him aside.

"Get back," he said. Then he added a word. "Sir."

Never in my twenty-four years as an army brat had I heard a captain snap out an order to a general. I braced myself.

Then my father smiled. "Sorry, Sam," he said. "Come on, Nicky. Let's get away from the door. I forgot I'm not allowed to answer it."

He led me into the living room to tell me why I had been summoned home. It seemed my parent had received threatening phone calls. One had mentioned me. The CID had thought it would be easier to keep an eye on the two of us if we stayed in the same spot for a while. Sam, who had just been assigned to the CID in Frankfurt, had been equipped with false shoulder patches and installed in our house in the disguise of a new general's aide working on a special project. He and a burly new housemaid were, of course, our bodyguards. And no matter how high my father's rank, Sam was in charge of the household.

The whole case was solved without any dramatics. A week later, Daddy recognized the threatening voice as belonging to a sergeant he had worked with years before. The man confessed and agreed to be hospitalized, and we were given permission to return our lives to normal.

But it was too late for me to do that. Sam had slipped into my life. He knew when to laugh, how to be steady and reliable without being dull, and how to order a general around when the general needed ordering.

We had long talks, planned our lives for the next fifty years, set impossible goals, gazed into each other's eyes, and traded tales of college antics.

Only one thing had bothered me, and it wasn't the prospect of twenty years of officers' wives' club functions. I had done my bit for youthful rebellion. Maybe it was my mother's death and the associated peep at mortality, or maybe it was Jacques and my realization that he wanted to mold me into a tool for world conservation instead of letting me mold myself. Or maybe it was just Sam. But the familiar circles of military life developed a nostalgic appeal for me.

After all, I had chosen an artistic career—one I could pursue anywhere in the world. And as an army brat I had been trained as an officer's wife from the cradle, absorbing the military trade along with my Gerber's. The travel associated with an army career could give me a professional boost, and I could be a genuine help to Sam. I knew more about climbing the ladder of military success than he did; he was a small-town boy.

In fact, that's what bothered me. Sam came from a small southwestern ranching community.

My mother came from a small town in the South. I had spent the eighth grade there while my father, then a colonel, had a hardship tour in Korea, where we were not allowed to accompany him.

It was the most miserable year of my life. The junior high crowd had already divided up, and the daughter of a Michigan native didn't fit into any of the adolescent categories.

My mother got tired of being needled about "runnin' off up North and marryin' a damyankee" and was unhappy. I made things worse by referring longingly to how things had been done at my school in Paris. I left the town at the end of a year, vowing never again to cross a set of city limits that enclosed fewer than 100,000 folks.

Sam had assured me that he felt the same way. He never intended to return to Holton, U.S.A., he said. Now, heading out over the Atlantic, I realized how little he had told me about Holton and about his family. As we drew nearer to the States, I became more and more fearful of what we would find when we got there.

Sam wasn't reassuring. He didn't say a word from Rhein-Main to O'Hare. I tried talking to him, but I got little response—not even an explanation of why he thought someone had attacked Big Sam. I finally settled for holding his hand. His grip made my fingers numb.

Our flight was late arriving in Chicago, but Sam grabbed a pay phone near the loading gate to call the Oklahoma City hospital. He told Bill we'd arrive in Dallas after midnight, and because there were no flights headed in the right direction until morning, we would rent a car and drive on to Oklahoma City. Bill seemed to object to this plan.

"I don't mind paying for it," Sam said. Then he listened.

"Does that mean Big Sam is better?" He frowned, his ear to the phone. "Okay, then. We'll just get the first flight out tomorrow morning and take a cab to the hospital."

He looked puzzled.

"What do you mean, you're leaving? Wait till I get there!" Sam's voice rattled against the walls of the phone cubicle. "We'll take care of that together."

He listened again.

"Look, Bill, I haven't done police work for the last six years without learning a little about how to deal with these local cops—including the Tarzan Thompson type. Wait till I get there."

He'd made it an order, and I could hear Bill's refusal to obey in the angry tone that leaked from the receiver.

"I am not doing a big-brother act," Sam said coldly. "I just want you to wait for me. If we see Tarzan together, we can get more done." He listened again, then shook his head. "I don't understand. If you're not going to see Tarzan, then who— Bill! Bill!"

He turned to me. "Damn! He hung up on me."

He muttered as he marched toward the departure gate, "If he wasn't going to see Tarzan, who was he going to see? Mom's taken a room at a hotel that's connected with the hospital. The doctors think Big Sam's condition has stablized—maybe—so Bill thinks there's little point in our arriving in the middle of the night. Bill's leaving, but I don't understand where he's going."

He still hadn't figured that out when we left Dallas the next morning on the last leg of our trip. I dozed a bit. When I woke, the plane was descending. I realized we must be over Oklahoma. I pushed up the window shade and looked out at an enormous expanse of blue, gold, and green.

The sky was huge. The land below matched it in size. It seemed completely flat. Its green and gold stretched to the edges of the earth, the horizon unbroken by hills or mountains. It was crossed by straight lines that might have been the canals of Mars and was dotted by shiny splotches of water, like dew caught in grass. The plane banked, and I saw a clump of skyscrapers in the distance. Nearer was a sea of rooftops in gray or brown masses. We came lower, and the canals of Mars formed into roads, and the dew in the grass became farm ponds and water hazards on golf courses. The houses lost their uniformity and became suburban dwellings with above-ground pools and terraced yards and pickup trucks and tricycles and doghouses and trees and shrubs.

If I had been expecting the Wild West I was in for a disappointment. Oklahoma City's airport was just like every other American airport. It had that stale airport smell and those plastic-covered chairs in rows and those ranks of businessmen waiting to grab our seats aboard the plane and rush farther northward for a day's business in Kansas City or Chicago. The airport restrooms were solid tile and stainless steel, impervious to graffiti, and a major construction project had the terminal topsy-turvy.

The cabdriver did wear boots and a western shirt. "Jawl heve a gud flight?" he asked. That was after he drawled, "Wear tu?"

He certainly handled the cab like a bronco, swerving from lane to lane and galloping along the freeways, but he was the most western thing we saw. Oklahoma City just looked like another big American town, moving to the rhythms supplied by the local disk jockeys—rock and roll as often as country and western.

The hospital was tall and brick and smelled as hospital-like as the airport had smelled like a terminal.

We found Sam's mom in the ICU waiting room. I had steeled myself for tears, but she was perfectly calm. She'd been lying down on a couch, and she touched her lips for silence when she saw us.

Marty Titus was fifty-six; she'd been in her late twenties when Sam was born. Her hair was streaked with gray, and she wore it long and braided, then wound up in a ball on the back of her head, as if she just didn't want to fool with it. She was tall, like Sam, but her slimness contrasted with his muscular look. Her eyes were an opaque gray that always seemed to be focused somewhere beyond her immediate surroundings. She wasn't beautiful, but she had a serenity that gave her style and dignity. She always wore tailored clothes, and that day she had on a navy poplin skirt and a shirt striped in white and red.

Her hands were her most unusual feature. They were big and broad and capable looking, with short, unpainted nails and knotted joints. I'd longed to photograph them as soon as I met her, but I hadn't had the nerve to ask. She was my mother-in-law, and her friendliness to me was like ice on a strange pond. One misstep might plunge me into hidden depths.

I did know one of her secrets. In Frankfurt—just a couple of weeks ago, but it seemed forever—we had visited the Städel Art Institute together. She hadn't had much to say about the exhibits. I had made one of my artsy comments about the significance of the texture of a painting there, and she had offhandedly explained that the artist had used a palette knife.

"You have to do that with oils," she said.

I looked at her narrowly. "Sam's been holding out on me. He didn't tell me you were an artist."

Her eyes dodged away from mine, and she smiled just a little. "I trained the boys not to say anything about Mama's aberrations."

Now she followed us into the hall outside the ICU waiting room. She hugged Sam, then me. "We're in an awful mess," she said.

"How is he?" Sam asked.

Marty shook her head. "Just the same. Would you all like breakfast?"

That *you all*—she said it more like "ya'all"—was almost her only sign of an accent. Sam and both his parents had that flat southwestern tone, but they certainly didn't sound like the cabdriver.

Marty showed us to the hospital cafeteria, and we went through a line to collect coffee.

"They have good cinnamon rolls. Why don't you have one?" Then Marty smiled pleasantly at the girl in the hair net behind the steam table.

"J'ount a roll?" the girl asked. Marty shook her head.

"You're eating right, aren't you?" Sam said sternly.

He was bossing again, but his mother took it with a smile. "I eat what I can, Sam."

She led us to a table, and we unloaded our trays.

"They won't let us in ICU for another forty-five minutes," Marty said. She sipped her coffee. "Sam, he hasn't gotten worse, but the doctors say they can't tell what's going on yet. If he hasn't shown any signs of recovering consciousness within another twenty-four hours—well, they'll do another CAT scan."

Sam stared at his plate. "How do they think it happened?"

Marty rubbed her hand over her forehead, and I realized that—hotel room or no—she was completely exhausted. "I don't know, Sam. He went off after lunch to check the cattle in the Wolf Creek pasture. When he hadn't come home at six-thirty, I asked Bill to look for him. I thought he might have had trouble with the truck or something."

She paused to stir the coffee—which she was drinking without cream or sugar—then went on. "God knows how long he'd been lying there. But the doctor—the doctor says he would have been unconscious from the first. Anyway, Bill jacked the truck up again and got it off of him. Then he went back to the Riches' place, and they called the ambulance."

Sam's voice was quiet. "The Riches' place. Two miles."

I shuddered. The thought of Bill, finding his father horribly injured, then having to leave him to fetch an ambulance dramatically brought home the idea of wide-open spaces.

Marty nodded.

Sam leaned toward her. "Mom, you know Big Sam would never have jacked up that truck without chocking the wheels."

"Sam, I know he has what amounts to a fixation on that subject—ever since that accident when he was young. But this was on a slope. And he had chocked the wheels. With rocks. The truck just got off balance somehow."

She put her hand on Sam's arm. "Bill felt the same way. He said it just couldn't have happened that way. He could hardly wait to get home and start convincing somebody that there was something fishy. But that's ridiculous."

"Why is it ridiculous?"

"Who would want to hurt your father?" Marty put her head in her hands. "Oh, I know he battles with people. He's blunt and outspoken. But not getting along is different from . . . from hate."

Sam took her hand. "People respect Big Sam, even if they don't get along with him."

They sat there, and I thought about what Sam had said.

Sam didn't get along with his father. He rarely spoke to him directly, I'd noticed when Big Sam and Marty were in Germany. If he talked about him, he called him "Big Sam," with never a "Dad" to match the "Mom" he called Marty.

Big Sam and Young Sam seemed to be operating under a truce. They were polite, they didn't disagree, and they kept their distance.

I had witnessed only one episode between them that hinted at any emotional involvement.

I had come upon them in the officers' club, when I'd slipped away from the rehearsal dinner for a minute. They were down the hall, nose to nose.

"Why won't you stay over another week?" Sam said. "You know Mom's dying to see the art galleries in Florence. She may never get another chance."

"I told her she could stay."

"You know she won't stay without you!"

"Godfrey Daniel!" Big Sam swung his arm up and down, and I pictured a cowboy hat hitting the floor. "There's stuff goin' on around that ranch that I don't understand. I got to get home and figure it out. I don't need criticism from you; I could use some help!"

Sam drew back coldly. "Sorry. I'm out of the ranching business for good." He turned toward the club's main bar.

"Sam!" His father's voice had been sharp.

But Sam hadn't looked around. He had quickstepped down the hall. He didn't hear Big Sam's final word.

"Please." The big rancher had said it very quietly.

I had backtracked into the dinner, unwilling to admit I had witnessed the scene. Big Sam was still trying to get my Sam back to the ranch, I decided. I was relieved that Sam wasn't considering it. I didn't see myself as a rancher's wife.

Now Sam leaned forward, about to start a major speech, but his mother clutched his hand.

She whispered urgently, "Hush!"

Then she looked over his head. "Why, here's Viola Mae. Sam, you get her a cup of coffee."

I turned around as Sam greeted the newcomer with a hug. She was a round, apple dumpling of an old lady, wearing a dull green polyester pantsuit. Her cheeks made me see why people who get brown from the sun are described as "tanned"; the face could have been made into a very serviceable pair of oxfords. But it was a happy face, dimpled and adorned with a sweet smile. Her hair was dark and straight and was cropped short. She carried a canvas tote bag, and a pair of binoculars of a classy German brand was nestled in its top. And she actually wore tennis shoes—navy blue with white soles and laces.

She came to the table and patted Marty's shoulder; then she shook my hand.

"Viola Mae Humphries," Marty said, introducing us. "A friend and neighbor."

The old lady plopped into a chair. "Just call me Viola Mae."

Marty spoke. "You got away early, Viola Mae. Have you broken that staying-up-all-night habit?"

Viola Mae's dimple deepened. "No, I kept my old habits. Today I simply happened to get up with the birds."

Marty smiled politely, then turned to me. "Viola Mae is one of Oklahoma's leading ornithologists."

"Oh, that explains the binoculars," I said.

Viola Mae gave me a sweet smile. Her eyes were a bright clear blue, and she didn't wear glasses. "Of course, my professional days are over, but I have my share of sightings."

Viola Mae did have circles under her eyes, but she seemed almost frenetically energetic as she sat at the table. She was batting her eyes, drumming her fingers on the table, and tapping her foot all at once.

She turned to Marty. "Has Big Sam had anything to say?"

Marty shook her head.

Viola Mae ducked her head nearly down to the tabletop and reached into the tote bag. The dimple appeared and disappeared. She groped in the bag, then pulled out a tissue. She wiped her lips and shook her head.

"I'm sure sorry to hear that, Marty. And for selfish reasons, of course. I kind of had in the back of my mind that I'd get Big Sam laid up in a hospital bed, where he couldn't keep from talking to me about this lawsuit."

Marty shook her head, but it was Sam who answered. He appeared at Viola Mae's shoulder with a cup, and he spoke before his mother could. "He's no better."

Marty looked at him and widened her eyes slightly. I saw Sam nudge her with his knee as he sat down.

"We mustn't kid ourselves," he said. "The doctors think any improvement is very unlikely."

Marty blinked, but she didn't contradict his report, a report a bit worse than the one she had given us. I imagine I blinked, too, but the nudge had told me Sam thought he knew what he was doing. I kept my mouth shut.

Viola Mae didn't seem to notice anything. "Well, it sure is a shame, Marty. You know we're all thinking about you, about the whole family."

Marty squeezed Viola Mae's hand. "Nicky, Viola Mae is taking the first shift. It's a Holton custom. When someone is in the hospital away from Holton, the neighbors divide up, and different ones come each day."

I wasn't sure what to reply to that, so I settled for "Oh?"

Viola Mae dimpled at us. "She's just joking, Nicky. It's not a formal system. We just keep track of who's planning to visit so that the family isn't swamped one day and all alone the next. And that way people can run errands, bring up laundry and things like that. Help out. Your mother-in-law's one of the most active members of the network. But I had bird business, so I volunteered to come today."

We sat and chatted for a few minutes—chatted about everything in the world except Big Sam.

Then Marty looked at her watch. "We'd better go back upstairs. It'll be time for another round of visiting soon."

"Oh, good," Viola Mae said. "I'm eager to see Sam." She pushed her chair back and bounced to her feet.

Marty spoke sharply. "You can't see him."

"I can't?" Viola Mae's cheerful face crumpled up like a paper bag.

"No. He's unconscious, and full of tubes and—" Marty swallowed hard, then smiled at Viola Mae. "He'd haunt me if I let an old girlfriend see him in such a state. It's also against the hospital's rules."

Viola Mae still looked crushed. "When I heard that Sam was still alive, even after that blow to his head . . ." She smiled again. This time the sweetness was tinged with something else. Was it sadness? "Well, I guess I thought he was just too tough to kill."

That remark was greeted with silence. I mean, what possible reply could there be?

Marty got up and left, and Sam caught up with her while Viola Mae was still gathering up her binoculars and tote bag. I could see Sam urgently talking to his mother.

"I guess I thought Big Sam must be better, with Bill leaving and all," Viola Mae said.

I decided it was time to change the subject.

"Are you a native of Holton?" I asked.

"Oh, my, yes," she answered. "Third generation. Went to school there, spent a lot of time there, even when I was working away. Lived there all the time since I retired. Known Big Sam all my life, too. We were grade-school sweethearts—way back in depression days."

We followed Marty and Sam down the hall to the elevator and caught up with them as Sam punched the UP button.

He turned and looked down at his mother. "I won't go up with you. Bill said you had a room in the hotel here. Can I take your car down to the ranch? Or would you rather I'd rent one?"

Did he mean we were leaving, leaving without seeing Big Sam? I was stunned.

Sam and his mother were staring at each other. Maybe they were reading each other's minds. Their faces sure weren't giving anything away.

Then Marty reached into her purse. She pulled out a ring that held two automobile keys, a bigger key, and a logo that featured the letters F, B, and H. She held it out to Sam.

"You're not coming up." It wasn't a question.

"I need to get down to the ranch and see what Bill's up to," Sam answered.

The elevator door opened, and Marty turned toward it without changing her expression. "Let it go, Sam," she said.

Sam stepped forward and took her arm. They stood looking at each other in the open door.

"I haven't forgotten everything Big Sam taught me," Sam said. His voice was low. "We've got to stick together. Bill and I need to work this out. I'll be back."

Marty was still completely impassive. "It's on the lower level, toward the rear."

It took me a moment before I figured out she was talking about her car.

Sam stepped back, and Marty and Viola Mae got on the elevator. Marty's expression didn't change.

"Come on," Sam said. "It's time to head for the ranch."

THREE

I WAS IN a quandary. I felt that we were being cruel, unfeeling, and wrong to leave Sam's mother.

I knew Sam wasn't cruel and unfeeling. But I didn't understand how he was acting, and I didn't know what to do about it.

Sam was determined to get to the scene of his father's injuries even if it meant neglecting his mother. Why? Why had Bill felt that same impulse? And why had Sam given Viola Mae such a gloomy report on Big Sam?

I chewed over these thoughts as I was trotting through the hospital parking garage, burning up in a light wool jacket suitable for European travel.

I caught up with Sam as he unlocked the door of a tan Chevrolet sedan a couple of years old. "Same old license plate," he said.

"Wait," I said. "Sam, we can't leave."

Sam stared at me. "Why not?"

"Darling, you haven't even seen your dad."

"What good would that do?"

"We've flown all this way to see him, and now you're heading off without going near his room."

Sam looked away from me and opened the door of the car. "Nicky, my father is unconscious. He wouldn't know if I was there or not."

"But what about your mother? She might like someone to... to talk to, at least! This Viola Mae said she wasn't going to hang around long. You're leaving your mother alone."

He took my arm and almost shoved me into the car. "I'm sorry I can't be two places at once. But I can't do anything to help here, and I might accomplish something down at the ranch."

"Should I stay with her?"

Sam paused in the middle of closing the door. He seemed to consider that suggestion. Then he shook his head. "No, I think she'd feel she should entertain you. You'd cramp her style."

"But why did you tell Viola Mae that the doctors weren't giving you any hope for Big Sam?"

"Because that's what I want her to tell everybody in Holton."

"Why?"

"Because I don't want whoever tried to kill him to come up here and try again."

He slammed my door, circled the car, and opened the door on the driver's side. We were both silent as he tossed his jacket and tie into the backseat and got in the car.

"One way or another, we'll be back tomorrow," he said.

I couldn't think of anything to reply. I had never felt so lonely in my life. Not even the first night at boarding school. Here I was, thousands of miles from my dad, the only real family I had, and the man I loved wouldn't talk to me, and I didn't understand his mother, and I didn't understand him, and he didn't trust even his family's oldest friends, and everybody talked funny, and the whole world was flat.

All I could do was go along.

The first stop we made was a complete surprise to me. It was a cement-block building in an industrial area. The planter in front of the building was filled with weeds, and the whole area looked run-down. A wooden signboard read MILLS LABORATORY.

"Wait here," Sam said. He got out of the car and strode into the building, leaving me to swelter in the heat. In about ten minutes he returned, followed by a short, balding man in jeans and a T-shirt that promoted beer. Sam carried a paper sack.

"I'll expect to hear from you tomorrow, then," the man said, watching Sam put the sack in the car. The man gave me a friendly wave as we left.

"Who was that?"

"Jack Mills."

"Oh," I said. "That explains everything."

"Uh-huh."

"Sam!" I was becoming exasperated. "What was that place?"

"A private lab," he said. "They do contract work."

"Crime work?"

"Sometimes."

We swung by the airport on the way out of town and picked up our luggage; then we got on another four-lane highway and headed out of Oklahoma City. The sign said I-44 SOUTH. We passed big yards filled with oil-field equipment, a lot of it surrounded by high weeds, and I saw my first pumping oil well. I recognized it from the pictures, since Sam wasn't volunteering any information. The terrain was still flat, though we did cross a river just south of Oklahoma City. It was lined with trees, some of them good sized.

The river didn't look too big to me, but Sam gave a little snort when he saw it. "Up some," he said. He was beginning to talk more like a native again.

The car's air conditioner added to my sense of isolation. The world flashed by at sixty-five miles per hour, and I might as well have been watching it on a television monitor.

I began to nod off, and Sam suggested I put my head down in the seat. When I woke again, the sun was beating through the windshield, and I was perspiring in spite of the air conditioning. The sky was enormously blue and held huge, puffy clouds. I realized we were slowing down.

I sat up and looked at my watch. Eleven-thirty.

Sam was turning the car off the four lane highway and onto a two-lane road. We were in open country, with no houses or businesses close by. The land had lost its flat look and now seemed to roll along. A low range of hills was ahead of us, against the horizon. The fields on either side were golden, with just a tinge of green, and coarse, tall grass bordered the road. A red brick house with white mock-Early American trim sat beyond the field on the right. A metal barn stood behind it, and in back of that barn was a green pasture filled with black cattle with white faces.

"Are we there?" I asked.

"Ten more miles of two-lane to Holton, then ten of asphalt and gravel to the ranch."

Sam kept his foot down, and we zipped along as if we were on the Autobahn. Once every mile or so we'd meet a vehicle, usually a pickup truck. The driver would lift one finger, and Sam would make the same secret signal in return. The drivers wore either cowboy hats or billed caps. Both styles shadowed their faces.

Golden fields, green pastures, neat brick houses, and clapboard country churches flashed by. We passed cattle— black, red, and white. We saw horses. Dogs looked at us from high weeds in the ditches or trotted across the road behind us. Now and then we passed an old house. Usually it was falling down and was either empty or stuffed with hay, but no one seemed to live in old houses. Once we saw an old red house with a white front porch, but instead of being built of bricks, it was made of strange, round red rocks. It looked as if someone had impaled softballs all over the walls, then slathered them with mud.

You always hear that there are no trees on the plains, but we never entirely lost sight of them. Scrawny saplings straggled in irregular lines across the pastures and marched in straight lines along fencerows. Taller trees with lush foliage grew in the creek bottoms. In a few cases we saw bigger trees in thick banks, usually close to houses. Sam said those were called windbreaks, or shelterbelts. They were planted as part of efforts to fight wind erosion, and they contained rows of trees, each row a different variety. I hadn't known there could be so many variations of green.

But dominating the whole scene was the sky.

It was deeply, brightly, unbelievably blue. Here and there were the biggest, most dramatic clouds I'd ever seen. They sailed the sky like battleships, commanding the humans below to realize their own insignificance. An airplane flew through one of them, a mosquito tolerated and ignored.

The effect was exhilarating and frightening. I pulled my prized Leicaflex out of my purse and tried framing some cloud shots through the window, but I knew the effect would be lost. I tried rolling the window down. It was like opening the door to an oven that was being used to bake a hurricane. I rolled it back up.

Sam tried a few conversational ploys. "Wheat'll be ready to cut in a few days," he said once. And, "Ponds look good. Hope we don't get any more rain for a couple of weeks." I was too overwhelmed with the earth and the sky to respond.

As we drew nearer to the low mountains, the land began to roll a bit harder. When we were at the bottom of the roll, it still seemed open, with all that sky up there. When we were on top of a rise, I had the sensation that I could see clear to the Gulf of Mexico. When I told Sam that, he nodded solemnly.

"Maybe so," he said. "It's downhill all the way."

If I wanted to forget the emergency nature of our mission, the speed that Sam drove kept it in my memory. We swung and swayed around the one or two curves in the highway. The low mountains against the horizon rapidly grew closer. Finally, we topped another rise, and I saw roofs beneath us. A town sat flatly, foursquare, nestled against hills on two sides.

"There it is," Sam said. "Holton."

I could take in the whole town at a glance. It was small. Little. Just like the horrible town where my grandmother had lived, where my mother and I had spent that miserable year. My heart sank.

We barreled around another curve, and Sam spoke again. "The end of the earth," he said. "Or the center of the universe."

As we came down the hill toward Holton, I could see that the town was laid out absolutely on a square—a square cut up into rectangles cut into smaller rectangles and dotted with trees. House lots of identical size were nested together into blocks—maybe a dozen lots to a block. The borders of each lot were clearly marked by fences or by hedges or by some other human paraphernalia. The blocks lined up to make the town.

In its center was a special square, a square with grass and trees and a big building. I didn't get a good look at it. I also saw a couple of buildings that were obviously schools and several with pointed spires. Two round white towers—far and away the tallest structures visible—sat at the right-hand edge of the town, and a water tower on the lowest of the hills was painted with the town's name, plus the initials of a selection of the Holton teenagers.

Then Sam hit the brakes, slowing our speed as we reached a sign that read 35 MPH, and we entered the town. The houses of Holton were nothing special—neat, shabby, old, new, brick, clapboard, mobile homes. They straggled along the street independently, each one unrelated to its neighbors.

"Maybe we'd better drag Main," Sam said. "Bill might be downtown."

He glanced over at me and grinned for the first time since we'd left Germany. "For that matter, maybe we'd better get a hamburger at The Hangout. We might as well make a public announcement that Sam Titus and his new bride are in town."

"A public announcement?"

"Yeah. The Hangout's the root of the Holton news network. Once you've appeared there, it's official."

He drove to the central square. The large building, of course, was the Catlin County Courthouse, a white structure that might as well have had 1933 written on every block of stone. One side of it faced the business district. Across the square, behind the courthouse, I could see the houses and trees of a residential area.

Sam pulled the Chevrolet into an angled parking slot across the street from the courthouse. A half-dozen pickups and a couple of midsize sedans were parked in a clump in the middle of the block. There were plenty of empty parking spaces.

A metal sign proclaimed THE HANGOUT in red letters not much larger than the COCA-COLA that shared it. It hung on a cement-block building with show windows all across the front. I could see people sitting at tables inside. Nearly all of them were men, and like the pickup-truck drivers we had passed, they all wore cowboy hats or billed caps.

We crossed the sidewalk, and Sam opened the door for me. I was about to meet the good ol' boys.

We might as well have been wearing spangles and have swung in the door on trapezes. A drum roll or a trumpet fanfare would not have been out of place.

Every eye turned toward us. Every voice hushed.

Then a terrible crackling sound came forth. "Well, if it ain't Young Sam," it squawked. "Come in here, youngster."

A tall, skinny woman with her hair teased eight inches high approached us. She wore a white uniform covered with a purple flowered apron. The apron was trimmed with green piping in a nauseating shade. Her face was thin and her nose enormous. Her ears were quite striking, since they were roughly the size of Dumbo's, and were adorned with big plastic rings that almost matched the nauseous green of her apron's trim.

She put out a paw and patted Sam's arm. Then she croaked out another greeting. "I don't believe I'd a know'd you, Young Sam, if you had'na been drivin' your mama's car. It's been a long time since you come back to the old hometown."

Sam reacted to this fearful greeting by grinning. "Hi, Ollie," he said. "This is my wife, Nicky. I've been telling her about your hamburgers all the way down the road."

That came as a surprise to me, but I tried to do my gracious army-wife routine. Maybe it would work in Small Town, U.S.A. "How do you do?" I said, and I stuck out a hand for shaking.

Ollie looked at my hand suspiciously. She nervously wiped her own hand on the purple-and-green apron before she took it. "Well, how do," she said, looking into my eyes deeply. "Look at them big brown eyes. Sam, you shore picked out a purty woman." Then she leaned over to him conspiratorily. "Kin she cook?"

Sam laughed. "She's a good cook, Ollie, but not even Nicky can make hamburgers like Lou's. How about getting him to put a couple on the grill for us?"

Ollie beamed with pride. She turned toward the counter, earrings swinging. "Lou, you ol' fool!" she rasped loudly. "Git busy and git them hamburgers cooking!"

Ollie's place was taken immediately by two grizzled men. Both of them wore straw hats, jeans, boots, and white shirts with western detailing on the shoulders. I wondered if they were twins; they looked a lot alike, but they weren't quite a matched set. Sam introduced them as neighbors, Maynard and Millard Smith.

We made royal progress among the little restaurant's dozen or so booths and tables, moving toward the back of the room. Sam stopped to shake the hand of each midafternoon coffee breaker and to tell each person that his dad's condition was unchanged. He seemed to move along aimlessly, but now and then his eyes flickered; after the third flicker I realized he was making for a specific spot at the back of the room.

Where was Sam going? I kept up my friendly new-bride act, but I began to long to see what was back there. Finally, I could stand it no longer, and I simply turned around and looked.

Sitting in the back booth was a big man in a western hat, a white hat with a wider brim than the utilitarian ranchers' hats hanging on the rack near the door of The Hangout or on the heads of the men in the booths. The hat had a fancy snakeskin hatband, too, and this man's western shirt was a bright red. A pair of crocodile boots extended out into the aisle. He was a handsome man, if you like them slightly greasy and with thick, sensual lips and bedroom eyes.

When I first saw him, he was staring at Sam, a slight smile on his face. But then he switched his eyes in my direction. The smile grew broader, and he deliberately looked me up and down. Then his heavy-lidded eyes closed and opened again in a come-hither signal.

I turned my back on him and took Sam's arm. The man in the booth gave me the willies.

But Sam was definitely headed in his direction. He patiently answered all the questions from others in the room, then turned slowly toward the back booth, where the greasy character sat.

When we got there, Sam guided me into the empty seat and slid in beside me.

"Hello, Tarzan," he said. "Glad I ran into you."

Now I saw the star on the red shirt. This was Tarzan Thompson, the sheriff of Catlin County. I was surprised. I had pictured the sheriff as a grandfatherly old codger— maybe not too smart, but salt of the earth. This guy wasn't more than thirty-five or forty years old.

"How ya doin', Sam?" Thompson said. "I wanted to talk to you."

Actually he said, "Ah wonted to tawk to yew." But I'll translate.

"Sorry to hear your dad's not any better," Thompson said.

"Miracles happen," Sam replied. "Did Bill come to see you?"

Thompson turned to face Sam. He pulled his feet under the table, managing to nudge my ankle as he resettled the boots. "'Scuse me, ma'am," he said, giving me a toothy smile. Then he turned back to Sam.

"He came by the office 'fore he went up to the City, but I was out. What's wrong with that boy, anyway?"

"I haven't managed to see him since all this happened, but I think he's pretty upset. He and Big Sam are close."

Thompson grinned. "Unlike the other Titus boy."

Sam shrugged. "I've had my differences with Big Sam, but I'm not going to let anybody do something like this to him, Tarzan."

"Something like what?"

"Like knocking him in the head and leaving him to die."

Thompson snorted. "You gonna start on that song and dance, too? It's stupid, Sam. Your daddy had an accident."

Sam shook his head. "No. He wouldn't have jacked up that truck without chocking the wheels. An uncle of his was killed—"

Thompson interrupted. "Don't give me that bull about a childhood accident. Bill and I went all over that on the phone."

Sam shrugged. "It's true. Bill and I had it drilled into us when we were kids. Big Sam is nuts on the subject."

"Maybe so. But he was out there in the middle of nowhere, and he had chocked the wheels. With rocks."

"He should have had a regular pair of chocks in the toolbox. He always carried them."

"Well, there weren't any there. He musta left 'em someplace. He did the best he could. But the truck was on a slope, and it rolled and fell."

"He wouldn't have worked on it on the slope. He would have driven to a flatter surface."

"On the rim?"

Sam nodded. "On the rim."

Tarzan Thompson put his head back and laughed. "That's rich!" Then he laughed again. "You think Big Sam Titus would'a deliberately ruint a tire. Sam, you been gone too long, boy. You've forgot that Big Sam's tight as a pair of new boots."

"I haven't forgotten." Sam's voice was very quiet, but it sounded rock firm. He stared steadily at Thompson, and the greasy sheriff stopped laughing.

"What made the tire go flat?" Sam asked.

Thompson scowled. "How the hell would I know? I didn't take it to the shop."

Then he leaned across the table. "Listen, Sam, I've had enough of this crap about what was just an accident. If you and Bill want things to be different, you're gonna have to come up with some evidence."

He sat back and turned his grin on me. "Sorry, ma'am, to fight with your husband. But you might as well know—you've married into the most bullheaded bunch in Catlin County."

I guess that I had been more than halfway convinced that Sam's suspicions about his father's accident were wrong. But Tarzan Thompson had convinced me Sam was right.

Sam hadn't forgotten how his father's mind worked, no matter what Thompson said. His relationship with his father almost haunted him. He knew the man.

Besides, Thompson's blustering was unconvincing. He might as well have admitted right out loud that there was something funny about the accident. He was just too lazy, or maybe too dumb, to investigate it.

I opened my mouth and started to say as much, but a loud bang reverberated through The Hangout.

I saw Thompson's eyes widen, and his mouth form a grimace. "Dammit."

We all looked around. A pretty young girl, blond, with delicate features, was standing in the open doorway, still holding the heavy glass door she had banged into the wall. She looked all around the room, and her eyes grew bigger and bigger.

Then she put a hand to her forehead in a helpless gesture. "Where's Bill? His mother's car's out front. I thought he'd be here. Has anyone seen Bill Titus?"

FOUR

SAM SLID OUT OF the booth and approached the girl.

"Hello, Brenda."

Brenda? Then I realized. Brenda Titus. Bill's wife. Sam's sister-in-law. Mother of the grandchildren whose pictures Marty had showed us before the wedding.

"I drove Mom's car down. Bill came in his truck," Sam said.

Brenda's eyes grew even wider. "Oh, Sam! I'm so glad someone's here. Where's Bill?"

"He's around someplace, Brenda." Sam took her by the arm and gently guided her in my direction. "Come back and meet Nicky."

Brenda was a tiny, ultrafeminine girl. I really couldn't call her a woman; her delicate good looks, her blond curls, her mannerisms, her talk, and the very way she cocked her head to look up at Sam were all childish. Marty hadn't had much to say about her, I remembered. I didn't think they'd have a lot in common.

By the time Sam and Brenda reached our booth, Tarzan Thompson had disappeared. I think he must have slid out through the kitchen, vanquished by the sight of an emotional wife.

Sam seated Brenda beside me, then scooted into the opposite side of the booth.

"You don't have the kids with you, do you?"

"Oh, no. They're over at my girlfriend's."

Brenda turned to me. "Oh, Nicky, I'm so glad to meet you. Big Sam said you were pretty as all get out, and Marty said you were smart as a whip. Now I see what they mean."

I tried to make the appropriate replies.

"Well, Big Sam and Marty had to hit it lucky some-time," she said. She had a much broader accent than Marty's. "Heaven knows I was a sure 'nuff let down for 'em."

I didn't know what to say to that one, but luckily Ollie and her purple apron appeared at the end of the booth.

"I forgot to ask what y'all want on your hamburgers. And how 'bout you, Brenda? You want a hamburger?"

Brenda allowed herself to be persuaded into a cheese-burger with mayonnaise, lettuce and tomato. When Ollie returned to the kitchen, she leaned over the table toward Sam.

She lowered her voice. "Where is Bill?"

"I haven't talked to him since I got back here," Sam said. "Where'd he go this morning?"

"This morning! I haven't talked to him this morning. Don't you know where he is?"

Sam shook his head. "No, I talked to him from Chicago last night. He was going to head down to the ranch then."

Brenda gasped. "Last night! Oh, surely not!"

"That's what he said. He left Mom at the hospital about ten-thirty."

Brenda's face seemed to crumple. "Oh, no! Oh, no!"

I put my arm around the girl's shoulder. "What's wrong, Brenda?"

She buried her face in her hands and rocked back and forth, moaning. Tears were rolling out from under her palms.

I opened my purse and found a little packet of tissues I had bought in some airport within the past twenty-four hours. She accepted one, still sniffing and moaning, but the act of drying her eyes seemed to calm her. She gulped twice, hard, then looked up at Sam. She spoke in a dull, dispirited voice. "Bill's left me. He's left me and the kids."

It was lucky I was sitting on the inside of the booth. If I had been able to get out without climbing over Brenda, I might have simply gotten to my feet, walked out of The Hangout, and taken a bus for New York. I was beginning to think I had fallen into a soap opera. Dying father, stoic mother, family feuds, lecherous sheriff, cryptic remarks, a husband who had gone incommunicado, and now somebody else's marital problems. All we needed was a paternity suit and a case of amnesia and we could sell it to daytime television.

But since I couldn't get out of the booth, I hugged Brenda with the arm that was already around her shoulders. "Come on, now. You're just upset."

She shook her head, but the appearance of Ollie forestalled another outburst. She settled our hamburgers before us, then looked closely at Brenda. "You okay, honey?"

Brenda nodded, and Sam answered for her. "She's just hungry, Ollie. She'll be better when she gets some food down."

After a bit more nudging, Brenda did eat. I think Sam was right; she really was starving. Certainly she cleared away a large hamburger. And Sam was right about Lou and Ollie's hamburgers, too. They had just the right amount of grease. Delicious.

As we ate, Sam asked Brenda about her children. Little Billy, she said, was four now, and Lee Anna had just turned two. Billy went to nursery school, and he already could write his name. Lee Anna had potty trained herself. Brenda said she couldn't get over it. She'd had to work like a dog with Billy, and Lee Anna took care of the whole thing with no problem.

The talk seemed to calm her down. Sam let her finish her hamburger before he tried to talk about Bill again.

"Brenda, I don't see how Bill could have left you," he said.

"Sam, we had a terrible fight. You just don't know how awful it was. He slammed out without a word," she said, fumbling for a tissue.

"When was this?"

"It was the day your father got hurt. I guess after Bill left he went over to your folks' house. That's when Marty sent him to look for your dad—and he found him hurt so bad."

"Did you see him after that?"

"Yes, I tried to talk to him at the hospital here, but he just shrugged it off. He said he couldn't worry about it right then. He had to go to Oklahoma City with your mother."

She inhaled, and her breath was quavering on the brink of another sob. "We never got to talk, to settle it. We had to let the sun go down on a quarrel. And that's a thing you're never supposed to do."

She touched her eyes with the new tissue. Sam frowned and stared off into space. He had a way of using his glasses as a shield, and now he retired behind them.

"It really sounds as if he forgot the whole thing, Brenda," I said. "He was more worried about his dad than about the quarrel with you."

She shook her head. "You're tryin' to make me feel better, Nicky. But I've gone over it and over it. I called him at the hospital, and I tried to settle it, but he wouldn't discuss the matter."

Sam leaned forward. "Then he didn't come home last night or this morning?"

Brenda shook her head again. "No, Sam. If he's left the hospital, he should have come home. That's why I know he's left me."

Sam's lips tightened. "Brenda, Bill might leave you. Strange things have been known to happen. But—tell me the truth, now—would he leave the ranch?"

Sam sat back and looked at her steadily.

Brenda blinked. She seemed to consider the question seriously. "Well, I admit it's hard to imagine him leavin' right here before time to cut wheat," she said. "But, Sam, if he didn't leave me—well, where is he?"

Sam didn't answer. Instead, he got to his feet and pulled out his billfold.

Brenda looked up at him with her baby-doll gaze. I wondered if her eyes automatically closed when she lay down.

"Bill always admired you," she said. "Did he give you a hint on what he planned to do?" She put her hand on Sam's arm. He looked at her steadily.

"Where is he?" she repeated.

"That's the question that's bothering me," Sam answered.

Sam took money out of his billfold. He gestured toward the cash register. "Come on. Let's get out of here. We'll make some calls."

Instantly, I felt relief. Sam knew someone to ask, somewhere to look. He could find Bill.

Brenda and I followed him out onto the sidewalk. The sun was really beating down now. Standing there in the dry heat, I felt like a potato sitting in a 400-degree oven, with my insides gradually getting soft.

Sam turned to Brenda. "How about the bank? It seems like Bill might go by there. Who does he do business with?"

"Brock Blevins."

Sam nodded and wheeled right. Only a dozen or so people were on the sidewalk. We passed a clothing store, a hardware store, and two empty buildings before we came to the corner. I saw the old-fashioned bank building across the street.

It was a two-story building of red brick. The corner was chopped off to give it a cater-cornered entrance that didn't face either the courthouse or the side street. Massive red pillars—of sandstone, I think—stood on either side of the door, supporting a heavy archway of matching stone. A cupola crowned the entrance corner, capping it with a frothy white gazebo. It looked like a wedding cake perched on a mausoleum.

Sam gave a low whistle. "When did they take the bank back to its pioneer look?"

"Oh, a couple of years ago," Brenda answered. "I think it looks kind of dumb. I mean, why go back to that old-fashioned stuff?"

Curlicued letters on the glass in the door identified the building: FIRST BANK OF HOLTON. I gathered that it was also the only bank of Holton. I recognized the bank's logo from the "FBH" on Marty's key chain.

Inside, the bank retained its period look, with grilled cages for the tellers. Luckily it did not retain its period temperature. The air conditioning was going strong, and it felt good.

Sam strode across the bank lobby to an office in the rear. It had a picture window that overlooked the lobby, and I could see him step inside and shake hands with the man at the rolltop desk.

"That's Brock," Brenda said scornfully. "He thinks he's a big man in Catlin County."

Brock Blevins did have a distinguished look. He was sixtyish, with a dignified stance. His hair and his eyes were a matching light gray, and he wore a beautifully cut gray suit—the only suit I had seen so far in Holton.

Blevins came out and shook my hand and greeted Brenda like an uncle telling a sassy niece happy birthday. I almost expected him to pat her on the head and slip her a dime for her piggy bank.

"Sam, I don't have to tell you how upset we all are about your dad," he said. "Is there anything you need? I know these things can get expensive. If your mother needs funds transferred, needs a line of credit—well, just tell her to write any kind of a check and we'll honor it.''

"Thanks, Brock," Sam said. "We may well have to take you up on that. But right now we've got another problem. Has Bill been here?"

Blevins frowned. "Bill? Isn't he still in Oklahoma City?"

Sam shook his head. "He left last night. We thought he might have come by here."

Blevins's frown deepened, and he used his left hand to pull his chin to a point. "Well, I really would have expected him to come here, but no."

"You'll get your money, Mr. Blevins," Brenda said curtly.

"There's no problem, Brenda," Blevins said. "I know how prudent Bill is."

"Yes, and I know how impatient you are," the girl answered. "Bill told you you'd get your money as soon as wheat harvest was over."

"I know, Brenda. And that's just fine." Blevins's voice had grown quite oily. He turned back to Sam. "Bill's affairs are in perfect order with the bank. It's your father's that are a little more complicated. Just what is his situation?"

"Financially?" Sam said. "I have no idea."

Blevins smiled, and Mazola dripped. "Oh, no, Sam. I meant his health. Do the doctors indicate that he'll regain consciousness soon?"

"They don't think so." Sam's voice seemed to grow tighter each time he answered that question. "Nobody's making any rosy predictions. But about his financial situation—is there any immediate problem?"

"No, no!" Blevins was emphatic. "Everything we're involved in is completely secured."

"Secured!" The word seemed to take Sam by surprise. "Does that mean he owes money that's due right away?"

Blevins shook his head and held up his hand in a calming gesture. "Everything's fine, Sam. Just get Big Sam well. That's the important thing. We'll arrange something."

For the first time, Sam seemed to wilt. "Tell me the worst, Brock."

Blevins managed to look as if the subject pained him a great deal. "Well, he signed a promissory note on the old Fields ranch. The Smith brothers sold out in January, to avoid foreclosure. I think he intended to make a payment against the principal before he went for permanent financing. While he was in Germany, did he tell you what he intended to do?"

"He didn't mention it. When is the payment due?"

"June fifteenth."

That was less than two weeks away.

"I'll talk to Bill and my mother," Sam said. He turned toward Brenda and me. "Come on, Brenda, Nicky. Let's head for the house. Maybe Bill's been out there."

We went toward the door, followed by Blevins.

"We're perfectly prepared to arrange permanent financing on the Fields place," the banker said.

"That's twelve hundred acres. What was the amount of the loan?"

"Three fifty an acre. It totals $420,000."

My heart skipped around in my chest, but Sam only nodded. "I'll be talking to you." He pushed open the door and held it for Brenda and me while we went back out into the bake oven.

I turned to him. "Sam, what was all that about?"

"It's about nearly half a million dollars," he said. "Let's get out of here."

I was completely confused. For one thing, I hadn't had any idea an Oklahoma rancher whose son had once described him as "just country folks" would be involved in half-million-dollar deals. I started to ask Sam to explain, but

I saw his eyes flicker toward Brenda, and I shut up. He must not want to talk in front of her.

We walked with her to a year-old Ford Taurus with an infant seat in the back. She said she would pick up her children and meet us at the house. We waved her off, then turned toward Marty's car.

"Sam," I started. "What's going on?"

"Later," he muttered. His face looked dark. "It's the Smith brothers."

Standing beside Marty's car were the two old men I had met in The Hangout, Maynard and Millard. They still looked almost like twins.

Their differences were plain, however. They were average-sized men, but one of them was slightly smaller than the other. The smaller one stood a step in front of his brother, and his slanted eyes squinted out from under a rancher's hat of finely woven white straw. He was fingering the heavy metal buckle of his western belt. The larger brother's eyes were round and vapid. He stood with his hands limp at his sides, an identical hat square on his head.

The brothers' weather-worn faces had pointed chins and wide cheekbones. The combination reminded me of night-prowling animals. The smaller one might have been a flying squirrel and the larger an exotic nocturnal monkey. I guessed their ages at past seventy.

As we approached, the smaller one smiled ingratiatingly and spoke. "Young Sam, is it true what you was sayin'? That your daddy ain't up to handling his own business now?"

"For the moment, Millard."

The squirrel face screwed up into a worried expression. "Well, then, are you and Bill handlin' things?"

"I hope I can stay out of it. Mother and Bill know more about what's going on."

The worry deepened. "Your daddy and I had a deal."

Sam and I were touching shoulders, and I could feel his arm tense. When he spoke, his voice sounded curt. "Did you have it in writing?"

Millard gave Sam a sidelong look from under his hat brim. "Since when do neighbors need to put anything in writing?"

"Since things happen and other people need to know what's going on. What's this all about?"

"Our place. The old Fields place."

"Oh." Sam didn't relax. "Brock Blevins just told me that Big Sam bought it in January. I didn't know anything about it."

"Well, we're still livin' out there. He promised to sell it back to us."

Sam didn't answer, and I looked up at him. A rather sardonic smile crossed his face. "I find that hard to believe."

"Are you calling my brother a liar?" The bigger brother took a step forward and scowled, looking up. Sam topped him by several inches, but for a moment I thought Maynard was going to punch Sam.

Sam shrugged. "I know Big Sam," he answered. "He doesn't like to sell land, that's all."

The smaller brother gave a high whinny. "That's fer damn sure!" he said. "Calm down, Maynard. Young Sam's right. Big Sam will do nearly anything to hang on to a piece of property, once he's got his hands on it. He's a hard man, Big Sam." He smiled his ingratiating smile again and looked at Sam with that sly look, as if he were hiding under his hat brim.

"But he's fair, Big Sam is," he said.

Sam nodded. "Yes, he's fair, and if he ever did anything dishonest, I didn't hear about it. What did he tell you about the ranch?"

"He said that if we got the money together by July first we could buy it back. And we're gonna have it."

Sam sighed. "Look," he said. "I don't know what's going on here. If he doesn't get better, then we'll have to take some sort of legal steps about running the ranch. I don't know how it works. But it will be up to Mom." He stopped, then added, "And Bill, I hope."

Millard smiled again. "Just as long as you know your daddy promised us."

Sam shook his head. "No, Millard. Mom and Bill will have to decide what's best. If you didn't have it in writing, all bets are off."

The low grumble came from Maynard. "All you Tituses are just alike. Hard. Hard as rocks. Hardheaded. Your grandfather was the same way. It don't mean a thing to you that our granddaddy homesteaded that place. It's nothin' that our sweat and blood went into that land!"

His voice was rising, and his brother touched his shoulder. "Maynard! Stop!" he said, giving his sly smile. "You ain't bein' neighborly."

"When were the Tituses neighbors to us?" Maynard said. His brother's calming action seemed to simply spur him on. "What did the Tituses ever do but connive with the bank to grab our land!"

Sam took my arm. He leaned forward between the two brothers and took hold of the door handle. He turned his back toward Maynard and his ravings.

"Listen, Millard," he said, ignoring the tirade that continued from Maynard. "I'll talk to you sometime when Maynard's not having a bad day, but right now Nicky and I have got to get out to the house."

He brushed the two elderly brothers aside and opened the door. Then he put himself between Maynard and me and almost shoved me into the car. As Maynard continued his ranting, Millard stood by, smiling sweetly. Sam went around the car and climbed in behind the wheel. Maynard followed him.

We had left the car windows down, and Maynard leaned over and put his head almost inside the car, right up in Sam's face. "Rotten! Mean as snakes! That's what you Tituses are! I told your grandfather as much back in the Dust Bowl, and I told Big Sam so just this week! You'd better watch your step, Young Sam! You'd better watch—!"

But Millard had caught his brother's arm. "Shut up, Maynard," he said quietly.

Almost as if a switch had been flipped, Maynard stopped talking.

Sam didn't look up. He started the motor, leaned over and turned on the air conditioner, then rolled up his window without another glance at the Smith brothers and backed the car out of the parking place.

I had found Millard and Maynard scary. "Whew!" I said. "What a pair."

Sam looked over at me. "Actually, there are a lot of ordinary, everyday people in Holton. I'm sorry we didn't run into any of them."

"What's the story on those two? Are they twins?"

"Yes. I guess they're at least seventy-five now. I think Maynard must have had brain damage at birth. He's always been that way. They were delivered by some old granny in a soddy."

"A soddy?"

Sam looked at me and smiled. "A sod house. You know, the plains equivalent of a log cabin."

"Oh, I thought all that was in the olden days."

"Millard and Maynard always tell the soddy story as if they're proud of it, but Big Sam says it means their family was really poor. Everybody else had a frame house by then."

"Does Millard always do the real talking?"

"Yeah. And yells 'sic 'em' at Maynard."

I took all this in.

"Okay," I said. "Let me see if I have this straight. The bank was about to foreclose on the Smith brothers' ranch which is called the Fields place."

"Right. They inherited it from their mother's family."

"Your dad bought it, agreeing to pay nearly half a million dollars for it."

"Four hundred and twenty thousand—which probably went to get Millard and Maynard off the hook with the bank. I doubt they saw a penny."

"But where would Big Sam get that kind of money?"

"The bank."

"You mean he has that much in an account?"

Sam laughed. "No way! A ranch is a business, Nicky. If ranchers want to expand, they borrow, just like a…a pants factory or an ice-cream store."

I took that in in a minute, readjusting my view of my down-home father-in-law. "And Big Sam has that kind of credit?"

"You heard Brock. The loan is secured with property the Titus Ranch owns free and clear."

I digested that before I spoke again. I hadn't realized I'd married into money. Big Sam and Marty didn't act rich.

"Okay. But Millard claims that your dad said they could buy the ranch back if they got the money together by the first of July."

"Which I doubt."

"Why?"

Sam looked straight ahead at the asphalt street. He clenched his fist a couple of times. But his voice was calm when he spoke.

"Two reasons. First, Big Sam has a desire to own land that really comes down to avarice. Once he gets hold of an acre, he keeps it. Second, the Smith brothers are lousy farmers, and Big Sam knows it. Our land, the Titus land, is always kept in great shape. Once Big Sam got the Fields place away from Millard and Maynard, he'd have big plans for building the pastures back up and putting in Bermuda on the back eighty. He wouldn't want them to get their hands on it again.''

"And you feel the same way."

Sam barked out a laugh. "Maybe I do. God knows that twelve hundred acres of weeds and erosion has been a thorn in the Titus side for years. But basically I just don't want to get involved with the Smith brothers right now. Right now I want to concentrate on Bill."

"Bill." I mulled that situation over for a minute. "You told Brenda that Bill was around—someplace."

"There's no call to scare her yet. We'd better stop at the Co-op. I can get gas, and Bill might have dropped by there."

"What's the Co-op?"

Sam glanced over at me and blinked. Then he grinned. "You sure are a city girl, aren't you? The Co-op is a cooperative, owned by all its customers. Farmers and ranchers use it to buy feed, gasoline, diesel fuel, and such stuff in bulk. If Bill needed gas when he got down here, he might have stopped by."

The Co-op, I discovered, was the site of those skyscrapers I had seen as we entered town—the round white towers six or seven stories tall. It had a gravel drive, several gasoline pumps, and a loading dock.

But the skinny kid who manned the Co-op cash register said he hadn't seen Bill. He yanked the visor of his blue cap down over his eyes and shook his head when Sam asked.

"Shure haven't seen 'em," he said. "But, listen, I'd shure be glad to fix that tar offin yer daddy's truck. I told Bill I'd do it before he left for Okie City, but he said not to. My offer's still gud. I could swing by there on my way home from werk." Or anyway, that's how it sounded to me.

But Sam also turned his offer down. "We may take you up on it later," he added. Then he got back into the car and started the engine.

"Maybe there'll be some sign of Bill out at the house," he said.

"What do you think has happened to him?"

Sam shook his head. "I don't know," he said. "But what I do know is that the idea of Bill running off and leaving the ranch is just as crazy as the notion that Big Sam would jack up a truck on a gravel slope."

I reached forward and adjusted the air-conditioning vent. All of a sudden I was chilled clear through.

FIVE

WE DROVE along a flat stretch of road. The mountains were still there, on our right and behind us, but to the left and in front the horizon was broken by only a few scattered trees. The trunks of the trees didn't grow up straight toward the sky. They all leaned slightly, and all in the same direction. Their foliage bulged in that same direction. When I commented on this, Sam explained that they were shaped by the strong prevailing winds.

"You can use any tree around here as a compass," he said. "They all lean northeast."

That particular day was going to leave the trees even farther out of plumb. The wind was blowing hard. I could feel it buffet the car, and the farmhouses and barns seemed to nestle down into the prairie, pushed over by its force. Powered by that same force, the massive clouds paraded across a clear blue sky.

After driving a couple of miles Sam slowed and turned right onto a gravel road. "About five more miles," he said.

A small, ramshackle house sat on the corner. Bales of hay were oozing out its windows. I pointed to it.

"What's happened to the big, old-fashioned farmhouses that you see on postcards?"

"Big old Victorians?"

"Yes. Did you Oklahomans tear them all down?"

"Nope." The mouth under Sam's glasses smiled. "Us Okies weren't around to build them. This part of the state wasn't opened to white settlement until 1901. And people don't come in and build big fancy houses the first couple of years they're homesteading. We missed the Victorian era."

"Until 1901? I hadn't thought of that. But why are all the old houses stuffed full of hay? Doesn't anybody live in an old house?"

"The Tituses do."

Sam's voice had become curt. When I looked at him, his mouth was set in a hard line, and he was hiding behind his glasses again. I opened my mouth but decided to keep quiet. His parents' home and his father's tightwad attitude were obviously emotionally charged for Sam.

In a mile or two, he slowed again, then pointed out my window. "That's the east eighty of the Fields place," he said. "See what I mean? It's completely overgrazed."

I looked out at a pasture that was dotted with scrubby cedars and some short, sprawling trees with lacy leaves. They wouldn't give much shade.

"Well, the trees don't look like much," I said. "But do you want trees in pastureland?"

"No. The fact that those cedars are even in there shows the land is overgrazed. Good grassland would keep cedars out. And the mesquites need to be taken out, too."

"Is that the lacy-looking tree?"

"Right. A real junk tree."

My photographer's eye began working again. "They're interesting shapes," I said defensively.

The land began to roll a little again, and as we topped a rise, a house popped up on the left.

Sam nodded toward it. "That's new," he said. "It must be Bill and Brenda's. They were living in a house trailer the last time I came home." He slowed, and I could read the TITUS on the mailbox.

It was a one-story, red-brick house, probably three bedrooms and a bath and a half. It had an incongruous set of dovecotes under the eaves, and miniature Tara pillars overwhelmed the five-by-ten front porch. All the trim was painted white. Halved whiskey barrels held a riot of marigolds. Two big trees I recognized as cottonwoods stood behind the house, and a couple of scrawny saplings had been planted inside the front fence. It was no architectural marvel, but it looked cheerful and cared for, and suddenly I liked Brenda a little better.

Sam craned his neck to look back after we passed the house. Behind it were a barn and an open metal shed that held several pieces of farm equipment. A swing set stood under the cottonwood trees.

"No truck," Sam said. "Bill's not there."

We drove on, but Sam had slowed down. "Listen, Nicky. I ought to warn you that the folks' house isn't much."

"That doesn't matter, Sam."

"Mom wrote me that they did some work on it, but she said she wanted to surprise me. That probably means a paint job. Like I said, anytime Big Sam gets two cents together, he buys land. He's not interested in houses or such.

"And I finally figured out that my mother's not too interested, either. She kind of does minimum housework; then she works on her painting. And leaving in a hurry like she did— Well, it's just an old house."

"Don't worry, Sam. I was raised in military quarters, remember."

"Yeah, I saw the military quarters your dad has."

"Sure, since he's a general. We didn't rate anything like that when I was growing up. And I hope I'm not stupid enough to judge people by how fancy their homes are. There's nothing wrong with an older house."

"There are a few things wrong with the Tituses' older house." Sam's face was dark. "The Titus house was built back in the twenties, when people were still trying to make a living on 80 or 120 acres around here. In the twenties people in Catlin County were poor. Then the Dust Bowl hit— and times got even harder. That's when Big Sam was a kid here—and his folks lost their farm. In the fifties people figured out it took a larger piece of land to farm profitably. Things picked up, but the less productive farmers were shoved out."

"And their houses were abandoned?"

"Right. That's what happened to the Titus house. But when Big Sam was able to buy back the first piece of the land his grandfather had homesteaded in 1901, he cleaned the hay out of the old house and patched it together. Then he and Mom got married, and they've lived in it ever since. But it's still just a 1920 bungalow—that used to be stuffed with hay—with the wind blowing through the cracks."

He slowed and turned right onto a gravel drive. A line of poles carried wires up another of the small hills to a complex of buildings at the top.

"That's it." He spoke glumly.

Golden fields of wheat were on either side of the road. A quarter mile ahead and at the top of a rise, a house and barns and a grove of trees were silhouetted against that clear blue sky and those fantastic clouds.

I looked at the scene, then shook my head. "Sam, I don't know how luxuriously your parents live, but you can't beat the setting."

The house was white with black trim, a one-story bungalow with a wooden porch clear across the front and an attic window above the porch. It was surrounded by a four-foot cyclone fence. There wasn't a lot of shrubbery, but a bush of some kind was beginning to bloom in the fence corner. A row of poplars grew outside the fence on the west, and a rope swing hung from a large tree that shaded the east side of the house.

We drove past the house, and I saw a white metal barn, its yard surrounded by a fence made of pipes, also painted white. Two round tin structures with conical roofs stood beside the barn. They were connected to each other by pipes that rose out of the center of each cone and met about thirty feet in the air. I'd seen these at a lot of the farms and ranches we passed, and a giant version had loomed up near the Holton Co-op.

"What are those things with the funnels on top?" I asked.

"Grain bins."

"What are the pipes for?"

"The pipes? Oh, you mean the legs. They're used to load and unload grain from the bins."

"Then the pipes—the legs, I mean—are sort of like vacuum-cleaner hoses?"

Sam laughed. "No," he said. "The grain is moved by augers."

I thought about that one. "Isn't an auger a screw?"

"Yeah. It pulls the grain up to the top something like an automatic ice machine pulls out an ice cube. Going into the bin, the grain is moved by gravity."

He wheeled the car abruptly to face a low metal shed that was open on the long side. Several exotic vehicles and pieces of equipment were neatly lined up under the roof. A bright blue pickup truck was at the end, and Sam pulled the Chevy into an empty space beside it. He took off his glasses and rubbed his eyes.

I got out and looked over the piece of equipment next to me. It was green and had enormous wheels in back and little wheels in front. Three exhaust pipes stuck up from the hood, and a cab with four glass sides perched over the big rear wheels.

"What's that?" I asked.

"What's what?" Sam walked around the car.

I pointed at the strange vehicle. "That."

Sam frowned. He kicked the big tire. "That?"

"Yes. What is it?"

He grinned. "That, my city-slicker bride, is even less complicated than an auger. It's a tractor. Surely you played with a toy tractor in your sandpile outside some of those army quarters.''

I imagine I frowned, because Sam's grin faded. I touched the glass cab.

"This is what surprised me," I said. "I never saw one glassed in like that.''

"Oh. That's for the air conditioning.''

"Air conditioning? In Oklahoma the tractors are air conditioned?''

"In Oklahoma everything is air conditioned. Even Big Sam got a window unit for the living room.''

Then Sam grinned. "Want to see Big Sam's cow ponies?''

I looked around, puzzled. "Horses? Where? They wouldn't be in the barn in weather like this.''

Sam crossed to the end of the machine shed, stopped beside a waist-high heap of tarpaulin, and yanked the protective sheet aside. "Here they are. Trigger and Champion.''

Two all-terrain vehicles stood in the corner of the shed.

I could feel my eyes widen. "Horses?''

"Yeah. Big Sam isn't one of your old-time horse-loving ranchers. He uses ATVs to herd cattle. They'll go anywhere but the roughest country. For that kind of work we hire real cowpokes—and they bring their own horses.''

I laughed. "No mustangs? No cayuses?''

"Not on the Titus Ranch.'' I helped Sam as he carefully draped the tarpaulin over the ATVs again. Then he opened the trunk of the car and took out the suitcases.

I got out the few things we had tossed into the backseat—our jackets and my carry-on bag. I hoped Sam was right about the air conditioning. Away from the car's cool air I was already beginning to sweat, and the wind was blowing dust.

Then I heard the roar of a motor. I turned and saw Sam was looking toward the sound.

"It's a pickup," he muttered, "but it's running too ragged to be Bill's."

A beat-up tan truck barreled around the corner of the house and skidded to a stop, spraying gravel. More dust blew over us.

A bleached blonde leaned out the window. "Hi, y'all! Brenda here?"

She stuck her hand out through the window and opened the door from the outside. "Goddam handle's broke," she said casually. "You may not remember me, Sam. God knows I don't really remember you, though I rarely forget a big, good-looking feller." She cast a seductive smile in Sam's direction as she jumped out of the truck.

"I remember you," Sam said. His voice was expressionless. "Nicky, this is Brenda's mother, Mrs. Schrader."

The blonde laughed and reached over and patted Sam's chest. "Oh, Sam, you're all out of touch! My name's Baker now. Bobbi Baker."

She stamped the feet in beaded moccasins, dusted her hands over a pair of skintight jeans that covered a tiny behind, and tucked in a western-style shirt of electric blue with a silver stripe. It gapped between the second and third of the pearl snaps that ran down the front. She wasn't overly endowed; her shirt was just too small.

"Did I beat Brenda here?"

Sam nodded. "You just about beat us. We haven't been inside yet."

Bobbi Baker grinned and wriggled her behind. "You haven't been here since the big remodeling, have you?"

"No."

"Well, you'll be surprised." She pointed toward the house, and we followed her gesture.

"I'm surprised already," Sam said. "They've put a room in the attic."

The back of the house looked completely different from the front. To begin with, on this side it was two stories high, with lines of windows like an old-fashioned sun porch stretching completely across the whole width of the downstairs and across the narrower width of an attic room. A deck was at the right end of the upstairs, cut back into the roofline.

"I thought all those windows on the north would freeze 'em out, but Big Sam put in the most expensive kind of insulated glass, and it's not a bit cold," Bobbi Baker said. "Then they moved the back door around there on the east side so the wind won't blow straight in. And wait till you see the circular stairs. And the new bathrooms!"

She marched toward the house, leaving the gate in the cyclone fence gaping. "I thought your mama would want some fancier kind of fence, but she said she just wanted something to keep the cows out of the yard. She wanted to be able to see through it, she said."

Sam's mouth grew tighter as he set down a suitcase to close the gate.

A sidewalk cut diagonally toward the house, meeting a little patio with a wooden bird feeder mounted on a pole at one corner. A brick planter stood along its edge, and Bobbi Baker began to dig among the geraniums in it. "I'll just find the key right quick," she said.

"I have a key." Sam's voice was sharp. I thought this woman's patronizing attitude about his parents' home had annoyed him. I was annoyed, too.

Sam unlocked the back door, and he and Bobby engaged in a little maneuver to settle who was going in first. Sam won, blocking Bobbi to let me in.

Inside was a large kitchen. It had a dark floor of wide boards that had been given a permanent finish of what I guessed was acrylic. Counters and work space were on our left. Simple unbleached muslin curtains were hung on wooden rods with wooden rings along the row of windows. On the right, a wooden circular stairway spiraled upstairs, and next to the back door an antique church pew perched over a couple of chairs of work boots. The cabinets were natural oak, and the walls were painted a warm brown that leaned toward terra-cotta.

The only thing "country" about it was a collection of wheat weavings, and those were just wheat—no ribbon or calico trimmings.

The room looked as if it belonged in *House & Garden*.

"Isn't it cute!" Bobbi Baker cried.

"It's beautiful," I said. I was reproving her, and I didn't much care if she knew it.

But Bobbi Baker wasn't interested in my opinion. She concentrated on Sam. "Your mama sure likes things plain. I told her I was goin' to get her one of those cute kitchen witches to hang over the sink, but she said she hadn't planned to use anything but that wheat weaving in here. Said it was partly a wheat farm, after all."

She rippled out a giggle and patted Sam's arm. Sam almost winced. He put the suitcases down near the stairway.

A round table sat in the center of the kitchen, holding a pile of place mats. Two high stools marked places for Billy and Lee Anna, and a finger painting was displayed on the refrigerator door. The magnets that held it in place were topped with hand-carved wooden buttons.

"How is it changed?" I asked Sam.

He didn't seem to hear me, but Bobbi answered my question. "It's completely different. That back area, that was a screened porch. All it did was make the kitchen dark. And there wasn't any upstairs. And there was no pass-through."

She pointed to the wall of the kitchen where a window opened to the living room beyond. Sam deftly dodged around her and moved into the front part of the house.

Bobbi was hard at his heels. "See, they threw the living room and dining room together. The new dining-room set is real nice, if you like the old-fashioned styles."

The "old-fashioned" style was a traditional harvest table with a drop leaf along each of its long sides. It was close to the kitchen, ready to turn that end of the room into a dining area. Simple Windsor chairs sat beside it.

The wooden floors extended through the living room, and now Bobbi took advantage of their smooth surface to whirl on one moccasined toe.

"But they saved most of the living-room furniture," she said. "I just adore that suede stuff they had the chairs covered in."

The living room was also furnished in earth tones. The furniture was traditional, with club chairs and a camelback couch. There wasn't a ruffle or a pattern anywhere, unless you counted the homespun look of the couch upholstery or the abstract design of the custom-made area rug. The "suede stuff" on the chairs was a rich rust color.

"Now, me," Bobbi said, "I'd have picked some nice flowered drapes, you know, with all this plain stuff. But your mama, Sam, she said she thought these went with the house better."

The curtains weren't quite as artless as the muslin in the kitchen, but they gave much the same effect—simple curtains that stayed inside the window frames. The one painting was an abstract. Plants were massed in a tray on the dining table, all of them in plain clay pots.

The room had real class, unlike the woman who was giving the tour.

Sam was pretending she wasn't there. For that matter, he seemed to be pretending I wasn't there, either. Was something besides Bobbi annoying him?

"They kept that same old fireplace," Bobbi said.

The fireplace was on the east wall. It did look like the 1920s—small, with a simple design in brownish red brick.

A collection of wooden candlesticks marched along the plain oak mantel, with the tallest on the left and the smallest on the right. Another abstract painting hung off center, over the shorter candlesticks. The asymmetrical arrangement was correct, my art classes told me, but it was unusual. I was also quick enough to notice that the custommade area rug was another version of the painting.

"Your mama said your daddy saw that painting at some art fair," Bobbi said. Her voice was disapproving. "She claimed your daddy insisted on hangin' it there."

Sam took a close look at it. He gave a very small snort, then turned his back and walked away.

I looked at the painting closely. It was an acrylic with muted shades of orange, pink, purple, and blue running from side to side. The name BETHANY was neatly printed in the corner.

"It's beautiful," I said.

Bobbi was looking at it doubtfully. "Well, if you like that sort of thing," she said.

Then she whirled again. "And look—those are the old dining-room doors," she said. "They made that front bedroom into an office."

Sam strode across the room to a set of french doors and threw them open.

The room beyond held filing cabinets, a desk, and a computer. Bookshelves lined one wall, surrounding yet a third abstract. Sam looked the room over and frowned. He went back through the living area and entered a hall that opened off the dining end of the room. I followed. He seemed madder than ever, and I wondered why.

"Isn't that bathroom scrumptious?" Bobbi's enthusiasm was growing a bit hollow. She had seemed finally to notice that Sam was snubbing her.

But he still didn't reply as he stood in the hall, looking into a bathroom that was a mix of modern and old-fashioned. The tub was a genuine antique, with giant ball and claw feet, and the toenails on the claws had not been painted gold. The floor was the same wood that had been used in the kitchen and through the living room and office. An old-fashioned shower was mounted in the tub—the type with a shower curtain going all around on a pipe. The curtain wasn't looped up in a coy fashion; it just hung there ready to keep water off the floor. More muslin was at the window, still on wooden rings and looking as if it had been done that way on purpose, not as an economy measure. The only decoration was a quilted wall hanging, an amusing white-faced bull standing knee-deep in a farm pond.

"Look at this!" Bobbi stepped into the bathroom and opened louvered doors on the right to display a washer and dryer. "Elegant and handy!"

Sam glared at the appliances, then went back to the bedroom.

"They put the back bedroom and the old lean-to room together," Bobbi said. "Sam, you must have nearly frozen out on that back porch in January."

Sam gave her a look that was barely civil, but he finally spoke. "I made out fine."

Bobbi rolled her eyes and turned toward me for the first time. "I like to fainted when I learned Sam had slept out there in that funny little room. He had to go out on the porch to get into it. And Big Sam wouldn't put a heater out there because he was afraid of fire."

The new bedroom was long enough to hold a queen-sized bed, a double dresser, a couple of easy chairs, and a television set. The bed was centered under the wall of windows, again covered with muslin curtains.

The bedroom color scheme varied from the rest of the house; instead of accenting the earth tones with rust and ocher, it used cream and a clear cobalt blue. It held another painting, this one a bit more realistic. Bare branches were visible against its striped background, which evidently represented a cloudy sky.

Bobbi popped her head between us. She reached for Sam's arm again, but he moved away.

"I was floored when they picked that bright blue for the bedspread," she said. "Your mama's so practical, and that blue's goin' to fade something fierce."

"That's Big Sam's favorite color," Sam said.

His voice almost choked up. Could he be dropping his unemotional front? I followed him into the room and took his hand. He barely squeezed it, then moved away.

"What's this?" he asked. He crossed the room in a couple of long strides and opened a door in the right-hand wall.

I trotted along after him, and we were again standing in the kitchen. Brenda's Ford was driving by the back door.

"There's Brenda!" Bobbi yelped. She shoved past us and went out the door. We followed.

When we reached the car, Brenda and her mother were facing each other. Brenda's face was flaming, and Bobbi was smirking.

"Shut up!" Brenda hissed. Then she looked toward us. "Hi, Nicky. Hi, Sam."

The kids were squirming in their seats, and Brenda opened the back door to get them out. They climbed down, two handsome little towheads. Then they both had attacks of shyness at the sight of strange relatives.

"Come on!" Bobbi squawked. "Billy! Lee Anna! Give your uncle a kiss!" Both the kids flattened themselves against the side of the car, obviously intimidated by this large person peering at them through his big spectacles.

Sam knelt down, but he was still taller than preschool level. "I don't think we're quite on kissing terms yet," he said. "How about a handshake?"

In a minute Billy reached out and tapped his hand. Then he jumped back, rather as if he had touched a snake on a dare. Lee Anna stuck two fingers in her mouth and edged toward her mother.

Sam laughed and stood up. "We'll get acquainted," he said.

Brenda reached into the front seat and pulled out a paper sack. "I brought y'all some lettuce and eggs and stuff," she said. "Marty asked me to clean out her milk and things that might spoil, so there's nothing much here."

"Oh, thanks," I said. I took the sack.

Bobbi smiled, and saccharin dripped. "Brenda, I need to talk to you, honey."

Brenda pursed her lips. "Go play on the swing, kids," she said.

Sam and I took the hint and went back in the house. I stuck the groceries in the refrigerator. Sam pointed to the stairs.

"Let's see what's up there," he said.

We climbed up into the prairies.

That's the only way to express it. You could tell about the room—twelve by twenty, with glass on two walls—but that doesn't describe it.

It was like being in a tree house, maybe. Rocking in the treetops with an unobstructed view right into forever. The winds were tossing the trees around the house, and their limbs were close outside the windows, yet we were looking beyond them at grassland and mountains and sky and clouds. We were part of the outdoors, yet protected from it—immersed in the scene, yet observers.

The room was almost unfurnished; it held only a couple of worktables and some director's chairs. A sink and counter were in one corner, and a line of cabinets stood along one wall. Sam opened one, and I saw it held shelving built under the roof.

"Sam," I said, "this is a studio."

His face was stony. "A tribute to Mom's compulsion," he said.

"What do you mean by that?" I asked.

He didn't respond. He walked across the room and opened the french doors that led to the deck.

I followed him. "Whew!" I said. "Talk about heat."

The afternoon sun was beating on the deck. It had been hot enough under the trees in the yard. It must have been 130 degrees on that deck.

Sam turned without a word and looked around. He reached for a narrow rope, and I saw that a canvas awning could be pulled down to shade the deck and keep the sun out of the studio. He studied the apparatus, then lowered the awning and hooked it down securely.

Before he could finish, the wind blew Brenda's voice up to us. "No!" she cried. "I won't talk to her! No! Not now! Not ever!"

Bobbi's voice was no longer sweet. "You're so damn eager to get rid of me I thought you'd be ready to do anything to run me out of town."

"Just let me find Bill!"

"Bill's already given you the turndown, thanks to his nosy papa. And don't think I didn't tell that old man what I thought of his interference."

Sam and I looked at each other. He nodded toward the french doors, and we went back inside.

"Goodness!" I said. "Brenda's mother is quite a trial."

To my surprise, Sam smiled. "She's pitiful," he said calmly, "but I've always found her role in the human comedy sort of entertaining."

"Entertaining! You like her?"

"Well, no. But she's harmless. I can put up with her now and then."

"You could have fooled me. You snubbed her in every room in the house."

Sam became deadpan. "I didn't realize I was being rude," he said.

"You've been acting as if you're angry. If you aren't mad at Bobbi Baker, what are you mad about?"

"I didn't realize I was mad," he said. Then he gestured toward the back of the studio. "Let's see what else is upstairs."

He turned and walked into a hall I hadn't even noticed, a hall that led off the studio toward the front of the house. In the hall was a dormer window, surrounded with bookshelves that actually held books. In a bathroom across the hall a vanity and cabinets had been built around a matching dormer. That bath had a stall shower.

At the end of the hall was a bedroom. It had a long closet that used the space under the eaves and a window that looked down toward the road. I realized that this must be the attic window over the porch. The bedspread was a handmade quilt. A smaller quilt—an antique silk one—hung from a brass rod mounted on the wall above the head of the bed.

Away from the sun that had been beating into the studio, the upstairs was cool. In fact, the whole house was cool. Obviously Big Sam's window unit for the living room had been replaced by central heat and air conditioning.

"Sam, this whole place is super!" I said. "It may have been makeshift when you were growing up, but now it's great. I love it all. They did a wonderful job of remodeling."

"Yes," Sam said.

He turned and walked back toward the studio.

The house was comfortable, beautiful, practical, and in perfect taste—obviously a carefully designed dream house for his parents.

Why did it distress Sam so much?

"Sam!" I expect my voice was sharp, but what the heck. Sam knew I had a temper when he married me.

He kept heading for the stairway.

"Sam!"

He stepped onto the top step.

"Sam!"

This time he turned. When he spoke, his voice was smooth and even, something like a newly shaved ice rink. "Yes, Nicky?"

I refused to be intimidated. "You're avoiding your duties." I walked over to the stairway and stood on the main level, facing him, so that we were nose to nose.

"Hug," I commanded.

I'd made a flippant request, and I'd expected a flippant hug. But his embrace was powerful. Sam buried his face in my neck. He took two deep breaths, his arms tightened around me, and I could feel his body tremble.

We stood there a long moment, clutching each other. Then Sam swallowed hard and raised his head. His face held no hint of the emotion his embrace had revealed. He kissed the end of my nose, then turned and started down the stairs again.

I spoke quickly. "Sam, you keep telling me you quarreled with your father, but you never tell me exactly what it was about."

Sam stared at me silently. His face grew iceberg hard. "It was a lot of things," he said. "It centered on philosophical differences on the handling of material possessions."

He turned and started on down the circular stairs.

"Sam!"

He took five steps down, an action that swung him around facing me once more, then stopped. He still looked like a hazard to North Atlantic navigation.

"That's not much of an explanation," I said.

Sam shrugged. "The final battle before I changed my major from agriculture to political science and law enforcement was over a clothes dryer," he said.

"A clothes dryer?"

"Yeah. I thought he should buy Mom one. He said he couldn't afford it. The next day he bought four hundred acres of pastureland. That caused Brock Blevins to point out in my hearing that the Titus Ranch was one of the two or three largest spreads in Catlin County. The land, stock, and equity were then worth around two and a half million."

He stared at me bleakly. "I realize there's a difference between land values and cash money. But I got to thinking that if my mother was a partner in one of the most successful ranches in Oklahoma, she didn't have to be hanging blue jeans on a line in freezing weather and living in a dump."

Sam made a gesture that took in the whole house. "I guess Big Sam finally came around to my way of thinking," he said.

He stalked on down the stairs.

SIX

WHEN I WENT downstairs after Sam, Brenda was standing at the back door, and her mother's truck was rattling and banging down the drive. Brenda's eyes were reddish, but she spoke fairly calmly.

"Marty called when I went by our house to check the mail," she said. "She wants you all to take the upstairs room. I'll run up and get you some towels, but she said there were sheets on the bed."

"Oh, I can get the towels," I said. Sam picked up the suitcases and without a word carried them up the curving stairs.

"I hope everything at the house is all right," Brenda said. "Marty had to leave so sudden. I came over and straightened up a little and cleaned out the refrigerator."

"It's just fine—beautiful and sparkling clean."

Her eyes filled with tears. "I should have done more, but I've just been so worried about Bill."

I wasn't quite sure how to answer that one. What if he really had left her? But I tried to sound confident.

"Oh, the house is just great, and I'm sure Bill's all right," I said. "He'll drive up that road anytime now—looking for you."

Brenda didn't seem too reassured. She gulped and stepped out on the back porch to look at the children. "Let Lee Anna swing now," she told Billy. She lifted a hand to her face, and I wondered if she hadn't wiped away a few more tears.

Sam came back down the stairs, still looking solemn behind his glasses, and Brenda came inside.

"Sam, where do you think Bill can have gone?" she asked.

"Bill was always one to take care of business," Sam answered. "I have a feeling he's gone to see someone about a cattle deal or something."

Brenda looked doubtful. "Maybe so. But I don't know of anything he had hanging fire."

"How about the wheat harvest?"

Brenda's face brightened. "Oh, that could be it!"

"I'm sorry to be so dumb," I said, "but exactly what would Bill be doing about the wheat harvest? Hiring extra help?"

Sam shook his head. "No, custom cutters."

I'm sure I looked totally blank at that, because he smiled. "There are people who make a living harvesting grain, Nicky. A combine—which is the machine used to harvest wheat and other types of grain—is so expensive that most farmers don't bother to buy one anymore. They hire a custom combiner, also known as a custom cutter. He'll own several combines and big grain trucks. He hires crews for them every summer. They start in Texas along in May and move north through Oklahoma, Kansas, Nebraska—even on into the Dakotas and Wyoming as the summer goes on. Some of them wind up cutting wheat in Canada in September."

Sam turned to Brenda. "Who do they usually hire?"

"Big Sam and Bill changed last year," she said. "The new man was from over at Walters. His name is in the computer."

"Computer?" Sam raised his eyebrows. "I hope they've got a good user's manual."

"Oh, I can run the computer," Brenda said. "That's the one thing I'm good at around here. I enter all the information on the computer for them."

She gave a proud smile and headed toward the office off the living room.

Sam would have followed her, but I stopped him.

"Do you really think some wheat cutter will know where Bill is?" I spoke softly so that Brenda wouldn't hear me.

Sam's eyes dodged away, refusing to meet mine.

"I hope so," he said.

"You don't think Brenda's right? That he's gone off?"

Now Sam looked straight at me.

"I feel sure that's not right," he said. "Bill might leave Brenda, but he'd never leave the ranch."

"Never is a strong word."

"It's not strong enough to express how Big Sam and Bill feel about the Titus place," Sam said. "Big Sam was ten when his family lost the farm in the middle of the depression. Frankly, my grandfather made a better living as a carpenter in Oklahoma City. But Big Sam never gave up the idea of getting back to the farm—to this particular farm. He worked like a dog, saved his money, put off marrying until he was in his thirties, lived hand to mouth, and worked my mother like a slave, all so he could own this particular piece of land. It's like holy land to him."

He reached up and straightened his glasses. "He raised us on the sanctity of the Titus land, and Bill was the one he indoctrinated most successfully. Bill really believes that the world will come to an end the day the Tituses don't own this particular patch of rocks and grass."

Then he shrugged. "I guess Big Sam almost made me a true believer. I escaped by the grace of laziness."

"You're not lazy, Sam. If you've escaped—"

An eerie sound echoed through the house, a tortured cry somewhere between a moan and a shriek.

"Brenda!" Sam said.

We both turned and almost ran to the office.

Brenda's blond head was bowed against the computer screen, and she was sobbing. Her arms were around the monitor.

"Brenda!" I cried. "What's wrong?"

I knelt beside her and put my arm around her. She leaned back in her chair, the picture of hopelessness, and gestured toward the screen she had been embracing.

A message stood out in green letters.

"Brenda or Sam," it said. "I don't know who will find this, but don't worry. I've got to get away for a few days. I just don't know which way to turn. Don't worry. Give the kids a kiss and tell them Daddy will be home soon."

The last word stood on a line by itself:

"Bill"

THE AFTERNOON turned into a nightmare.

Brenda was hysterical. Sam was made of stone. The kids were upset and whiny. The wind was blowing, and the temperature outside was nearly 100.

I tried to cope with Brenda, the kids, the wind, and the heat, but I didn't know what to do about Sam.

I kept going over and over Bill's note in my mind. How could Bill have left? How could he have abandoned Brenda when she obviously depended on him so much? Or was that it? Had her dependence driven him round the bend?

But those beautiful kids? How could he leave them—even for a few days?

I grew very angry with Bill. How dare he behave in such an irresponsible fashion?

This thought made me mad at my own husband. How had he had the gall to assure Brenda and me that Bill was somewhere around the ranch, that Bill would not have left? Had it simply been wishful thinking?

Little of this came through as rational thought that afternoon. All Sam and I did was run from one crisis to another.

First the children heard Brenda crying, and they ran in and joined in the wailing. Sam and I helped Brenda into the downstairs bedroom and got her to lie down with a cold cloth. Then we enticed Billy and Lee Anna into the kitchen with a promise of cookies and juice. Lee Anna responded by wetting her pants. Thank God for the wonderful acrylic-covered floors.

We barely had Brenda's wailing down to a low moan when a cheery "Howdy!" sounded from the back door and a plump gray-haired lady bounced in.

"Hai, Sa-um," she drawled, pulling each word out into two syllables. Then she grabbed me in a bear hug. "Ah'm Nora Rich, and yer Nicky. Mary Martha thought you were wonderful and jes right for Yung Sa-um. And look at those purty curls and those big brown eyes!"

It took me a second to realize that Mary Martha was Sam's mother, Marty, but if I showed my confusion, Nora Rich ignored it.

"I saw the car go by when I was in town," she said, "and I grabbed a dish of King Ranch Chicken out of the freezer. I'd hate for Mary Martha to have to cook the minute she got back from the hospital." She managed to make "grabbed" into "gray-ab-ed" and "ranch" into "ra-inch."

God, I thought. Just what we need. A caller. There was a jar of instant tea sitting out on the counter, and I offered to make her a glass.

But Nora Rich didn't linger. She saw we were in a mess—though Sam and I didn't volunteer any information about Bill—and found out that Marty was still at the hospital. She gave us each a sympathetic pat and bounced out again.

"Yew call me!" she hollered. "Take ca-ure!"

Before she could get out of the drive, a red pickup came racing into it. It dodged around Nora Rich's sedate sedan and roared up to the house, skidding to a stop in a cloud of dust and gravel out by the machine shed. A young guy with dark, wavy hair jumped out and almost ran up the back walk. He wore tennis shoes and jeans. Period. No shirt. No hat. No socks.

Frankly, he was built. And his tan would have knocked out Southern California.

The beach boy jumped onto the back porch without bothering with the steps and stood in the open door.

"Yew Yung Sam?"

For a moment I thought he was speaking Chinese. Or maybe Tarzan Thompson had sent him. But Sam seemed to grasp his meaning, because he nodded. I conquered the urge to stick my head between them and say, "Me Nicky."

It seemed this hayseed he-man was Johnny García. He had been checking on the cattle and doing other Titus Ranch chores since Bill had gone to Oklahoma City.

"But I got to quit," he said, flexing a bicep.

Sam frowned. "We sure need you right now," he said.

Johnny García shook his head. "I hate to let yawl down, man. But I've got a slot on a harvest crew. They've already been on the road a week. I'm losin' overtime ever minute I'm sittin' here."

Sam grimaced. "I know you can't turn it down," he said. "What do we owe you?"

He and Johnny García hashed out salary and cattle care over glasses of iced tea. Johnny seemed a bit taken aback when Sam pointed out that he'd have to wait a couple of days on his check.

"I can't write checks on the Titus Ranch accounts, and Bill—" Sam's voice faltered. He swallowed and went on. "Bill's out of pocket for a couple of days. I'll have to get the check to Oklahoma City for my mother to sign."

I took the kids in the living room and read them a story from a book I had found in the office bookshelf, but Sam's remark had raised another specter.

Who could run the ranch?

I had always thought of the ranch as a home, but it was a business, too. A big business, I realized, remembering the news Sam had gotten from the banker. His dad owed the bank $420,000, and it was due within a few days.

Wow.

Did the ranch have $420,000?

With Bill gone, Sam couldn't even write checks to pay some insignificant sum to a hired hand. Could Marty? They might have to get Big Sam declared incompetent, get a court order to keep the ranch operating.

If Bill didn't show up quick, if Big Sam didn't regain consciousness—well, Sam could wind up in the middle of a legal hassle.

We might not be going back to Germany in two weeks.

We could spend weeks in small-town America. My emotions took me back to the eighth grade, and panic set in.

Then Sam came into the living room. He stood firmly. His face was blank, but the way he hunched over and leaned on the back of the couch displayed exasperation.

"Nicky," he said, "go ask Brenda if she can sign Titus Ranch checks. Johnny says she's been writing them."

I got up and started for the bedroom, and Sam reached out and took my hand as I went by.

"Thanks," he said.

He obviously didn't want to deal with Brenda in her present state of near hysteria. I felt sorry for him, I guess, since I didn't want to deal with her, either. But the request seemed to calm Brenda. It seemed she had been performing many of the functions of a bookkeeper, and she did have the authority to sign checks. She got off the bed and went in the office, then checked the number of hours Johnny García had said he worked, figured the state, federal, and Social Security taxes owed, entered all the figures in the computer, and gave him a check.

Then he and Sam went off in his truck to take a final look at some cattle whose health Johnny was concerned about, and Brenda began to collect her purse and her kids.

"I'll go home now," she said.

She refused to stay overnight, and she refused my offer to stay with her.

"No, we don't have a guest room," she said. "We just haven't fixed one up because my mother would probably move in."

She made the remark calmly, but it struck me as revealing. She hadn't made any other complaint or explanation to cover up her mother's behavior. Brenda's defenses were dropping fast.

She drove carefully down the road and turned toward her house.

"Bill Titus," I said aloud. "I've never seen you, but I might clobber you if we met face-to-face."

I WAS slamming clothes out of the suitcases and into the closet upstairs, still mad at Bill, when I heard the back door. I recognized Sam's quickstep pace up the stairs. He was still doing his Great Stone Face act.

"I'm ready to smack your brother," I said. "What kind of a jerk is he? How could he do this? Leave Brenda. Leave those kids? Leave your mom? Leave you!"

I think I had expected Sam to smile or otherwise show that he appreciated my loyalty. But his expression didn't change. I just saw his Adam's apple move, and I realized he was gulping down his emotions again. The thought almost scared me.

I tried to sound calm. "You know, Sam. You might be better off if you yelled and screamed a little about all this."

He had looked so stony that his reaction surprised me. He smiled. "That's your department," he said.

Then he pulled me close. I hugged him back, and we stood there in the middle of the floor, clutching each other.

"I've got too much to do to take on the yelling and screaming," Sam said. "You'll have to handle it. And right now you're going to have to help me do my part, too."

He released me and started for the bedroom. "The first thing is to change clothes."

"Sure. I've been hanging everything up."

"Did you bring your close-up lens?" he asked.

"I brought the macroadapter. Why?"

Sam kicked off the boots he had worn on the plane and began to unbutton his shirt. "If I'm going to turn into Sherlock Holmes, I've got to have a Watson."

I thought that one over. "For you I'll even grow muttonchops," I said. "But just what are you Sherlocking?"

"I want to look at the scene, at where they found Big Sam and his truck. Down at Wolf Creek." He stepped out of his khaki slacks and looked at the clothes I had hung in the closet. "Maybe I can find out what really happened."

"But what about Bill? Don't you have any idea where he's gone? Can't you find him and haul him back here to take care of his family?"

A look of pain flashed over Sam's face.

"I need some physical evidence before I can do that. I might find it at the scene."

He pulled a pair of jeans out of the closet, then hauled a semiworn straw western hat off the shelf. "Look at this. Imagine Mom hanging on to it."

He put the hat on. It fit perfectly. He turned around and faced me, wearing the hat and jockey shorts. "I really need help, Nicky," he said. "Would you mind changing clothes and coming with me?"

I put on jeans and got my close-up lens.

When I went downstairs, Sam was in his mother's car, his eyes shadowed by the hat and hidden behind his glasses again. I barely got myself and my camera equipment inside before he pulled off.

The scene of Big Sam's accident was nearly five miles away, on what Sam called the Wolf Creek Ranch. It did not border the original family holdings and was all pasture-land, he explained. It was on the other side of the mountain, a mountain owned half by the Tituses and half by Viola Mae Humphries. The Wolf Creek Ranch had a good water supply and was used for stock grazing, particularly in the summer, when ponds sometimes went dry.

I knew enough about rural mores to behave properly when we came to a gate. I got out and opened it, then closed it after Sam drove through. Beyond the gate was a road that looked like two parallel cow paths. Sam drove his mother's car along it slowly, bumping and jolting, heading toward the mountain.

"Wouldn't it have been better to bring that truck that was back at the house?" I asked.

"I didn't want to bring it back to the scene. And I need to go over it before it's moved again."

"Oh." That was the first moment I had realized that the truck at the house was the one that had fallen on Big Sam.

After a few minutes, Sam stopped the car, even though we had not come to the end of the road. We were definitely into the mountains. Big boulders and scrubby trees stood on either side. We were surrounded by cattle, great black beasts with white faces.

"Come on," Sam said. He got out, opened the back door, and took out a paper sack. I realized it was the one he had picked up at the lab in Oklahoma City. He started walking on down the road, looking at the ground.

I collected my camera and started to open the door. A giant cow was looking at me, its nose almost touching the glass.

"Sam!"

I had to call twice before he looked around. Then he came back. He came right up to that giant cow and yelled at it. "Git!" He whacked it on the nose.

The beast snorted and wheeled. She ran back up the road a few feet, then stopped beside her calf.

Sam opened the door for me. "Just shove 'em out of the way."

"Do they bite?"

"Only if you taste like hay. They're not carnivorous. Come on."

I followed him over a little hill and around a big boulder. Then I stopped and gasped.

"Oh, it's beautiful!"

A small lake, perhaps two hundred feet across, lay at the foot of a mountain. Giant boulders rimmed its opposite shore, and cottonwoods shaded a sandy patch on our side.

"Beautiful," I repeated.

"We used to swim here. When we got a little time off."

Sam resettled his glasses, then walked toward his left, still studying the ground. I followed.

"Step right where I step," he ordered. In a minute he stooped down. "Here. This is what I'd hoped to find."

He had come to a spot where water seeped out from under a rock, soaking an area about five feet across. Tire tracks marked the mud.

"Here, Nicky. This is what I need photographed," he said.

I looked at the tracks. They looked identical to me. "Looks as if your dad drove in here twice."

Sam shook his head. "I think one set belongs to Bill's truck. He and Big Sam always used to buy the same kind of tires."

I got out my trusty Leicaflex and twisted the close-up lens into place. Sam brought out a ruler. He laid it carefully beside the tracks, and I photographed both sets.

Then Sam pulled a sack of plaster of paris and a plastic dishpan from the paper sack he'd been carrying. He mixed the plaster with water from the pond and made casts of both sets of tracks.

For thirty minutes Sam went over the area. He located footprints, more tire tracks, then some stains I realized must be blood. He measured the depth of the tracks. He took little samples of dirt from various spots and put them in plastic sacks he labeled with masking tape. He made more plaster casts. He marked the sites of the various tracks and the bloodstains with sticks, sticks he had flagged with bits of tape. I took pictures of the entire scene.

He was so intent that I kept quiet and sat on a rock out of the way except when instructed to photograph or label something.

When I heard a rock rolling, I thought it must be a cow. But Sam stood up and looked at the hill behind me.

He didn't speak, but his eyes dodged toward me, then looked steadily toward a spot over my left shoulder.

I turned my head and looked, too. An armed man was standing behind me.

SEVEN

WE ALL STARED.

After my first moment of surprise I decided the man wasn't threatening us—yet. The weapon he held was a shotgun, and he wasn't pointing it. He was cradling it in the crook of his left arm.

But his right forefinger was on the trigger.

He was a squat, swarthy man with straight black hair. Only an inch or so of forehead showed between his hair and a set of bushy black eyebrows. His square face was at once wrinkled and lumpy, as if he'd been molded of Silly Putty, then squished. He wore a faded pair of blue jeans covered with black streaks, a blue work shirt—also covered with black streaks—and a pair of tough-looking round-toed boots that showed a few spots of brown leather between the black streaks.

I kept quiet after an initial squeak, and Sam, damn him, didn't turn a hair.

"Hello," he said. "Do I know you?"

"I don't know you," the armed man answered. "So I 'magine you don't know me. What you doin' here?"

"Just checking around," Sam answered. "I'm Sam Titus's son."

The man scowled, pulling his eyebrows into a single line of bristles. "You ain't Sam Titus's son," he said. "I know Sam Titus's son."

"You know Bill. I'm Sam junior."

The man took a few steps toward Sam and looked him over deliberately. His finger was sliding up and down the trigger, and I was holding my breath. I still didn't feel any confidence that he wasn't going to shoot us.

Then the stranger eased his hand away from the trigger and lowered the shotgun.

"I guess you got that Titus look," he said. "But not quite as mean around the mouth as the old man."

He pointed the barrel of the shotgun toward the ground. I took a deep breath, and I could see Sam's shoulders relax.

Our new acquaintance spat tobacco juice, then held his hand out to Sam. "I'm Dewayne Cudjoe," he said. "I'm the pumper on the Humphries' lease. Or I was."

Sam introduced me, and the two of them found boulders to lean against. They faced each other.

Cudjoe gestured at the ground Sam had been examining so carefully. "What y'up to?"

Sam shrugged. "Well, I'm a cop by profession. I just had to see the scene of Big Sam's accident with my own eyes. I guess you heard about it."

Cudjoe nodded. "Yeah. Tough. I was workin' over on the number-two well when I heard the ambulance go by. They come out here a-flying. How's your daddy doin'?"

"Not too good," Sam said. "I guess you're out this way a lot if you're the pumper for the wells on Viola Mae Humphries' place."

"Well, I was the pumper." Cudjoe raised his eyebrows and grimaced with his mouth. "I 'bout got fired over this lawsuit Miz Humphries filed. I'm still workin' for Slaughter Brothers, but I'm not a pumper."

Sam pulled a pocket knife out of his jeans and picked up a stick. He spoke mildly. "If you're not the pumper, what are you doing out here?"

"I guess I'm tryin' to figure out why I'm a fifty-eight-year-old roustabout." Cudjoe's mouth grew tight. "I swear

I handled that lease right according to Hoyle. I don't know what caused that leak.''

Sam whittled a shaving off his stick. "The well that caused the trouble—that the one right over the Humphries' fence?''

Cudjoe jerked his head to indicate direction. "There was some trouble with another one earlier, but now the problem's with the one 'bout a quarter of a mile over there," he said. "I was over there nosing around, and I seen your car come in. Never seen anything in here but the truck before, so I thought I'd check.''

"I appreciate you taking an interest," Sam said.

It was turning into a regular neighborhood-watch meeting, but I was still annoyed about being scared by a shotgun. So I spoke up. "Just what is a pumper? And why do they carry guns?''

Cudjoe and Sam both looked at me.

"A pumper is the man who takes care of producing oil and gas wells, Nicky," Sam said. "About the gun— Well, I never heard of a pumper carrying one before today.''

He looked at Cudjoe, and the older man snorted. He addressed his answer to Sam. "I been carrying the shotgun in the truck since we had all this problem over the supposed fire danger at the heater treaters. My boss don't believe me, but there's something funny about it.''

"I've been gone a long time," Sam answered. "I don't know anything about the lawsuit.''

"It stinks." Cudjoe spat again, then stood up. "I'll be goin'. Fool lawyers'll probably tell me I shouldn't be speakin' to y'all outside a court.''

He and Sam shook hands again. Cudjoe's face was cloudy as he picked up the shotgun and once more rested it in the crook of his arm.

"Listen," he said to Sam. "People are goin' to try to tell you I had it in for your daddy. We argued all the time—I admit it. But that don't mean I wanted anything bad to happen to him.''

He scowled, then spat expressively.

''There's some I couldn't say that about,'' he said. ''Bein' shifted back into a roustabout is no joke at my age. And I don't like bein' told to be glad I've got any kind of a job.''

Sam and I strolled back up the hill with Cudjoe and watched as he trudged away, winding in and out among the giant boulders along the base of the mountain. Now I could see some sort of oil-field tanks across the pasture, along with the up-and-down motion of a pumping well.

''What do you think of him?'' I asked Sam.

''I don't know. Farmers and ranchers always tend to look at the oil-field workers with a jaundiced eye, and the oil-field workers feel the same about farmers. That doesn't mean anything.''

He started back toward the pond. ''Come on. Let's get that evidence and head on home. If we get back to the house, we can check the truck before dark. And Mom may call.''

After an hour crawling under the truck in the machine shed, taking pictures with a floodlight improvised from a desk lamp with a 200-watt bulb, I was whipped. And starved. A lot had happened since we had that hamburger at The Hangout.

''I'm just about out of film,'' I said. ''Two more frames. I hope you're nearly through.''

''Just the tire.'' Sam hauled the muddy flat tire, the one his dad had supposedly been trying to change, across the truck bed and close to the light.

I leaned against Marty's sedan. ''Sam, there's one thing I've been curious about. You've collected all this evidence—dirt samples, tread marks, and such. You've done a complete scene-of-the-crime investigation. Now what are you going to do with all this stuff?''

"Send it to the lab."

"What lab? You're not a policeman here. You have no authority. Do you think that sheriff—Tarzan Thompson—will send it off for you?"

"Not likely." Sam concentrated on the tire.

"Then what?"

He ran his hand carefully over the tread. "You've heard of the 'old boy' network, haven't you? That's why we dropped by the Mills Lab as we left Oklahoma City. I knew Jack Mills in college. He'll do it for me for half price."

"Oh." I stood up. "I'm totally whacked out, Sam. What are you looking for on that tire?"

"Luckily, Bill stopped that kid at the Co-op from fixing the flat." He stopped. "Here it is."

"Here what is?" I looked over his shoulder.

"What caused the flat." Sam fingered the head of a nail that fit neatly into a crack in the tire's tread.

"Hand me those pliers," he said.

Using the screwdriver and the pliers and making appropriate stops for me to use my last two frames of film, Sam pulled the nail free and looked it over. It was a tough item—at least four inches long, with a broad head. It was shiny and perfectly straight.

I looked at it as seriously as Sam, but it didn't send me any messages. Finally, I shrugged. "I can see how a thing like that would cause a flat."

"Right. Very interesting."

Sam carefully tucked the nail into a plastic bag and began to make out a label.

I was confused. "What's so interesting? What do you see on it?"

"Nothing," Sam answered. "Not a scratch. Not a speck of mud."

I was too whipped to ask any more. Sam sighed then, and I realized he was exhausted, too. After all, we'd come halfway around the world since the phone rang—way on the other side of the Atlantic—on a few hours of sleep in a Dallas motel.

It was eight o'clock and nearly dark when we went back in the house. Nora Rich's casserole tasted wonderful, along with a salad from Brenda's lettuce and tomatoes. I called Brenda and repeated our offer to stay with her. She sounded teary, but she declined.

I was putting dishes in the dishwasher and thinking about a shower when the phone rang. Sam took it in the office.

I could hear his deep tones for five or ten minutes. Then he reappeared in the kitchen. His face was carved of oak.

"That was Mom," he said abruptly. "They ran a CAT scan on Big Sam this afternoon."

I couldn't guess at the report from his face. "And?"

"No change. The doctors say there's nothing to do but wait and see. Mom's talking about moving him back to the Holton Hospital, or even to a nursing home."

I went to him and put my arms around him. He slid an arm around my back, but his mind seemed to be far away—at least as far as Oklahoma City.

"That could be dangerous," he said. Then he stroked my hair absentmindedly, kissed me on the forehead, and moved out of my arms.

"I'm getting in the shower," he said. He walked back to the circular stairway and started up it. On the first turn, the one that left him looking at me, he stopped.

"I can't go back to Frankfurt," he said. "Not in two weeks. Maybe not ever."

He walked on up the stairs, his tread heavy, leaving me standing in the kitchen with two empty arms.

Rebuffed.

Forty-eight hours earlier we had our lives all planned out. Another fifteen or twenty years traveling the world as army officer and wife. A couple of bright, good-natured kids.

Sam rising to head of the CID. Me winning fame and fortune as a talented photographer. Then retirement in some cosmopolitan spot with a terrific climate, spectacular scenery, and a whiz-bang cultural life.

Now we were back on the ranch—a spot Sam had sworn he never wanted to see again—baked and buffeted by the interesting climate of the Southwest, surrounded by the exciting scenery of the prairies, and stimulated by the cultural thrills of Small Town, U.S.A.

And Sam was considering staying. Talk about culture shock.

I heard the water start upstairs. Just as well, I thought. I needed a few minutes to get my head on straight. Then I'd be ready to argue this out with Sam.

I walked through the living room and went out on the front porch. The dramatic clouds were gone, and a brilliant full moon floodlit the wheat field in front of the house. The wind had dropped to a breeze, as Sam said it nearly always did at sundown, and the temperature had become mild and pleasant. I sat in the porch swing and rocked back and forth gently.

Big Sam could be dying, but I had heard plenty of horror stories about people turned into vegetables by head injuries. He might face years, years of living death.

A tear ran down my face at the thought, but I confess my grief wasn't just for Big Sam. His injury could turn into living death for Marty, for Bill, and for Sam and me, too.

Bill had disappeared. I had asked Sam if a missing-persons report would help, but he had said no. The note left in the computer indicated that Bill had left of his own accord. The authorities would not be interested in helping find a guy who had a fight with his wife and took off.

The ranch was a big operation. Just what part did Brenda and Marty play in it as a business? Were they co-owners? I knew all that would have to be sorted out with lawyers and court orders.

And what about the $420,000 owed to the bank?

I could see that Sam would have to stick around long enough to get all that settled. And I could see it might take more than his two weeks of emergency leave.

But surely Bill would be home soon. He was the rancher in the family. Why did Sam say we might never go back to Frankfurt?

I contemplated living in Holton—eating at The Hangout, cashing checks at Brock Blevins's bank, chatting with Millard and Maynard Smith down at the Co-op, trading casserole recipes with Nora Rich, explaining to Brenda the best way to wipe her nose, and wearing jeans tight enough to compete with Bobbi Baker.

On the other hand, I could look at birds with Viola Mae Humphries, and Marty obviously could teach me a lot about art.

And I could watch those clouds and their shadows on the hills and try to photograph the effect of the moonlight rippling through the wheat.

I considered the moonlight, the wheat, and the ripples for a moment.

Then I pulled out a tissue and blew my nose. No, army posts often had surroundings that were worse than Catlin County, but they had one advantage. The people were my kind of people. They might not be any smarter or richer or nicer than the natives of Holton, but they had traveled, and they knew about living in foreign countries, and they were ready to welcome newcomers and new experiences. And they were ready to help each other.

They were not narrow-minded, small-town bigots like the ones who had made my life miserable in the eighth grade.

I'd have to explain all this to Sam.

Suddenly I longed to feel his arms around me. If he'd only hold me, he wouldn't need to say anything. I'd be able to make him understand. He wouldn't need to make love to me. Just hold me. Let me hold him. With my face buried in his chest, I'd be able to explain how frightening all this sky was, how scared I got when I looked at the eerie beauty of that vast wheat field, how strange all the people were—and how strange he had become, silent and closed in, not at all like the guy I married.

I loved him. I wanted to help him, and he was pushing me out.

I moved slowly and carefully, as if my emotions would spill if I jiggled my insides. I went inside and locked the front door. I turned out the living-room lights, checked the kitchen, and locked the back door. Then I walked up the circular oak stairway, still moving as if I were balancing a water jug on my heart.

In the bedroom the lamp was dim, and Sam was already in bed, his back to the door. I went around the bed, pulled off my sneakers, and lay down facing him.

Sam didn't move. The silence in the house grew thick. Then it was broken by a low rumble.

Sam was snoring.

I leaned over him. He snored again. I kissed his forehead, and he jumped all over and opened his eyes. "Huh!"

Then his eyes focused on my face. "'Night, Nicky," he said.

His eyes shut.

I was alone.

"Well," I told the vanity mirror a few minutes later, "he talks in the morning, too."

But that next morning wasn't a good time to talk. It was barely beginning to be light when I heard the telephone.

I don't know how long it had been ringing before I woke up and staggered into the studio to answer it.

"Damn, these country folks get up early," I muttered as I reached for the receiver. "Hello."

"Sam! Young Sam!" It was a woman's voice.

"I'll get him. Just a minute."

"It's a fire! Tell him quick!"

Sam was thrashing around by then, and I called to him. "Hurry, Sam! Someone wants to tell you about a fire."

He rushed in and grabbed the phone. I ran from the window to window, looking for flames. I saw no sign of a fire, but I didn't find that reassuring. I scrambled into my jeans and a T-shirt. If we were going to flee, I didn't want to do it in the slinky black nightgown I'd pulled out the night before.

"I'll be right there," Sam was saying. He dropped the receiver and hurried to pull on his jeans. "It's the Wolf Creek Ranch," he said.

"Where your dad was hurt?"

"Yeah. That was Nora Rich. Her husband saw the fire. He's gone over to get the cattle out."

"Did she call the fire department?"

Sam looked at me and shook his head. "There's no fire equipment closer than Holton," he said. "The volunteer fire fighters will come, but there's not a whole heck of a lot they can do."

We ran out the back and this time Sam jumped into the pickup. I barely made it through the right-hand door before he backed out of the machine shed.

The truck's tires threw gravel as he started down the drive. "You'll have to stay out of the way," he said.

I'm always sarcastic on the way to a fire before the sun is up. "Yes, sir, Captain Titus," I answered. I gave a snappy salute.

The ride to Wolf Creek was terrifying, but by the time we had driven a few miles, the sky had grown lighter, and I could see smoke rising. Then we topped a rise, and I saw a line of flames. They weren't high, not a raging inferno, but the line went up hill and down dale, extending over the horizon.

"Damn!" Sam muttered.

Then, to my amazement, we heard a siren.

I looked back. "Sam, the fire trucks are here!"

"I guess they got some new equipment."

Two fire trucks, both of them tankers, came around us, but one of them turned off on a road that went to the right. It wasn't going toward the fire. Sam followed the first truck and swung in at the gate I remembered from the previous afternoon. It was already open.

The fire truck shut off its siren and slowed, and after we were inside the gate, I saw why. Cattle from the Wolf Creek pasture were coming toward us, and the firemen evidently thought the noise might stop their progress. I could see headlights, and I realized that Nora Rich's husband must be leading them toward the gate with his truck.

Sam swung the truck in beside the pickup. A man in a billed cap scooted across the seat and looked out the window at us. He looked as scrawny as Nora had looked plump.

"Young Sam, there's a bunch more over in that southwest corner!" he said.

"I'll get 'em," Sam said, and we went bumping across the pasture. The line of flames slanted down toward the road, and our path took us toward them.

Cows and calves had bunched up in a corner of the fence. Smoke was drifting around them, but they seemed to regard it placidly.

Sam stopped short of them. "I'll get out and cut the fence," he said. "You drive the truck on through the gap. The cows have been fed from this truck, so I think they'll follow it."

He jumped out, and I slid over into the driver's seat. Sam slammed the door, and I could see his reflection in the side

mirror as he dug in the metal tool chest right behind the cab.
Then he ran past the window.

"Stay in the truck!" he shouted over his shoulder.

I looked at the truck's controls. Manual transmission.
Thank God I had driven a Volkswagen for years. But what
pattern did the transmission follow?

Already the cattle were surrounding the truck. I could see
Sam in the headlights. He had reached the wire fence, and
a huge cow was butting him in the back. Sam ignored her
and began to work on the wire.

Then a cloud of smoke came between us. I looked back.
The flames were closer. A lot closer. They were so close that
now they did look like a raging inferno.

Then I heard a "Hi! Hi!" and looked back at Sam. He
had cut the fence and was herding the cattle through the
break.

That break in the fence looked mighty good. I eased the
clutch in and slid the gearshift into what I thought was first.
I let the clutch out and goosed the gas.

The truck choked and died.

EIGHT

I DON'T RECALL SWEARING. I imagine I did, but I turned the key over in the ignition at the same time. The motor caught again. It was the most beautiful sound I'd ever heard.

I eased the clutch out and gave it a little gas.

Same song, second verse. It choked and died.

This time I peeked over my shoulder while I cranked the key. I wished I hadn't. The inferno was getting really close. The motor caught.

I took a different guess at the position of the truck's first gear, and I eased out the clutch. The motor died again.

I looked forward. I could see Sam coming toward me, but there was a herd of cattle between us.

Sam was yelling, "Leave the truck! Leave the truck!" He waved his arms, motioning for me to come on.

I put my hand on the door handle, ready to jump out, but as I turned, my knee whacked into something.

The emergency brake. Sam had set the emergency brake when he got out of the truck. I released it and cranked the key.

The clutch did its job. The truck jerked and jumped, but the motor kept running, and the pickup moved forward.

I had been concentrating so hard on the gears and clutch that I nearly ran over Sam.

He had kicked a whole herd of cattle—or at least a dozen or so cows and calves—out of his way and almost reached the truck, but I had my head down, and I hadn't seen him. When the pickup finally began to move, I looked forward and saw his face looming out of the smoke, oozing toward me like a ghostly hood ornament. I gave a startled yelp, but

Sam merely sidestepped smartly and swung into the right-hand door as it went past. I followed the cattle, bouncing and jouncing across the rocky pasture while he hung on.

Sam didn't say anything until we were through the gap in the fence and out on the road and away from the thickest smoke. Then he spoke very calmly. "Just head on down the road slowly," he said. "The fire isn't likely to jump the gravel."

I was shaking. I would have been delighted to hand the truck over to him. But before I could say, "You drive," or any of the other witty remarks I was considering, he was gone. He simply stepped off the truck and disappeared into the smoke. I looked back at where I had been and, like Lot's wife, nearly turned into a pillar. The flames seemed to be all over, though the smoke was being blown away from me.

The cattle kept following the truck along the road, back toward the gate where we had left Mr. Rich with a similar bovine bunch, and I drove along slowly. Sam walked behind them, keeping any stragglers moving.

In a few minutes one of the fire trucks came toward us, sailing out of the smoke like a tugboat. Men were walking beside it, wearing small water tanks on their backs and spraying the grass in the ditches.

The cattle and I were moving slowly, and soon Sam joined me. He just walked up and climbed through the right-hand door. I offered him the driver's seat.

"You're doing fine," he said. He was irritatingly calm.

Eventually we reached a gate on the right-hand side of the road, where Mr. Rich was waving his arms and herding the cattle into a pasture. Nora Rich, wearing a tight pair of polyester slacks and a loose shirt of some kind, was on the bed of a truck behind him, offering fire fighters ice water out of a giant can.

I got out of the truck gladly and readily agreed to go back to Nora's house with her.

"We'll fix these fellers a little snack," she said. "Road ought to stop the fire pretty quick."

Back at Nora's I cleaned up a bit—it's wild what smoke can do to a head of curly black hair—and tried to help. Nora pulled packages of cinnamon rolls and bacon out of a seemingly bottomless freezer on her back porch, and she set me to thawing bacon in the microwave oven, then frying it in two big electric skillets. She plunked the rolls into the oven to warm.

Her kitchen belonged to a devoted cook. She owned a blender, a mixer, a double oven, a deluxe can opener, a food processor, and dozens of other appliances. The hall closet, I discovered when she sent me for a platter, was filled with enough china, silver, and tablecloths to feed thirty-five people a sit-down dinner. I wondered if she had a large family that held lots of reunions.

She also had an ample supply of paper plates, paper napkins, and paper towels, and she set about cooking breakfast for twenty or so drop-in guests with zest.

In about forty-five minutes the guests started to arrive. They may have smelled like smoke and sweat and have been so grimy most of them refused to come inside, but I thought they were beautiful. Even Millard and Maynard Smith looked good. They seemed to be in somewhat better moods than when we had parted from them outside The Hangout.

Nora set up a buffet on the patio in back of her newish brick house, and the fire fighters washed their hands to the wrist at the backyard hose, then wolfed down everything in sight.

I circulated through the crowd with a coffeepot in each hand. The conversations were pretty interesting.

"That big cow just jumped over, and the water caught her right in the patootie. Ran like a rabbit."

"My wife's gonna kill me. I got dressed so fast I just now realized I'm wearing my new pants. Had 'em on to go to the movies over to Lawton last night, and I just grabbed 'em up in the dark.''

"I barely caught the truck. I couldn't get the damned old pickup to start, so I ran down the road and thumbed as y'all come by. Thought Ol' Harry was gonna run me down.''

"Well, seeing you jumping around in the lights like that would make anybody hit the ditch. I thought it was a beached whale. Thought we'd found ourselves a prize cat-fish a-floppin' in a bar ditch.''

It was all good-ol'-boy stuff except for a rather odd little piece of conversation from a couple of the men who had driven in on the second tank truck. That was the truck we had seen turn off before it got to the fire but which later showed up on the scene. They were drinking coffee while they refilled the truck from the Riches' farm pond. I came up behind them, sneaking around in my sneakers, and they apparently didn't hear me.

"I don't know what her problem was,'' the taller one said. "She's gettin' crazier than a bedbug.''

"Than a loon, you mean,'' his short partner said. They both laughed.

"Yep, she is plumb cuckoo,'' the first one said. They laughed again, and he went on. "Every bird in Catlin County couldn't empty that spring-fed pond. I don't know what she's savin' the water for. But I'm not fightin' over it.''

"Yeah, she's cuckoo,'' his partner replied. "It can't be PMS—not at her age.''

They snickered, and I coughed so they'd know I was there. Both of them jumped, and there was an embarrassed clearing of throats as I refilled their cups.

"Sure is good coffee,'' one assured me.

"I was really glad to see you guys show up,'' I answered.

Both of them shifted their feet and looked at the ground. Then the short one spoke. "We'd of been there sooner, but we stopped to top off the tank truck. First place wouldn't let us use the pond. Luckily, we had plenty of water, as it turned out.''

The only thing missing from all this was Sam. After another half hour he finally showed up, following a car driven by Sheriff Tarzan Thompson.

Every inch of Sam was covered with smoke, dirt, ashes, and gunk. The sheriff, on the other hand, was sparkling clean. His shirt displayed creases the laundry had provided, and he wore a white hat that would have graced Hopalong Cassidy. In the current grimy crowd he was definitely a sight.

I hadn't asked anybody where Sam was, since I didn't want to appear to be a worried wife, but I was really glad to see him. I edged up to him, but we had no time for any personal greetings. We were immediately surrounded by the fire fighters.

Questions such as ''All out?'' and ''Whadja find out?'' echoed over the crowd.

But the questions dried up when a second pickup pulled in. It was loaded with esoteric bits of pipe, giant wrenches, and other strange tools, and the sign on the door read SLAUGHTER BROTHERS OIL COMPANY.

The firemen fell into an uneasy silence as Dewayne Cudjoe got out of the truck. He wasn't carrying his shotgun, but he stood as if he were ready to shoot off his mouth. It was hard to get the verbal drop on Tarzan Thompson.

''You sorry bastard,'' the sheriff said. ''You sure took your time gettin' here to cut that line off.''

Cudjoe's eyes became as beady as raisins. ''I pretty well ignored your speed limits,'' he said, ''but it just flat takes forty minutes. Believe me, I wish I was closer so I could figure out who's been tampering with that well.''

''Tampering!'' Tarzan yelled out the word. ''Tampering! That's stupid.''

"I know it's stupid!" Cudjoe yelled back. "I also know I've checked every connection, and that saltwater line is not leaking. Yet there's salt water all over the ground."

"Salt water? Salt water!" Tarzan's voice was derisive. "Salt water never caused a fire."

Cudjoe dropped his eyes and his voice. "I said it was stupid," he said sullenly.

Then he turned to Sam. "I'll call the office and tell them what's happened. They'll be in touch with you." He got back in his pickup and started the motor.

Before he could pull out, Nora ran over with an offering of coffee and a cinnamon roll. Her action seemed to make Cudjoe look more hangdog than ever, but he accepted the coffee, swung the truck around, and drove on off. I felt sorry for him. Pipe was sticking out the back of the pickup, and the weight dragged the truck's back bumper down; even his pickup seemed to have its tail feathers drooping.

Thompson drew himself up and began to orate. "It's that same problem Viola Mae and the Tituses have had for a year or more, and I hope they sue the pants off of 'em," he said.

Mr. Rich spoke up. "That right, Sam? The fire started over at that well?"

Sam reached over and took a plastic cup I was handing him. "Looks like it," he answered. "I'm no fire expert."

Thompson snorted. "It doesn't take an expert to smell a gas leak. Anybody with a nose can tell when that raw gas is burning."

Mr. Rich leaned between Sam and the sheriff. "That right, Sam?" he repeated. "I didn't smell nuthin'. D'you smell gas?"

Sam nodded. "Seemed like I did."

"See!" Thompson crowed. "You Tituses and Viola Mae Humphries need to make that oil company eat dirt!"

Sam sipped his coffee and shrugged. His attitude seemed to exasperate the sheriff.

"I don't get you, Sam!" Thompson was almost shouting. "How can you keep so calm after that bunch burned your pasture, nearly burned up your cattle? You gonna do something about it?"

Sam gave him a look that could have quenched a bigger fire than the one we'd just seen, but his voice remained calm and even.

"It's pretty hard to burn up cattle as long as there's a fence they can break through. As for the burnt pasture, what am I supposed to do?" he asked. "As a lawman, you're surely not suggesting I go punch somebody—assault them over this?"

"Naw, what would that gain? But you might join Viola Mae's lawsuit."

"I can't. My mother might want to do that, but I have no standing in the matter."

"No standing?" Thompson sounded confused.

Sam shook his head again. "I'm not a partner in the Titus Ranch. Just Big Sam, Bill, Brenda, and my mom. They'll have to decide what to do."

Then Sam turned away from Thompson. "Oh, Nora," he said. "Have you got any more of those rolls I see people eating?"

He walked through the crowd without seeming to notice it was there and helped himself to one of Nora's cinnamon rolls.

Tarzan Thompson was left sputtering. Sam's refusal to be pushed into making wild statements about lawsuits and irresponsible oilmen had left the sheriff as flat as stale beer. He seemed relieved when his radio made a noise, and he grabbed the excuse to drive off in a cloud of dust and sirens.

Sam stationed himself near the trucks pulled up in the yard, and I noticed that he managed to speak with every man as the fire fighters left.

When the crowd thinned out to the Riches, Millard and Maynard, Sam, and me, Sam unbent enough to sit down on the patio wall for one last cup of coffee.

He turned to Mr. Rich. "I'll try to get those cattle out of your pasture before the day is over," he said. "I should be able to put them on the Fields place."

I heard a low rumble.

Maynard Smith stepped forward. "You Tituses—" he began.

Before the older man could launch a tirade, Sam swung around without even standing up and cut Maynard off at the pass.

"Maynard," he said, "I'm too tired to argue over this. Right now that land belongs to the Titus Ranch. I expect Big Sam intended to work on it a bit before he turned cattle on it, but today it's the only place I can put that herd."

Maynard stopped talking and scowled. Then he took a deep breath and plunged on. "Clear back when I was a kid—"

Sam spoke again in that firm voice. "And I don't want to hear any more about how my grandfather acted back in the depression," he said. "My grandfather went broke just like everybody else in Catlin County."

Maynard growled again. He knit his brows and opened and shut his mouth. "You—you," he began.

Sam bit him off again. "You said it all yesterday."

Sam's firm reaction seemed to stymie Maynard, so Millard came to the fore.

He smiled slyly, squinting his foxy eyes in the morning sun. "Sure, Maynard, that's enough," he said. "Young Sam has a real sense of family. He knows what's gone on over the years between the Fields and the Tituses. He'll stand by what his father said."

"But, Millard," his twin said plaintively, "if he puts them cattle on our place—"

"What goes on can come off, Maynard," Millard smiled more slyly than ever. "July first is comin', and we'll have our say."

He raised his hat to Nora Rich in a gesture that parodied politeness. "Miz Rich, thank you kindly for the breakfast. We appreciate it."

He turned toward a rusty pickup. "Come on, Maynard."

Maynard pouted. "But, Millard—"

"Come on!"

Maynard muttered, but he allowed his brother to stuff him into the driver's seat of the truck, and the Smith brothers drove off. But the truck stopped with an angry jerk at the end of the gravel drive, and Maynard leaned out the window.

He shook his fist at Sam. "I'll get you yet!" he yelled. "I won't forget how the Tituses treated the Fields. I told Big Sam the same thing, and I'm repeatin' it."

The truck moved off down the road, and Sam, the Riches, and I watched its departure silently.

I was the first one to speak. "Is he dangerous?"

Sam sipped coffee again. "I never heard of him actually hitting anybody."

Mr. Rich stood up. "Naw. He ain't dangerous, Miz Titus. He's all talk."

It took me a moment to realize I was Miz Titus.

I still had my doubts about the Smith brothers. "This is the second time he's acted like that in twenty-four hours. I can't help wondering if he really means it." I looked at Sam. Actually I was wondering if Maynard could have been the

one who attacked Big Sam, but I hesitated to say anything
in front of the Riches.

"When he was a young man he fought a bit," Mr. Rich
said. "In those days he wasn't so mouthy. Then he got older
and figured out that nobody wants to hit an old man. That's
when he began to talk so wild."

Sam slid his arm around my shoulder. "He might bust
somebody in the snoot, Nicky, but he's not tricky enough to
carry out any kind of a plot."

That comment stopped me. It seemed to me that getting
busted in the snoot might be exactly what had happened to
Big Sam. So what did Sam mean by the second part of his
statement?

I tried to read his mind. He must mean that Maynard
might have slugged Big Sam but the older rancher wasn't
smart enough to make it look as if the truck fell on his victim.

That made sense. But the other twin, Millard, was smart
enough—and sly enough—to fake the accident. I opened my
mouth to explain this, but Sam gave me another squeeze.
This one clearly said, *Shut up.* Then he added one that said,
Please.

I kept my mouth open a moment. This was Sam's turf. If
he didn't want to talk in front of the Riches, it was his pre-
rogative. I wouldn't cross him.

Sam stood up. "Nora, you sure know when a guy needs
food," he said.

Nora smiled all over her plump face. "I always think
things look better after you've had something to eat," she
said. Then her face grew troubled. "But about Maynard—
I think he's the least of Sam's problems right now, Nicky.
I'd be a lot more worried about—well, Sam's dad and the
fire and that lawsuit. When is Bill coming back from Oklahoma City?"

Sam sipped his coffee before he answered. "Bill's gone." He made it sound permanent.

Nora Rich stared. "Gone? What do you mean?"

Sam used his most curt voice as he described Bill's departure and the note Brenda had found in the computer.

Nora Rich rolled her eyes and covered her mouth with her hand.

"I declare. I declare," she said. "It just defies all reason."

That pretty much summed up the way I felt about it, too.

"So I guess any decisions on the ranch will have to be made by my mom," Sam finished.

"What do you think your mother will do, Sam? About the lawsuit, I mean?" Nora asked.

Sam drank the last of his coffee and meditated a long moment. "I'll talk to her, but I don't think she's too interested in this just now, Nora. I haven't even told her about Bill yet."

Nora clucked. "I know, I know. She's just concentrating completely on your dad."

"Seems as if everything's happening at once," Sam said.

"Well, you're due some pressure from Viola Mae on this lawsuit," Nora said. "She's turned into a fanatic about those oil wells. Plumb ungrateful, I call it. They supported her all those years."

She turned to me. "Nobody else around here has any wells, you know. Everything else they drilled was a dry hole. We all envied her for years."

Sam put his cup in a garbage bag at the corner of the porch. "I'll try to talk to Viola Mae later," he said. "But first I've got to move those cattle. Then I've got to explain all this to my mother, and I'd better do it face-to-face. Viola Mae's at the bottom of my list for today."

When we got back to the Titus house, however, Sam discovered that he was at the top of the list for Viola Mae.

We hadn't locked the back door as we ran out before dawn, and when we came into the kitchen, we saw a note taped to the cabinet with a piece of black electrical tape.

"I told my lawyer we'd be in his office at 2 p.m.," the note read. "I'll come by to pick you up at 1 o'clock. Ta! Vi H."

"Damn." Sam said.

He walked up and down the kitchen a minute, then sat down on the bench beside the back door and pulled off his boots. "Damn," he said. "I've got to move cattle and then go to Oklahoma City. I can't fool with Viola Mae."

"Then call her and tell her you can't go."

"She doesn't have a phone."

"No phone?"

"Nope. Scares the birds, or something. You'll have to go over there."

"Me!"

Sam nodded serenely. "Yeah. We can't just not show up. She's an old family friend, after all."

"But why do I have to do it?"

"You can go over there while I'm moving cattle." Sam looked down and patted the dirty T-shirt he wore.

"I guess I'd just as well wear these clothes. There's no sense in taking two showers." He put his boots back on.

"But, Sam! I've barely met Viola Mae. I can't discuss family business with her."

Sam walked to a wall telephone and pulled a sheet from a notepad hanging beside it. "You were telling me you're an official member of the family now. I'll draw you a map."

Five minutes later I had my instructions. Go to Viola Mae's place, five miles around the mountain. Pull in the drive. If she isn't at the house, try the barn across the road.

"She calls it her lab," Sam said.

If she isn't at the lab, honk the horn and hope she shows up.

"Take a book," Sam said. "You may have to wait. That's all there is to it," he said firmly. Then he kissed me. Convincingly.

"Thanks," he said. "Moving the cattle will take a couple of hours, so you have plenty of time to take a shower before you go." He took his hat from the church pew by the back door and went out.

In a few minutes I saw him drive past the house in the blue pickup, hauling a trailer with high, slatted slides. He waved at me as he drove by.

Some bird was singing in the side yard. That was the only sound except for the rushing wind.

All alone on the prairie. Suddenly I felt a certain kinship with Sam's pioneer great-grandmother.

NINE

AN HOUR LATER I was whizzing along a gravel road in Marty's tan sedan with Sam's map beside me. The mountain behind the Titus Ranch house was now on my left, and I was swinging around it. Ahead I saw one of Sam's landmarks, a standing rock rather like a miniature mesa. This was known as the Chest of Drawers, Sam had told me.

I saw the reason for its name immediately. The layers of the rock formation cast horizontal shadows that made it look as if it had drawers. A few scrubby trees on its sides could even be interpreted as drawer pulls.

Past the Chest of Drawers the elevation dropped, and the vegetation grew thick and green. This was a swampy area, Sam had said, and was the feature that had turned Viola Mae's farm into a bird sanctuary. As if to punctuate the point, a white water bird of some kind flew in front of the car and landed near a small pond, then stilt-walked along the edge on the sticks it used for legs.

I drove on slowly. A gravel road marked by a small sign appeared on the left, just where Sam's map had showed it would be. HORSE PEN CREEK BIRD SANCTUARY, it read.

The road led back toward the mountain, through the swampy area. I turned in and drove on the length of a city block. An animal—an opossum to judge by its naked tail— ran across the road in front of me. It stopped at the edge of the road, cowering.

I brought the car to a standstill so I could look at the animal. The poor thing may have felt he had no place to hide. The land on both sides of the road was swampy, and the whole area was completely flat. The biggest thing to break the flatness was a blue-gray mailbox that was sticking up at the right-hand edge of my peripheral vision.

A mailbox? Wouldn't a mailbox be back where I turned off?

I turned my head and looked. That was no mailbox; it was a giant bird.

It stood on stilts like the white bird's, but it was much larger and was a grayish blue color. It had a white head, and a jaunty black feather hung down its back. Its breast was speckled. If I had had the nerve to stand up beside it, its head would have been even with my rib cage.

The bird ignored me. It turned with immense dignity and, lifting its spindly legs high, slowly walked away from the road and into the swamp. Impressive.

When I looked back at the opossum, it had disappeared. I drove on.

The road branched in about a quarter of a mile, with a dirt track leading toward a wooded area on the left. The right-hand branch was marked HEADQUARTERS, and I drove another quarter of a mile before I saw the house. It was a rock house, apparently made of native stone, and it nestled in front of a grove of cedars—real cedars, not the scrubby kind that Sam had objected to in the pastures of the Fields place.

A blue metal building stood beside it, and a small green pickup and a bright yellow school bus were parked next to the building. The bus was labeled FIRST BAPTIST CHURCH OF HOLTON. A cardboard sign in the back window proclaimed BIBLE SCHOOL and gave the dates.

I breathed a sigh of mingled relief and annoyance. If a Bible-school class was visiting Viola Mae's operation, she was sure to be there. But she might be unable to talk.

I parked the car and got out. Everything was quiet. I peeked in the door of the big blue building. It was a true laboratory; I could tell by the smell of formaldehyde and the microscope at the end of one table. It was filled with work-tables, storage cabinets, lab equipment—even a refrigerator and two freezers, a chest type and an upright. But it was empty of people. I checked my watch. Ten-thirty. I hoped Viola Mae and the Bible school would be back soon. I climbed back in the car. A big outdoor thermometer on the outside of the blue building told me it was ninety-four degrees hot.

In about ten minutes I heard the clatter of children's voices and saw a group of youngsters coming from behind the cedar grove. They trooped toward the house and lab, some running ahead and some falling behind and all of them talking like mad. Two women trailed along behind the group, herding the kids as inexpertly as I had herded cattle earlier.

Viola Mae's cropped dark hair was surrounded by children, and as she drew nearer, I could see she was smiling her sweet, dimpled smile. She wore a khaki vest that was covered with pockets, and her binoculars hung around her neck. She waved at me happily, then stopped and clapped her hands. The children gathered around.

"If you can be quiet, we'll visit the lab," she said. "But it echoes inside that building, so we must keep our voices down, or we won't be able to hear. People who can't stop talking had better stay outside."

She wheeled around and waved to me again. "Come with us, Nicky," she said.

I wasn't sure I could stop talking, but I joined the group and followed her inside the blue building.

Several small cages stood on tables along the back wall, and one of them held a black bird with a brown head. Viola Mae picked the cage up, and the bird hopped about frantically.

"I'm sure you recognize this, after our tour," she said. "It's one of those nasty cowbirds I've been trapping."

"What will you do with him?" one child asked.

"I'll study the parasites he carries, both internal and external," Viola Mae said. "Parasites are things such as mites and fleas."

"Yuck."

Viola Mae smiled her dimpled smile, and her blue eyes twinkled. "I agree. Yuck. That's why you shouldn't touch wild birds. They do carry mites. You can even get diseases from them."

"But you touch them, Miz Humphries," a freckled boy said.

"Yes, but I use rubber gloves and other precautions." Viola Mae put the cage down and moved to a cabinet with shallow drawers. "Now these," she said, "are skins. I prepared all these myself." She smiled proudly this time, and she opened the top drawer.

It was filled with birds of all colors and sizes. They were all dead.

Somehow that came as a shock to me. I had been picturing Viola Mae, with her sweet smile and her binoculars, as looking at live birds and making notes on their behavior in a polite little notebook, perhaps turning away modestly from their mating habits. It seemed monstrous that she would have drawers filled with dead ones.

They were stuffed, of course. She picked up a bird of a lovely blue color. "An indigo bunting," she said, beaming. "One of my best specimens."

She held it out and let each child look at it closely, warning them not to touch it. Then she turned around and placed it on my open palm. "Isn't it lovely?" she said. "I can't help bragging on that one a bit."

It was a mockery of a beautiful little bird. It was only a few inches long, and its feathers were a vivid blue, with slightly darker feathers on the wings. Its tiny bill was a shiny black, and tufts of the cotton that stuffed it protruded from its tiny eyes. A string attached a tag to a tiny foot. HORSE PEN CREEK BIRD SANCTUARY, WOOD DUCK LAKE, it read. JULY 15, 1988.

I could see its value to a scientist at once, of course, but I found it sad. I didn't know what to say, so I simply held it and looked at it. It weighed hardly anything.

The freckled boy seemed mystified, too. "If you're going to stuff birds," he asked, "why don't you put them up on branches or something? Why do you keep them in drawers?"

Viola Mae gave a cheerful chuckle, not unlike a chirp. "These are not meant to be displayed as mounted birds are," she said. "These are study skins. They're used by scientists. You see"—she paused to pick up another bird—"each one is tagged with the location and date it was taken. Students can use them to examine the birds closely. This one was taken at Horse Pen Creek Sanctuary on October 10, 1970. Can you tell me what it is?"

A chorus of voices rang out identifying it as a dove.

"My dad shoots those," the freckled boy said proudly.

"Huh!" a dark-haired boy said. "My grandma says you shouldn't shoot doves. They're the Lord's birds. It says so in the Bible." He glanced back smugly at the Bible-school adult, a plump woman in a blue pantsuit. His freckled classmate flushed.

For a moment I thought we'd have a theological dispute, but Viola Mae handled the disagreement smoothly. "Yes, Jimmy, that's an interesting folk belief about doves," she said. "And in the Bible it does say the Holy Spirit descended on Jesus in the form of a dove. Some people have interpreted that to mean that doves are special birds, but others have thought that passage referred to the Holy Spirit only in a spiritual sense."

She smiled again, showing her dimple. "Your teacher can correct me if I'm wrong, but I think that's a topic on which doctrine indicates we should each follow our own conscience. There are a lot of points in life upon which we must each decide what's right and what's wrong. Sometimes we have to do it on the spur of the moment.''

The dark-haired Jimmy looked as if he might argue the point, but Viola Mae quickly whisked the dove and the indigo bunting back into their drawer. ''Who has a question?'' she asked.

After a discussion on what to do if you found a baby bird, the children were led away to their bus, calling their thank-you's from the windows as it drove away.

Viola Mae waved sweetly. Then she turned to me. ''There's nothing like a morning with a Baptist Bible-school class to make you long for a can of beer,'' she said. ''How about it?''

I laughed. ''Talked me into it.''

She went back into the lab, opened the refrigerator, and pulled out a six-pack of Coors, the cans still wrapped in their cardboard box. ''Darn things,'' she muttered, struggling to pull the cans out of their packaging. ''But I won't buy the ones that use plastic rings. They kill birds, you know, because people throw them away and birds get them hooked over their heads. But these boxes could kill *me* someday. I may die of thirst trying to get a little Colorado Kool-Aid.''

I reached over as the first can came out of the box. ''Here. No one is allowed to graduate from an American college without learning how to cope with beer-can packaging.'' I pulled my own can out, then opened the refrigerator to return the other cans to the shelf.

I found myself looking at another dead bird, lying flat on its back in a plastic sack. Gross.

I quickly slammed the door and turned to my hostess. ''Sam sent me over to say he won't be meeting you at the lawyer's office this afternoon.''

Viola Mae's face twisted into a picture of disappointment. "Oh, dear," she said.

I quickly rehashed Sam's reaction to the fire and explained his reasons for refusing to get involved in the lawsuit.

"So, you see, he has no legal standing in the matter," I concluded.

"Yes, but morally—" Viola Mae looked up at me and smiled. "I won't harangue you, Nicky. Let's go over to the house. At least we can get acquainted a bit."

Instead of a living room, Viola Mae had an office. The main room in the rock house had a couch and a coffee table, true, but it was dominated by a gray metal desk. A home computer sat on the desk, and an old rolling typewriter table beside it held a typewriter. Over the desk was a row of framed diplomas, and I stopped to look them over. Viola Mae, it seemed, held several degrees—bachelor of science, master of science, another master's, and a doctorate.

I waved at the wall. "I don't think people around here understand your credentials and background. This is very impressive."

Viola Mae laughed and sat down on the couch. She stretched out her short legs and put her feet, tennis shoes and all, on the coffee table. She pulled up the legs of her dull green slacks.

"BS, MS, piled hip-deep," she said. "It's too hot to impress anybody."

Then I realized that Viola Mae's house and lab were wide open to the summer heat. While there was a window air-conditioning unit in the office-living room, it was not turned on. The windows were all open, and a hot, dry wind was blowing in, ruffling the edges of weighted papers on the desk and depositing dust on the books. I wondered why she didn't turn on the air conditioner, but I didn't like to ask.

She swigged her beer and motioned toward the diplomas. "I was a science teacher to begin with," she said. "Then, when I turned thirty and realized I wasn't getting anywhere, I started on the advanced degrees in biology. I taught at Southern Oklahoma State University before I retired."

"Where is that?"

"Oh, it's just about thirty miles from here. My parents died about the time I started teaching there, and I was able to live here and commute. That's when I got the idea about starting the bird sanctuary." She dimpled her cheek. "Really shocked your father-in-law."

"Oh?"

She nodded and ran a hand through her close-cropped hair. "Yup. Of course, historically man has seen the land and all nature from the viewpoint of Genesis. You know, that God created all the world to benefit mankind. That's always been Big Sam's viewpoint."

"But not that of a scientist?"

She shook her head vigorously. "Nope. The ecologist sees man as just another competing species. Of course, I'd known Sam since we started first grade together at Horse Pen School. He was absolutely appalled that I would allow my land to be unproductive, to simply sit there and not produce income." She smiled.

I contemplated her statement for a moment. "But it wasn't unproductive for you, was it?" I asked. "It must have given you the basis for your scientific papers and studies."

Her dimples deepened. "Exactly! I didn't need the money from the ranch nearly as much as I needed the research material."

"Which reminds me... What was that king-sized bird I saw wading along the road as I drove in? A big bluish gray guy."

Viola Mae sat forward abruptly and smiled all over her face. "You saw one of my great blue herons!"

"Well, I don't know my birds, but that name sure describes what I saw."

My hostess was beaming. "I'm so pleased that you saw one of them. They've been incidental visitors before, but this is the first year they've nested at Horse Pen Creek. I'm terribly excited about them."

She leaned back on the couch and gulped beer from her can again. "A lot of the neighbors—including Sam—find my excitement over a mere bird hard to understand."

I gestured down the road the bus had taken. "They must have come around, since I see the community is taking advantage of the special facilities you can offer. You handled the children beautifully."

"I didn't teach thirty years without learning a little something, even though I didn't teach children that young." Viola Mae allowed her dimple to be a bit complacent. "I remember Young Sam when he was that age. I could tell he was really bright. I tried to recruit him as a scientist, but I was afraid Big Sam would tie him to the land."

I could feel my lips tighten. "Well, he wasn't able to," I said.

Viola Mae looked pained. "Oh, I didn't mean—" Then she smiled again. "Poor Big Sam. He's always been so bullheaded that nobody can get along with him. Except Marty. He's quarreled on a regular basis with all the neighbors and with his boys and with his business associates and with his fellow county commissioners."

I blinked a couple of times while that one soaked in. "County commissioners! Fellow county commissioners?"

Viola Mae drank beer. "Oh, yes. Hadn't Young Sam told you his daddy is a county commissioner?"

"No. And I'm amazed. If he's so quarrelsome, how did he get elected?"

She dimpled. "Well, it was a fluke. Old man Henry died in office, so they had a special election. Caught the local politicians unawares. It came up to the end of the filing period, and nobody had put in papers for the job but Millard Smith."

"Millard Smith!"

Viola Mae took a gulp of beer and nodded as she swallowed. "You've met him already, I see. One of the Smith brothers. Anyway, at the last minute somebody must have gotten on the telephone, because Big Sam dashed down to the courthouse and filed right at five o'clock."

"Giving Millard another reason to dislike him."

"I don't think that bothered Sam much. Anyway, Sam turned out to be real fair—equally obnoxious to everyone. He's also obnoxiously honest. He was able to run for re-election last time without even drawing an opponent."

I shook my head and drank some of my own beer. "I liked Big Sam when I met him, but he was rather on the gruff side. Not at all what I'd expect a local politician to be."

"Well, they have Brock Blevins for smoothness."

"The banker?"

Viola Mae nodded. "I see you've met him."

"Well, yes. And he's certainly smooth. How many commissioners are there?"

"Just one more. A man named Harley Bolinger. He's more on the traditional commissioner pattern. A wheeler-dealer."

"What will happen now? I mean, the doctors don't think Big Sam will be able to... to handle his own affairs, much less handle county business."

Viola Mae pushed her short dark hair back again. "I hadn't thought about that. They'll have to do something, and I sure hate the thought of leaving it up to Brock and Harley."

"Why?"

She drank her beer thoughtfully. "Well, it's sort of hard to put your finger on. But the last time I talked to Sam he was real upset—upset over some sort of county business."

She pulled her feet off the coffee table and sat up straight. "Maybe I ought to pass the word about that on to somebody in authority, but he didn't really tell me anything. Maybe he told Marty the whole story."

"What did he say?"

Viola Mae leaned forward and widened her eyes wisely. "I was over at the SOSU library—"

"So-sue?"

"S-O-S-U. Southern Oklahoma State University. We all call it that. It's better than So-So U." She smiled. "Local joke. Anyway, I was over at the SOSU library, and I ran into Sam. He was looking something up in the state statutes. I was surprised to see him—after all, there's a county law library in Holton."

"Did he say what he was after?"

"Not really. Just asked me to keep my mouth shut about seeing him and muttered something about county business."

I drank from my beer can. "Well, if he was a commissioner, county business was his business."

"Yes, but why sneak into the SOSU library to look something up when he had a law library closer and had a district attorney he could ask for advice?"

We drank beer and mulled that one over.

"Well, it probably wasn't important," I said. "And as you said, maybe he told Marty or someone else."

Viola Mae gave one of her dimpled smiles. "Yes, he and Marty have always presented a united front. I introduced them, you know."

"No, I didn't know."

"Yes, Marty was a new history and social studies teacher at Holton High School. This was in the early fifties. I was teaching there then. They went off to Wichita Falls and got married in 1955. She taught until the boys came along. Young Sam and Bill are just two years apart."

I drank the rest of my beer and stood up. "I've got to get back," I said. "Thanks for the refreshments, and where do I put the can?"

Viola Mae bounced to her feet. "I'll take it," she said. "I recycle, of course." She grinned. "Holton would be disappointed if I didn't."

She put my beer can next to hers on the coffee table and followed me out to the car. Her binoculars still dangled over her plump bosom, and her blue eyes sparkled. She was delightful, I thought. She had plainly picked the role of town eccentric for herself, and she seemed to be having fun acting it out.

"Thank you very much for the beer and conversation," I said. "I needed both."

Viola Mae beamed. "Come back anytime, Nicky. If I'm not here, I'll be out with my traps."

I guess I looked blank, but she laughed.

"Oh, you didn't hear about my current research project, did you?" she said. "I'm trying to kill two birds with one stone—metaphorically—by trapping cowbirds. This provides the specimens for a study I'm making of internal and external parasites in cowbirds, and it's helping to reestablish a habitat for Bell's vireos, which are often victims of cowbirds."

"Then you don't simply let nature rule the sanctuary?"

"Not when it comes to cowbirds. They're nasty creatures. They lay their eggs in other birds' nests, you know, just as the European cuckoo does."

I nodded. "I have a lot to learn about Oklahoma birds, I guess." I climbed into the car. "I have a lot to learn about

Oklahoma in general. This morning I nearly burned up Big Sam's pickup, not to mention myself, in that fire.''

Viola Mae gasped. "Oh, that's the last thing I'd want!" she said. "What happened?"

I laughed and described my problems with the gears and the emergency brake. "It came out all right," I said. "Neither the truck nor I was barbecued. But it was a bit scary."

Viola Mae looked at me closely. "Well, that should have given Young Sam a good idea of what his daddy and I have been fighting with the oil company about. I know that after he talks to Marty the Tituses will want to join the lawsuit."

"I really don't know," I answered. "I always thought an oil well was a good thing to have on your land. Of course, you hear about oil spills and such."

She pursued her lips. "Well, the income has always been enough to offset the threat of pollution on my land," she said. "But since this new production company bought the wells, I've had nothing but trouble."

I climbed into the car, and Viola Mae waved as I headed back down the road. The talk with Viola Mae had been interesting as well as enjoyable. I'd found out a bit about my in-laws' courtship, learned a few local jokes, and made the interesting discovery that Big Sam was involved with local politics.

If Sam thought his dad had been attacked—and he'd convinced me that it was true—the political angle could open up the suspect list to everyone in Catlin County. But what about Big Sam's trip to the college library for apparently secret research? I resolved to tell Sam about that immediately.

It was nearly noon as I turned into the road to the Titus house. I hoped Sam was back from moving cattle. I'd fix us sandwiches while he cleaned up, then tell him what Viola

Mae had said while we ate. Next we could head for Oklahoma City and his report to Marty.

But when I drove up to the Titus house, the pickup and
the big trailer were still missing from the machine shed. A
different truck, a beat-up tan pickup, was sitting in the drive
behind the house. Its cab was empty.

I parked Marty's car in the shed and stared at the tan
truck. I knew I'd seen it before, but I'd seen a lot of pickups in the past twenty-four hours. Whose was it?

In answer to my question, the back door of the house
swung open, and a thin woman with masses of bleached-
blond hair stepped out on the porch.

"Yoohoo!" she yelled. "So you're finally home!"

It was Brenda's mother, Bobbi Baker.

"Damn," I muttered. Then I forced my mouth into a
smile. "Hi, there!" I called.

She met me at the back gate.

"Sam's not with you?"

"No, he's moving those cattle, the ones that were in the
pasture that burned."

"Well, I want to talk to him." She turned and went back
toward the house. "I'll wait," she said firmly.

I went after her, discovering that I was extremely annoyed. I didn't like her demanding attitude. "What do you
want to see Sam about?"

"I'll talk to him direct."

She swung the kitchen door open and waltzed into the
back hall.

"How did you get in here?" I asked. "I know I locked
that door."

She didn't even look around. "Oh, I know where they
keep the key. Remember, I looked for it yesterday. Under
the geranium." She gestured toward the counter, and I saw
a key. It was on a metal ring and was marked by a red plastic logo that read CO-OP.

I reached over and picked up the key.

"Well, while Sam and I are staying here without Marty, I think the key won't be under the geranium." I put the key in the pocket of my jeans.

Bobbi whirled around and looked at me. Her eyes narrowed. Then she laughed. "Oh, really?"

I nodded. "Yes, really. If you want to wait for Sam, you're free to, of course."

She laughed again. It wasn't a pleasant sound. "Thanks a lot, honey."

"However," I continued, "Sam is going to come in here in high gear, because he wants to go to Oklahoma City. So I think you're wasting your time."

"Wasting my time!"

"Yes. I suggest you leave a message with me, and either Sam or I will get back to you tonight."

Bobbi looked at me a long time, then gave a humorless chuckle. "You little turd," she said conversationally.

That one was hard to answer. I certainly didn't think I could match her in a name-calling contest.

Finally, I stepped back and gestured toward the door. "If you don't like the company, you're free to leave."

She looked me up and down. "Well, if you don't beat all," she said. "Little Miss Namby-Pamby. Butter wouldn't melt. And it turns out you can hand it out just like your snooty mother-in-law."

Suddenly she leaned her face close to mine. "Bitch!" she said.

I tried hard not to jump or to let my gaze drop. I reached behind me and felt for the door handle. I turned it and stepped aside, then swung the door open. "Sorry you have to leave so soon," I said. "I'll tell Sam you came by."

Bobbi barked out another unpleasant laugh. "Not only a bitch, but a rich bitch. Trust the Tituses. They know how to pick 'em. Just like Bill went for that Brenda, though why she wanted him, I don't know. But she did. 'Hold out, baby.' That's what I told her. 'Hold out.' That's the way to catch a Titus. Look at the old man. Slept with ol' Viola for years, but when it came to marrying—oh, no. Left her flat and took up with a cool customer, a gal who can turn rain into sleet just by lookin' out the window. You're gonna fit right in the family circle, honey bun."

She moved into the doorway, and I allowed myself to hope she was leaving. But she turned for one last shot.

"Tell your husband, the iceman—my God, you make a pretty pair!—that I'm not buying that crap about him not knowing where Bill is. He'd better get hold of that good-for-nothin' creep and tell him to get his butt home. Because Bill's got my money tied up—my inheritance—and he'd better get home and straighten the whole thing out, or I'll sue him and Brenda and take everything they've got."

She stepped back, shaking her fist, and nearly fell off the step. "And don't think I won't do it!" she yelled.

She whirled and discovered herself almost nose-to-nose with Sam, who was standing on the patio behind her.

Sam stood his ground. It was Bobbi who jumped all over. "Goddam it! Where'd you come from?"

She looked at Sam, then looked back at me. It was amazing to watch. I had the feeling I could read her mind. She automatically considered vamping Sam, and she gave him a tentative smile. Then she began to wonder how much of her tirade Sam had heard, and the smile froze on her face. Meanwhile, she was caught between Sam and me, and neither of us was saying a word.

Finally, she just pushed by Sam and went out the back gate, leaving it swinging.

Sam closed the gate, then watched as she drove off down the drive, spraying gravel.

TEN

WE FINALLY LEFT for Oklahoma City at one-thirty, after only two more problems. Both came via the telephone.

First I called to check on Brenda and her kids. Her "Hello!" was eager, and her reaction to my name was dispirited. I felt terribly sorry that I wasn't Bill.

She had just put Billy and Lee Anna down for naps, she said.

"You try to lie down, too, Brenda," I advised.

"Oh, no! I've got to get some work done around here," she said. "I'm washing the kitchen windows, and the curtains are in the dryer. I can get a lot done while the kids are out of the way."

I thought about that one for a minute. Emotional crises can bring on odd reactions, but I hadn't expected spring cleaning. However, that wasn't what I had called about.

"Do you have a key to this house?" I asked.

"Yes."

"I'm taking the one from under the geranium with me, and I wanted to be sure you can get in if you need to."

There was a moment of silence; then Brenda took a deep breath. "Did my mother come over there?"

I paused. I hadn't planned to describe our fight. "Yes. But she's gone now."

"I've told her and told her not to bother Marty. I think moving that key is a good idea. Tell Marty hi." Brenda hung up.

Almost immediately the phone rang. A brisk female voice was on the other end of the line. "Mr. Slaughter is calling from Houston for Sam Titus," it said.

"Mr. Titus can't come to the phone right now," I answered. "May I take a message?"

"Just one moment." Click. I was on hold. The kitchen clock ticked off forty-five seconds before a new voice, a masculine one, came on the line. "Is this Mrs. Titus?"

"Yes."

"Well, we want to make a settlement on the fire as quickly as possible. We don't want any more unpleasantness."

"I can have my husband call you."

"We'll have a man out there later this afternoon."

"We won't be here."

"Now, Mrs. Titus, as a partner in the Titus Ranch, you can see—"

I broke in at that. "You're talking to the wrong Mrs. Titus, you know."

He paused. "Who is this?"

"This is Mrs. Sam Titus, Jr."

"Oh. I didn't know there was a Sam Titus, Jr."

"Oh, yes. He's alive and well and taking a shower because he's been fighting fires and moving cattle all morning. And as soon as he's dressed, we're leaving for Oklahoma City on important family business. So you leave your number and he'll call you tomorrow."

"Then Sam Titus, Jr., is a partner in the Titus Ranch?"

I sighed and decided to be cautious. "Just leave your number, Mr. Slaughter."

He finally hung up, and I reprogrammed my brain into the unfamiliar housewife mode. I made bologna sandwiches and thought about all the many reasons I should stay away from Oklahoma City.

I was worried about Brenda, and I could go by and check on her, I thought. I should go to the grocery store and do a bit of stocking up. I should stay by the telephone in case Bill called. I could fix a nice dinner and have it ready when Sam got back. I could wash the clothes we had worn to the fire.

I could keep Bobbi Baker from breaking and entering. And I could avoid being an unwilling witness to an emotional scene when Sam told Marty that her son Bill had disappeared.

All the reasons except the last one were excuses, of course. Sam knew how much I loved hanging around the house, and the list wasn't going to fool him for a minute.

I didn't see how Marty could continue her facade of stoicism when she heard about Bill's desertion. I dreaded watching the wall crumble.

But I wasn't allowed to get out of the trip. Sam looked at me as if I were crazy.

"I need you to drive," he said.

"To drive?"

"Yes, Nicky. We need to take Mom's car back to her. I'll drive the pickup, and you drive the car. We'll have to make do with the pickup around here. Or I can drive the grain truck if we have to go different directions." He allowed one side of his mouth to grin. "After all, you've had your baptism of fire in that pickup."

I hit him with a slice of bologna.

But Sam and Marty made the emotional part of the day easy for me. As soon as we got to the hospital, before we went into the intensive-care waiting room, Sam stopped at the desk and located a private room he and Marty could use to talk.

"You go down to the cafeteria for about twenty minutes," he told me. "Then come back. And maybe you could bring some coffee."

It worked. When I came back, Marty and Sam were sitting knee-to-knee at a table. Marty was holding her face in her hands, but when she looked up, her eyes were dry.

We exchanged hugs. "Oh, Nicky, I'm sorry you've been thrown into all this mess," she said.

"I'm glad to be here," I answered. And I was surprised to find that I was telling the truth. As much as I had dreaded the situation, I wouldn't have wanted to miss something that was certain to have so much emotional impact on Sam.

Not that Sam was showing the effects of emotional impact. His eyes were like topaz, hard and cold, and his face was oak again. When I sat down with Marty's coffee, he stood up and paced up and down the little conference room.

"Sam said you'd talked to Brenda," Marty said. "How is she taking all this?"

"Energetically. She was washing windows."

Marty shook her head. "Poor Brenda. She's a compulsive cleaner, anyway. She'll scrub all the paint off her house, I guess. I imagine she's already spring-cleaned our place."

"Well, it looked real nice when we got there."

Marty smiled. "Let her, if she wants to. She'd been dying to get her hands on it ever since we finished the remodeling. I'm much too messy for her taste. I'm sure she has all the magazines in piles according to size and all the shoes lined up by color in the closets."

She sipped the coffee I had brought. "This is good, Nicky. Thanks." Then she turned to Sam. "I guess you'd better look for Bill, Sam. We have to find out what happened to him."

Sam was studying a picture of mountains and meadows that hung behind the table. It was generic art produced for conference and treatment rooms. Soothing but pretty blah artistically. He reached out and straightened it slightly.

"There's always hope, I guess," Sam said. "Maybe he took off for Dallas."

"No." Marty's answer was firm. "There's no point in kidding ourselves."

Sam turned around, and they exchanged level glances. Then Sam spoke. "I thought I'd look for his pickup."

His mother nodded. "It would be hard to hide."

"But not impossible," Sam answered.

Did they think the police would put out an all-points bulletin for Bill's truck when they wouldn't for Bill himself? I was all confused, but no one had ever mentioned one point I thought was vital to looking for a runaway husband. So I spoke up. "Did Bill take much money with him? Did he have credit cards?"

Sam and Marty looked at me. Marty looked amazed, and Sam looked even stonier.

Then Marty's face crumpled, and tears came to her eyes. "Dear God, I hope so," she said. "I only hope so." She put her head in her hands, and this time she sobbed.

I was absolutely astounded. What had I said? Why had she reacted this way? She had evidently taken the news of Bill's defection calmly. Now she broke down as they discussed the best way to look for him.

Sam shot me a look that would have killed a lesser woman. But I didn't understand what I had said that was wrong.

At this moment a timid knock sounded, and the door swung open. A gray-haired man, tall, portly, and wearing a well-cut gray suit, looked in. It was Brock Blevins.

The banker's eyes flickered over Marty, then turned to Sam. "I'm interrupting, Sam. I'll wait outside."

But Marty looked up and dried her eyes. "Oh, no, Brock. Please come in," she said graciously. "I'll get hold of myself, and I'm glad to see you."

Blevins came in and shook hands with Marty and Sam, then nodded to me.

"And how is Big Sam?" he asked solemnly.

"That's what I wanted to talk to you about," Marty said. "Sit down, Brock." She motioned toward the chair opposite her, and she and Sam exchanged nods. I knew they were agreeing to stick to the cover story on Big Sam.

She waited, rather like a queen giving an audience to the high chamberlain, until he was seated; then she spoke again. "I had a long talk with the doctors this morning, and we have to face facts. Big Sam has serious brain damage. The doctors see no treatment that is likely to help him regain consciousness. And if he did—well, Sam may be dead. That body in ICU may be just a husk with the kernel gone. We have to face that, and it won't help to put it off."

Blevins looked genuinely pained. He reached over and took Marty's hand. "Marty, I'm so sorry."

"I know, Brock. I know you and Sam were friends and that you'll need to grieve over this, too. But right now we have to discuss practical matters."

Blevins took his hand from Marty's and waved it airily. "Marty, we have all the time in the world to get Big Sam's business affairs straightened out. In the meantime—"

Marty shook her head firmly. "No, that's not the problem. Young Sam and I will have to discuss the business matters with our lawyer before we talk to our banker. I'm concerned about the county business."

"County business?" Blevins blinked, then gave a slight smile. "All right, I'll put on my county commissioner's hat. What is your problem?"

"I want you to find out what it takes to get Sam off the board of commissioners. Do we have to have him declared incompetent first?"

"I'll ask the district attorney this evening, if it's bothering you, Marty. But Harley and I can conduct business by ourselves. There's no particular hurry about replacing Sam."

"Perhaps not." Marty pursed her lips. "The second point is a bit harder to put your finger on. Had Sam said anything to you about malfeasance in office?"

It took a moment for her question to sink into my brain, and I noticed that Sam turned and looked closely at his mother. This evidently came as a surprise to him as well.

Malfeasance. The term always had a nasty ring to it. In the army it meant court-martial and dishonorable discharge. I guessed it could mean prison for civilian officials.

But why was Marty asking such a question? The only answer was that Big Sam must have suspected someone of malfeasance in office, and he must have talked to her about it. Was this the same problem that had taken him to the SOSU library? I had told Sam about that over lunch, of course.

Blevins was looking as astonished as I had felt. His gray eyes were wide open. "My God!" he said.

Marty frowned.

Blevins leaned forward. "He hadn't said a thing to me about it, Marty. Just what's going on?"

Marty shook her head. "Unfortunately, he was quite cryptic in discussing it with me. Or maybe I wasn't listening. Frankly, I always tried to ignore county business."

"Was Sam talking about some county official?"

"I think so," Marty said hesitantly. She turned toward Sam. "Did he talk to you about it?"

Sam shook his head. "When he was in Germany, he circled around some problem he was having a few times, but I never let him get to the point. I suppose it could have had something to do with the county."

Blevins leaned back in his chair and shook his head. "I don't know why I'm acting so surprised, local politics being what it is in Oklahoma."

Sam and Marty nodded solemnly, and I remembered that Sam had once mentioned that a series of kickback scandals early in the 1980s saw charges filed against county commissioners from nearly every county in the state.

Blevins looked at me and smiled. "We've always blamed our problems on the long years of Prohibition," he said. "It was really impossible to enforce the law to the letter in those days, and it got to the point only crooks would run for office. Prohibition's been gone thirty years, and I had hoped that things had improved. But God knows that running for county office is no way to enhance your reputation in Oklahoma."

Sam spoke up then. "I think you and Big Sam had well-established reputations before you took office," he said. "But I don't even know who the other county officials are right now."

"It's mostly the same old crew." Blevins studied his hands on the table a moment, then looked at Marty and smiled. "It could have been me he suspected, Marty. Sam and I were pretty close. If he didn't mention it to me—"

But Marty shook her head. "I don't think so, Brock. He always regarded you as honest, even when he disagreed with you, and I think I would have noticed if his attitude had changed."

It seemed to be a rather backhanded compliment. Blevins didn't look too pleased with it, but he didn't say anything in reply. Instead, he turned to Sam.

"Should I call in the OSBI?" he asked.

I must have looked blank, because Sam's eyes flickered in my direction, and he echoed Blevins's question in another form. "The Oklahoma State Bureau of Investigation? What would you tell them?"

Blevins gave an elaborate shrug. "I don't have the slightest idea," he said.

Marty shook her head. "I guess I shouldn't have brought it up."

"No! No!" Blevins was regaining his oily manner. "Of course you should have, Marty. I'm just not sure exactly what to do about it."

He turned to Sam. "Have you looked through your father's papers?"

"Just touched the surface. None of the ones at the house had anything to do with county business. Did he have a desk at the courthouse?"

"Of course!"

"Maybe you could look down there, Brock."

But Blevins had narrowed his eyes. He stared at the wall a long moment, then turned to Sam. "I think it would be better if you looked, Young Sam. After all, you're a trained investigator. And, besides, you're not involved in this. I'd better stay clear."

So that's how they left it. Sam was to meet Blevins at the courthouse as soon as it opened the next day. They'd pick someone from the county clerk's office, and Sam would inventory his father's papers with that person as a witness.

With that settled, Blevins left, and Sam and Marty had a business discussion. I sat in, but I didn't understand a lot of it.

The $420,000 loan due in a few days was a major problem, obviously. Marty wasn't exactly sure how Big Sam and Bill had planned to handle it. They wanted to make a payment against the principal, but now the ranch might have to settle for paying the interest, Marty and Sam decided. They could always extend at the bank for another six months. There was a lot of talk about the Federal Land Bank and other things I had never heard of.

We talked Marty into leaving the hospital long enough for an early dinner with us. She insisted on going at a time that didn't overlap visiting hours, which were strictly limited in the ICU. Sam grabbed the odd hour to take his scene-of-the-crime specimens to the lab. I stayed at the hospital with Marty.

Over dinner Marty told us she had already checked with the Holton Hospital and Nursing Center. They could take Big Sam as soon as the hospital released him.

I was relieved to hear it. I had had a picture of her trying to care for him herself.

But the nursing-home news worried Marty, I could tell. "It's a bunch of money," she told Sam. "Insurance won't cover nursing-home care."

Sam didn't bat an eyelash. "We'll manage," he said.

We walked Marty to the hospital's hotel for the night and headed down the interstate going south, toward Holton. The sun was dropping toward the horizon, but the temperature hadn't begun to come down. The truck's air conditioning felt wonderful. I turned my back to the sun, which was beating in the passenger's window, and looked at Sam.

His lack of emotion was worrying me. True, with so many family disasters going on, it was good to have a firm foundation, a guy we could count on to remain calm when all around him were losing their heads. But I had gone through my mother's illness and death only a year earlier. My father had tried that stuff, and it nearly broke him. We had gone through grief counseling. I knew, or thought I knew, how important it is to face up to your emotions when terrible things happen. But I didn't know how to tell Sam about it.

So far I hadn't even been able to talk to him about his— well, threat might be the right word—his threat to leave the army and stay in Holton. And now I had his attention for at least two hours. I could bring up any subject, and I couldn't think of anything to say. My concerns seemed rather petty compared to his problems. I just wished he'd share those problems with me.

Finally I decided to work backward from the latest bombshell.

"What about this malfeasance in office?" I said. "What do you think about it?"

Sam looked in his rearview mirror, then pulled out to pass a slower-moving car. "It's pretty vague. Mom didn't seem to have any idea on exactly who or what he was talking about."

"You and your mom and Brock Blevins were talking as if he meant one of the county officials."

"Yeah, but that's just a guess. County commissioners deal with a lot of people. He could have picked up a hint anyplace."

I thought about it. Who could Big Sam have suspected? One of his fellow commissioners? The district attorney? Would that explain why he looked a legal question up at the college library rather than asking advice from that official? Or could it have been Sheriff Tarzan Thompson?

Thompson would be my favorite candidate, I decided. The guy had crook written all over him. I said so.

"It could be anybody," Sam said. "It could be a city official in Holton. The mayor or one of the councilmen. It could be a federal official, for that matter—commissioners deal with judges and Department of Agriculture flunkies and federal marshals and bureaucrats of all types and kinds. Then there are state officials—the Highway Patrol and the National Guard and about a million more possibilities."

I sighed. "Do you think you'll find anything in his desk?"

Sam shrugged. "Probably not. But it's an avenue we have to pursue within the total investigation."

He sounded so official that it reminded me once more that he was a policeman. It also reminded me that despite the confusion of the past twenty-four hours, Sam was on a case—the case of the attack on his father.

Any official Big Sam had suspected of malfeasance had a really good motive to try to kill him. But other people looked suspicious, too.

"Big Sam had—" I started it out, but then I lost my nerve and quit.

Sam shot a glance at me. "Spit it out," he said.

"Well, your dad seems to have had so many enemies."

Sam gave a harsh laugh. "You mean I'm in good company."

"No! You and your father didn't get along. That's different from being enemies."

"Not much."

"But it is! Like that oil-field man—the pumper."

"Cudjoe?"

"Yes. He came right out and said he and your dad didn't get along. But I thought he respected your dad, and I don't think he wished him any ill."

"Killing Big Sam wouldn't do Cudjoe any good. He'd just have to deal with the rest of us."

"But the Smith brothers—they're scary."

"Huh," Sam snorted. "They're just blowhards."

"Maybe so, but Maynard has the temper that might make him attack your dad, and Millard is crafty enough to mastermind a cover-up."

"Yes, but I don't think Millard's crafty enough to keep Maynard quiet about it."

"Well, that's a point. How about Bobbi Baker? She sure had it in for your dad."

"Yeah."

"She's apparently trying to get money for a trip out of Bill and Brenda, and she blamed your dad for stopping the whole deal."

"I think that was just an excuse on Bill's part. Brenda would probably pay every cent they have to get her mother out of town. It's the same as blackmail, and I think Bill was smart enough to know they'd better not get started on the payoffs. There'd be no end to it. But he may have used some business arrangement with Big Sam as an excuse. The possibility of suing the oil company, maybe.''

"Which brings us to Viola Mae, who seems to be the only person in Catlin County who hasn't fought with your dad."

"Unless she's still mad because he jilted her thirty-five years ago."

I looked at Sam narrowly.

He looked back at me and gave a crooked smile. "I heard Bobbi dishing the dirt on Viola Mae and Big Sam. In a place the size of Holton nobody ever lives anything down."

He seemed matter-of-fact, but I wondered if the mocking smile was hiding some other emotion. "I find it hard to picture your dad and Viola Mae as lovers," I said. "Besides, she's stayed on as a family friend for thirty-five years. Surely your mother wouldn't have put up with that situation."

"Oh, I can see my mother making an old girlfriend into her own ally," Sam said. "And Viola Mae hasn't been around for all of those thirty-five years. She moved away not too long after my parents went off and got married. She came back about ten years later."

"Sam, surely you don't think—"

"All I know is that Big Sam and Viola Mae were considered a steady couple by Holton high society"—he gave the words a sardonic twist—"for about five years. Everybody expected them to marry, but it was never an official engagement or anything. As to their sex life— Well, I decided when I was about sixteen that I didn't want Big Sam asking me any nosy questions, so I guessed I'd better not ask him any. Certainly not any about things that happened before he married my mother. It's none of my business."

He was silent while he passed a semitrailer loaded with heavy equipment. "It's none of Bobbi Baker's business, either," he said bitterly. "But that's Holton. Small Town, U.S.A."

We drove another five miles before something else occurred to me.

For the second time, Sam had visited the hospital, but again he had not gone in to see his dad.

ELEVEN

THE NEXT DAY will go down in Holton history as the day of the Cuss Fight at the Catlin County Courthouse, also known as the Titus-Thompson Tourney. I'm still hearing about it, and like the supposed love affair of Big Sam and Viola Mae, I fear it will be haunting our descendants throughout the generations.

We had come in from Oklahoma City around nine-thirty at night, and Sam began going through his father's desk in the office off the living room. I tried to talk to him, but his mind was on desk drawers and file folders, not me. Finally, I slipped into my black nightgown, then went through the office and told him I was going to read in bed until he came up. He nodded, but he didn't look at me. I could still hear file drawers slamming and papers crashing downstairs when I fell asleep at one o'clock. I don't know what time Sam came to bed.

Then we both overslept, of course. We woke up at seven-fifteen, and Sam had to rush to meet Brock Blevins at the county clerk's office at eight-thirty, when the offices opened. Our plan was that I would go to the supermarket and shop to get ready for Marty's return while Sam was at the courthouse.

"I don't see how Big Sam's desk can hold more than an hour's worth of inventory," Sam said.

He found a plastic cooler for me to pack any frozen foods in, and we started out. I dropped him off outside that big white stone building on Holton's central square.

I didn't see how shopping could take more than thirty minutes or so, but I was wrong. I was spotted as the newest

Titus, and I had to report on Big Sam's condition to the checkers, the store manager, the minister's wife, the butcher, the baker, and about forty other people. Such a crowd gathered that I began to feel like a celebrity—"Young Sam's wife," the hit of the IGA.

So it was nearly an hour later when I pulled into an angled parking slot outside the courthouse. I was checking on the groceries in the back of the truck when I heard a siren coming my way. It grew louder and louder, and a black-and-white car with a flashy star on the door came wheeling down Main Street and circled the square, screaming like a kid having a tantrum. Tarzan Thompson was driving, and the face under his big white hat looked grim.

Thompson skidded into a parking place marked SHER-IFF, and the siren strangled and died. He almost fell out of the car and started for the courthouse, running. He stumbled over a row of bricks that lined a flower bed. He barely kept his balance, but he didn't lose any momentum.

The entrance to the Catlin County Courthouse is a half story up. The first floor is a half basement, and the main entrance is on the second floor. So Thompson had to mount a flight of fifteen steps to get to the door, and I think he managed to scuff his boots on at least five of those steps.

Since a sign reading SHERIFF'S OFFICE pointed around the corner, I knew Thompson wasn't going to his own bailiwick.

I had a feeling I knew where he was headed.

I'm not sure why I followed so quickly. If he was headed for Sam—well, Sam was certainly able to take care of himself with Tarzan Thompson. Maybe I just didn't want to miss the fun.

At any rate, I was only twenty feet behind Thompson as he burst through the main door, and I gained a little as he took the steps to the next floor, puffing a bit.

He didn't hesitate at the top of the stairs, but turned left abruptly and almost ran down the wide hall, his broad white hat bobbing as he bounced along, his cowboy boots clumping on the terrazzo floor.

Ahead, a modern-looking glass partition had been put up to create an office in what had originally been the end of the hall. Three utilitarian metal desks were lined up in it, and Sam sat behind the one at the back. A young girl sat at the center desk with her back to us; she turned as Tarzan crashed down the hall, and I saw she was holding a steno pad and three pencils.

The glass door in the partition was closed, and for a moment I thought Thompson was going to plow right through it. However, after fumbling with the handle a bit, he threw it open. The door banged into the glass wall with a clatter, but nothing broke.

"You son of a bitch!" Thompson roared. "What the hell are you doing?"

Sam had kept his head down during this dramatic approach, and now he lifted it. "Taking inventory," he said. His voice was calm, but it was clear and cold.

And it carried. People were already coming out of the other offices on the second floor. Secretaries were poking their heads around doorways. Cowboy-hatted retirees had left the bench just inside the main door and were climbing the stairway to see the show. Through one doorway I could see a woman rush to a telephone and start dialing. Uniformed men were coming down from the third floor.

So far it wasn't much of an exhibition, but Tarzan Thompson just seemed to be warming up.

"Taking inventory! Taking inventory!"

He stepped forward and shook his fist over the desk. "What's this shit at the lab? You goddamned SOB! You're passing yourself off as a county deputy, and by God! I'm gonna run you in over it!"

Sam looked incredulous. "What are you talking about? I'd never claim to be one of your deputies."

The emphasis on the "your" was slight, but it was there, and Thompson reacted as Sam probably expected.

Words such as "yellow-bellied," "snake," and "coyote" insulted the animal kingdom. Terms like "SOB" and "trash" insulted Sam's ancestry. "Liar," "lowlife," "scumbag," and "no-good" insulted his character. "Stiffnecked," "military crap," and "hot-shot army officer" insulted his profession. All this was interspersed with other words, profane and obscene. None of them were very imaginative.

The effect was frankly ridiculous.

Sam stood up, rested his hands on Big Sam's desk, and leaned forward. He appeared to be giving the sheriff his complete attention. A slight smile crossed his mouth. I don't know if anyone else realized that the hands on the desk were clenched into fists.

He stood there until Tarzan Thompson ran out of breath; then he raised himself to his full height and spoke almost casually. "I'm not sure what brought all this on, Tarzan. Was it the materials I sent to Mills Laboratory?"

"Yes, you goddamned—"

Sam spoke evenly and clearly, and Thompson broke off his tirade.

"I sent some evidence up as a private individual," Sam said. "The lab director is a friend of mine, from college. I assure you he's aware that I'm not a Catlin County employee, and he knows to send the bill to me personally. So what's the problem?"

"The problem? The problem! First you go gathering evidence behind my back, then you claim to be a deputy, then I get a call that you're digging through this desk, which is county property!"

Sam shrugged. "I was asked to inventory my father's desk by the chairman of the county commissioners, Brock Blevins. Blevins has that authority."

He gestured toward the young woman with the pencils and notebook. She'd been sitting there, apparently afraid to move, throughout Thompson's fit.

"As you see, Brock asked a deputy county clerk to make a record of what I find. I had not planned to remove anything except this." He reached in a drawer and pulled out an apple.

I could smell its rich, overripe odor clear out in the hall. A man standing next to me guffawed.

"As for the lab," Sam said, "if they think they received evidence from the Catlin County sheriff's department, somebody's mixed up. I made it clear when I talked to the director that you had done nothing to collect evidence in the attack on my father."

Now the man behind me gasped.

"Attack!" Thompson yelled again. "What attack! You and Bill are crazy on that subject! There's no evidence of any attack!"

Sam smiled. "We won't know that until the lab reports get back, will we?"

Thompson stood motionless for a moment, then took his hat off. He leaned over and used the hat to make a swipe across the top of Big Sam's desk. A desk lamp and a plastic rack went flying. They crashed into the glass wall, then hit the floor. The bulb in the lamp popped.

The poor girl from the clerk's office—she looked like a recent high school graduate—cowered and held her notebook over her face. She gave a sob, then cried out, "Oh, stop! Stop!"

I admit I took three steps forward, and the man behind me said, "That's enough!" loudly. Everyone else gasped and moaned.

But Sam remained impassive. He didn't even duck when the lamp went by. He stared at Thompson for what seemed to be a full minute. Then he spoke deliberately.

"I suppose you're trying to goad me into punching you out, Tarzan. Well, I don't plan on doing that. I don't give a shit about you.

"I don't give a shit about Catlin County, for that matter. But I know that what happened to Big Sam was no accident, and I mean to find out the truth. And if I want to investigate a crime that occurred on my family's property in a professional manner—the way it should have been done in the first place—I have a right to do that."

Then he slowly unfolded his arms, leaned down, and took hold of the cord to the lamp that Thompson had knocked galley-west.

"If you're not going to help, Tarzan, at least stay out of my way." He yanked the plug out and tossed it aside.

Thompson sputtered again, but the man behind me—I noticed he had a star on his shirt—stepped through the door and took him by the arm. "Come on, Tarzan," he said. "You've said all there is to say."

The big sheriff turned on his heel. He seemed stunned to see the thirty or more people who had gathered in the courthouse corridor to witness the battle. Then he lifted his chin and charged through the crowd.

A hubbub broke loose. Everybody but me began to talk. I felt weak, and I sort of staggered into the office. Several of the men gathered around Sam and pounded him on the shoulder, but he backed off.

"I don't have any quarrel with Tarzan," he said.

"Young Sam, you really believe somebody tried to kill your daddy?" one voice said.

Sam looked grim. "They succeeded, for all practical purposes," he said.

The deputy clerk was really in tears now, and the woman who had stood behind me in the hall was patting her. I gathered that the older woman was the county clerk. She ushered the girl out.

I was proud of Sam, of course. He had met the challenge from the obnoxious Tarzan Thompson and had bested him without sinking to Thompson's level. But the episode scared me, too. Thompson was going to realize that he'd been made to look like a fool and had been accused publicly of neglecting his duties. There were lots of methods of revenge. I remembered sitting on the front porch in the moonlight—all alone. No other houses in sight. I shivered slightly. There were a lot of possibilities for trouble out there on the Titus place.

A janitor materialized with broom and dustpan and cleared the broken lamp away, and people began drifting off. The older woman came back in. She had short, curly gray hair and gold-rimmed glasses. Her thin lips were pursed tightly, and her figure was less plump than imposing. Now she held a notebook and a pencil.

"Well, I hope you're through," she said firmly. "This is a business office, not a boxing ring, and I trust that you and our sheriff will remember that in the future."

"I hope so," Sam said. "Mrs. Milton, this is my wife, Nicky. Nicky, this is Sara Milton, who has been Catlin County clerk for her entire adult life."

Mrs. Milton looked me over and decided she could shake my hand. "I hope you can keep this husband of yours under control."

"Oh, he's always under control," I said. *That's his problem,* I added silently.

"Young Sam, are you finished with this inventory that I don't understand the reason for?" she asked.

"All except for the credenza," Sam said. He gestured toward a low oak storage cabinet behind Big Sam's desk.

Mrs. Milton waved the notebook. "Well, I had to send Sally home. I'll finish taking notes. Then I hope we will have had enough excitement for one day."

"Yes, ma'am," Sam said. He knelt and opened the door to the credenza. "It doesn't seem to have much in it."

He pulled out several boxes from the top shelves. "County envelopes. County stationery. Manila envelopes. Manila folders. Do you want me to count them?"

"Heavens, no! Get on with it." Mrs. Milton's pencil danced across the steno pad.

"There's a book. Hmm. *Modern Gas and Oil Production Techniques*. That's odd."

"I expect he was looking up something about that lawsuit Viola Mae Humphries was trying to get him into."

Sam flipped open the front cover. "He checked it out of the SOSU library," he said. "Maybe I'd better return it."

"I'll make a note of it." Mrs. Milton made more esoteric designs. "Is that all?"

"That's all on the top shelf. There's a cardboard box on the bottom."

"Well, haul it out, Young Sam. Let's get this over with."

Sam tugged, but the box barely moved. "Heavier than I expected," he said, and pulled harder. The box came out. "It's sealed."

It was a cardboard box about eighteen inches square. The sides were printed with a Pennzoil label, but it had been re-sealed with wide brown paper tape. Sam pulled out his pocket knife. He opened a blade and used it to slit the tape at the ends and down the middle of the box.

"He sure sealed it up firmly," he said.

With that he cut the last bit of tape and opened the cardboard flaps. He and Mrs. Milton looked inside.

"Well, forever more!" Mrs. Milton said.

Sam said nothing. He just frowned.

I moved to the desk and looked into the box.

It held a wooden box, more of a crate. It had no lid, and inside was a beat-up, corroded car battery.

Mrs. Milton gave an angry sniff. "Men! None of you ever grow up! I guess we'll be finding a dead frog and a sack of marbles in there next."

A car battery. I was totally confused. "Could he have wanted to return it to the manufacturer?"

Sam shook his head. He reached into the box and touched the broad head of one of the nails that held the crate together, then traced the manufacturer's name. "No, Big Sam swore by Delco. This is a Sears DieHard. And it died hard. It's obviously been used a lot."

"Maybe somebody brought it in with a complaint against a business," I said.

Mrs. Milton gave another sniff. "Not a county function. And besides, this battery's been used so hard I hardly think anybody could complain if it quit. Even I can see that water has dripped on it." She pointed to a trail of corrosion across the top and down the side. "Well, Young Sam, you have my permission to take this thing out of here."

Sam's face was expressionless. He ran a finger down the side of the little crate that held the battery. "I think I'll seal it up again first," he said.

"Whatever for?"

Sam opened the center drawer of his father's desk and took out a roll of masking tape. "I think it's better," he said. He was using his quiet but firm voice. I had seen an MP sergeant with stripes down to the elbow quail before that voice. Mrs. Milton gave way, too.

"If you think so," she said. "I'll make a note of it, of course."

As soon as it was sealed up, Sam asked Sara Milton to sign her name across the tape and cardboard. She scoffed, but she took a marking pen with a thick red point from Big

Sam's center drawer and wrote her name in big letters. Then she added the date below it.

I thought we'd go home then, but Sam said he had to report to Brock Blevins. He lugged the box containing the car battery across the street to the bank. It was nine forty-five, and the bank wasn't open yet. I knocked on the old-fashioned front door, and a teller came to let us in. Sam rested the cardboard box on Blevins's desk while they talked.

Sam's report didn't take long, since all he had to tell Blevins was that he had taken both Big Sam's desks apart and had found no reference to malfeasance in office.

I thought Blevins seemed relieved.

"Well, that's that, then," he said. "Can you think of anything else I can do?"

"Just keep your eyes open, I guess," Sam answered. "I'll ask my mom to think the whole situation over. Maybe she'll be able to remember something more about what Big Sam said."

Blevins nodded. "I'll ask around."

"No!" Sam spoke sharply. "I'd rather you didn't ask any questions, Brock. It might be dangerous."

"Dangerous?"

Blevins stepped over and closed his office door, although we could see through the glass walls that no one was nearby.

"Sam, I heard that you told Tarzan Thompson that your dad's accident—well, was no accident. Is that what you really think?"

"That's right, Brock."

Blevins sighed. He walked up and down in front of his desk a moment. "Sam, I know you quarreled with your dad—" He broke off and looked at me doubtfully.

Sam remained impassive. "Go ahead, Brock. Nicky knows I fought with Big Sam. She knows that the family is riddled with guilt."

Blevins frowned. "I'm no psychologist, Sam."

Sam nodded.

Blevins spoke again. "And I know you're a professional lawman."

"That's right, Brock. And my professional training tells me Big Sam's accident has a real fishy smell."

"You're sure that smell isn't just the Titus family guilt you mentioned?"

Sam didn't answer.

"I'm just asking, Sam. I just want to know that you've thought about it."

Sam stared into space for a long moment. "I've thought about it," he said finally. "I've thought about it a lot. And no matter how guilty I feel about quarreling with Big Sam, he would never have tried to change a tire on that slope."

"I'd known Big Sam for nearly fifty years," the banker said. "I didn't know he was hipped on the subject of cars falling off jacks."

"He didn't teach you to change a tire, Brock. He did teach me that. And he taught Bill. And Bill agreed with me. Big Sam would never have jacked that truck up on that gravel slope." Sam's eyes met Blevins's. "Never."

We said good-bye to Blevins then and left, with Sam still lugging along that cardboard box. He put it in the back of the pickup, masking it with the grocery sacks.

When I asked him why, he was evasive. In fact, he was back in the clouds, looking at me as if I were a stranger again. When we were halfway to the ranch, he suddenly spoke. "Nicky, maybe I'd better put you back on the plane for Frankfurt."

"Frankfurt! Why? What have I done?"

"Done? You haven't done anything. I have."

"Well, what have you done that would make me go back to Frankfurt?"

"I've brought all this out in the open. I've tried to shake the cage of the person who attacked Big Sam. I don't know what's going to happen next. I don't want it to happen to you."

"Sam, that's silly." Even as I said it, I remembered that I had sat in the county commissioners' office and shivered at the thought of Tarzan Thompson coming out to the ranch when Sam and I were there alone. And two nights before, I had been ready to beg Sam to take me back to Frankfurt.

But that was "we," not "me." I didn't want to go back without him.

"No," I said firmly. "I'm not going. You can't ship Brenda and your mother off someplace. I'm in no more danger than they are."

"If somebody thinks I've found something out, they may think that I told you about it. Mom's up in Oklahoma City, and I think she's fairly safe. And nobody would think I'd confide in Brenda."

The mention of Brenda made me feel guilty. "Maybe you wouldn't confide in her, but I guess we ought to stop by and check on her and the kids."

Suddenly, Sam braked the truck and spun the steering wheel. I was mashed against the door, and I could hear bottles turning over in the rear.

"What are you doing?" I yelled. "This isn't the road to Brenda and Bill's house!"

"I saw something red," Sam said. He drove about seventy-five feet down a gravel side road, then pulled in at a gate that led into a pasture. He opened his door and stood up with his head outside, gazing into the pasture.

"Sam, what are you doing?"

"I'd better check it out," he muttered.

He walked toward the gate, which was made of barbed wire stretched over badly trimmed poles apparently cut from nearby trees. The only latch was a wire loop. Sam lifted it.

I jumped out of the truck and caught up with him. "Sam! What are we doing here!"

He looked at me blankly. It was the same look he had had on his face that morning in Germany—was it only three days before? He wasn't even seeing me.

"Sam! Sam!" I said it desperately. I couldn't stand that look. It made me feel invisible. Sam was my whole life. How could he act as if I didn't exist?

He began walking across the pasture, toward a pond. The pasture looked awful. The grass underfoot was rough and crisscrossed by gulleys. The water in the pond was choked with algae and water lilies. The dam, which was on the far side, was overgrown with scrubby willows.

Sam struck out at a swift walk, headed toward the left side of the pond. I tagged along. He ignored me.

"Sam!" My voice was weaker. "Sam?"

I shut up then and simply followed him. He strode along, winding in and out among cedars and mesquites. He continued to ignore me, but his gait was so purposeful I knew he was on the track of something important. But what?

It'll probably be a cow, I told myself angrily. We circled the pond, and as we came near the dam, Sam began to walk even faster. He was almost running as we passed behind the willows that topped the dam.

Then he stopped, so abruptly that I ran into him.

It was like hitting a tree. He didn't react. He just stood there, staring at the hump that was the dam and at the trickle of water behind it. Then he gave a sudden leap, plunged into the willows, and climbed the bank.

"Sam!" I yelped it out.

Almost immediately he reappeared. He held a piece of scrap metal about three feet long. It had once been candy-apple red.

He slid down the dam and held it out. "Some old junk car," he said. "Shit!"

Well, he was speaking again, but why was he swearing? Sam rarely swore. Why would he curse a piece of scrap metal? I had to have the answer, even if it required desperate measures.

I waved my arms and jumped up and down. "Ahhh!" I screamed.

Sam's face whipped in my direction, but he remained calm. "What's that all about?"

"It's to make you look at me! You swerve off the road, nearly throw me—and the groceries—out of the truck. Jump out and run through some strange pasture, refusing to speak to me. All to pick up some lousy hunk of metal? Are you crazy?"

Sam's mouth took on its stony look again as he started back the way he had come. When he spoke, he tossed his answer over his shoulder.

"I saw something red," he said.

This time I caught him. I grabbed his arm and hung on. "So what? You said that before. What is so important about something red?"

I got him stopped, but Sam glared at me a long moment before he answered, and when he spoke, his voice was cold. "I thought it might be Bill's pickup," he said quietly.

"Bill's pickup?"

I loosened my hold, and Sam started walking away. So I grabbed tight again. "Wait, Sam! You and Marty said something about this yesterday, and I don't understand. If Bill left Brenda and took off for parts unknown, why would he leave his pickup around here?"

Sam turned to face me. He was still silent, but suddenly the stone of his face cracked. His face twisted in agony, and the muscles in the arm I was gripping got hard and tense. Then he closed his eyes, took a deep breath, and began to swallow.

He swallowed once, twice, three times, taking a long, deep breath between each gulp. And with each swallow his face smoothed out, eased, and remodeled itself into my strong, silent, calm Sam. When he spoke again, his voice was icy.

"Bill's dead," he said.

TWELVE

I DON'T KNOW HOW I got back to the truck. The next thing I remember is driving past Dill and Drenda's house. Drenda was on the porch, shaking a throw rug. Sam honked, and both he and Brenda waved. Casually.

"Oh, God!" I said. "Oh, Brenda! What will she and those kids do?" Then I began to cry. "Sam, you can't be right!"

He didn't even look at me. "Mom thinks I am." His voice was a monotone.

"But he left a message!"

"You know about the key under the flowerpot. Anybody could have come in the house and left that."

"But it was in the computer! They'd have to know the code."

"The instruction book was sitting right there beside the computer. I mastered it in about twenty minutes."

"But you have computer experience."

"Who doesn't these days?" His voice was totally calm, as if he were talking about a textbook situation, about strangers.

"Think of those people you listed off yesterday as having quarreled with Big Sam," he said. "Tarzan? He's probably got a computer link with the national crime line. Other officials? Even in a small county like Catlin County every official uses some sort of computer. Brock Blevins? The bank's full of computers. Bobbi Baker? When she works, she's a pretty good secretary. That means she can use a word processor and an accounting program. And since the oil people run a modern office, they'll have those, too. Even Maynard and Millard got a PC. Jack Rich mentioned it.''

His calm was spooky. Already I was having trouble remembering the agony that had crossed his face before he admitted his belief that Bill was dead. I cried silently until we pulled into the machine shed behind the house. Sam opened his door and climbed out, and I fished in my purse for a tissue and blew my nose. I had my head down, and Sam surprised me when he suddenly opened my door. We looked at each other a long moment.

"Oh, Sam! Sam!" I murmured.

He glared at me. That's the only word for it. His eyes might have been chunks of marble. Cold, hard—they seemed to shoot frigid beams at me, beams magnified by his glasses.

"Look," he said. "If Bill meant to leave Brenda, he wouldn't have gone off to think things over. Bill wasn't introspective. He would have moved into the guest room over here and kept an eye on his cattle. Let's face it. Bill's cattle would always be the most important thing to him. He wouldn't have left them to my inept care. The only reason he can be gone is that he is being kept away. And the only way to keep Bill away would be to kill him."

I began to sob.

"I shouldn't have told you."

"Oh, yes. I've hated being shut out. I'm glad you told me!"

Sam's voice was low and hard. "Well, you've got to get hold of yourself and forget it."

I looked at him numbly. The look on his face was turning my digestive system into an ice-cream freezer. I could feel the salt corroding the stomach lining.

His dad was at death's door, his brother might be dead, and Sam wanted me to forget all about it.

"How can either of us forget it? Don't you need help looking for Bill? What if he's still alive? What if he's a prisoner someplace?"

"Very unlikely." His voice belonged to a robot. "But if we aren't careful, the person who murdered him will get away with it."

For the first time it sunk in. We weren't talking about a traffic accident or a heart attack. We were talking about murder.

Sam went on. "That person is clever. He's eliminated two people and made the authorities believe no crime has been committed in either case. And I have no evidence to convince the authorities that I'm right. Tarzan Thompson—the OSBI—they won't do a thing unless that evidence I sent off to the lab shows something. And that's just a long shot."

"But, Sam—"

"So up at the courthouse today I threw out a challenge. I yelled it out in that fight with Tarzan. By now there's not a soul in Catlin County who doesn't know that I think someone tried to kill Big Sam and that I'm investigating it.

"But that's only an assault case. Bill's murder would be a lot more serious. And if we never find Bill's body, we may never prove he was killed. And right at this moment, all that killer has to do is lie low."

I blew my nose again. "So why did you challenge the killer?"

"I hope I shook his cage. I hope he'll make a move, some move that will make him stand out from the other suspects."

I leaned back and looked straight into Sam's face. "Do you think it will be more violence?"

Sam shook his head. "Not right away. I think he attacked Big Sam and killed Bill because they knew something. I think he'll make some attempt to find out what I know before he tries to do me in."

A cold hand clutched at my heart. "So you've made yourself into bait."

"Maybe so, but I'm on my guard."

"And your dad and Bill weren't?"

"I doubt they were." He shook his head slowly. "If Big Sam suspected somebody was up to no good, he would probably have confronted them. God knows he wasn't afraid of confrontation. He wouldn't have expected a physical attack."

"And Bill?"

Again Sam shook his head. "I know he wasn't expecting an attack. He told me as much on the telephone."

"When he called Germany?"

"No. When I called the hospital from Chicago. He said somebody knew something and he was going to see them. I told him to wait, but he hung up on me."

I thought back to O'Hare and that call in the middle of the night—was it two or three days ago? I remembered how Sam had barked into the pay phone, "Bill! Wait till I get there!"

Sam turned away. "I should have called back," he said stonily. "Just as I should have talked to Big Sam in Germany. He told me he wanted to ask my advice, and I refused to listen."

He turned and reached into the back of the pickup, lifting out the plastic cooler. I got out.

His voice would have called down a new ice age. "But you're going to have to act normal, to keep anybody from knowing this, Nicky. And you've got to start now, because I hear Brenda coming up the drive."

I grabbed the cooler out of his hands and fled to the house. I was still crying, and I didn't see how I could face anybody, especially Brenda.

I dropped the cooler on the cabinet and ran into the downstairs bathroom and locked the door. I washed my face. It was no good. Already I could hear Sam's and Brenda's voices in the kitchen.

Then I remembered my mother, lonely and desolate while my father did his final Vietnam tour. Whenever he got a chance to call home, her news was cheerful. After he'd hung up, she'd cry for two or three days. If she could be brave, I could, too. I'd show these southwesterners I was as tough as any pioneer.

I pictured Sam, standing in that pasture and literally swallowing his emotions. I put my hand on the sink and swallowed three times. Then I cleared my throat and practiced speaking.

"Hi!" Was my voice too bright? Well, it would have to do. I unlocked the door and went out.

Brenda's voice stopped as I came into the kitchen. I tried to sound cheerful.

"Emergency over," I said. "Whatever got in my eye is out now."

Brenda looked at me. "Oh, hi, Nicky."

"Hi," I said. "Are the kids with you?"

"No, my girlfriend came and took them to her house to play this morning. I was cleaning the living-room carpet. I just dropped by on my way to pick them up. I wanted to know about Big Sam."

"I guess Sam told you."

"There's no change, really," Sam said. "I'll get the other grocery sacks." He went back outside.

Brenda kept looking at me.

I gulped again. "Marty thinks they'll be ready to dismiss him later this week," I said. "She's arranged for the Holton Hospital to take him."

"Oh, dear." Brenda sounded forlorn. "That's not good, is it?"

"I know."

Brenda's face crumpled. "I'll never forgive myself."

"What do you mean?"

"Over the last time I saw Big Sam."

"What are you talking about?"

"The fight I had with Big Sam."

She had me interested. "You had a fight with Big Sam?"

"I guess it was silly, but it seemed so important at the time. See, my mother wants to go to California. She's chasing some man who's out there. So I had lent her some money." She pushed her blond hair back off her forehead. "See, my grandmother left me her house and property and didn't leave my mother anything. So Mama keeps claiming I did her out of her inheritance."

I nodded.

"So anyway, she wanted money. I didn't have enough, but I gave her what I had. And Big Sam found out about it."

"Oh." I thought about that. "He didn't approve?"

"Of course not. But what really got him was that I hadn't told Bill."

"Well, then, how did Big Sam know about it?"

"Oh, he's on the board at the bank, you know." I had forgotten. "I closed out the savings account, and it came up on some report at the board meeting. I guess Big Sam made some remark to Bill about it and Bill didn't know what he was talking about."

"Did he tell Bill?"

"No, but he came over and told me to tell him." Her voice quivered. "He wasn't ugly about it. I guess that made it worse. You know how short-tempered he could be, but this time I could tell he was trying to be nice. I think he felt sorry for me. Well, I just knew I was going to break down and cry, so I yelled instead." She took a deep sobbing breath, and I realized she was crying now.

"Brenda, don't worry," I said. "I'm sure Big Sam understood how upset you were. I'm sure he didn't blame you. And you mustn't blame yourself."

"I just can't help it! If I hadn't taken that money, then I wouldn't have had that fight with Big Sam. And it was that fight that made me have the battle with Bill!"

"Then you did tell Bill about lending your mother the money?"

"Oh, sure. But I was so upset I managed to mess the whole thing up even worse. See, instead of just telling Bill, I started out by complaining about Big Sam and griping about him putting his nose in our business.

"Then, of course, when I got to the part of the story when I admitted I had taken the money for the new couch and given it to my mother—well, Bill came all unglued, of course."

She wept silently, then choked out a few words. "We had an awful fight. And we never got a chance to make it up."

Sam came in the kitchen then, carrying a sack in each hand. He looked at Brenda, and his mouth tightened, but he had lost the icy look I had found so frightening. He plunked the sacks on the cabinet and went out again.

I moved over and put my arm around Brenda's shoulder. "Come on, Brenda. Sit down while I put up the groceries. Then we'll all have coffee. Or a Coke."

She shook her head and pulled away from me. "You can't understand, Nicky!"

"I can try."

"No! You can't understand! You had normal parents!"

She turned and ran out the back door. I followed as far as the porch. "Brenda!" I called.

"I'll come back later!" she yelled. She ran past Sam, who was taking something out of the truck's bed. She climbed into her little Ford and drove off, spraying gravel.

Sam walked up to the house, carrying that odd cardboard box, the one that held the battery. "What's wrong with Brenda?"

"She's feeling guilty. We can add her to the list of people who fought with Big Sam."

"If we want a list of suspects, I guess we can start with the Catlin County tax rolls," Sam said. "I'm going to put this box in the closet upstairs."

I looked at the box. "Sam, why is that box so important?"

"I don't know that it is."

"Then why are you taking such good care of it?"

"Just in case." He walked on past me and lugged the box up the circular stairway.

He was back down almost immediately. "I'm going out for a while. I'll be back for lunch."

"Wait a minute and I'll go with you," I said.

Sam shook his head. "Better not."

I stood on the back porch and watched him drive off in the pickup, a cloud of dust hanging on the road behind him. Then I was alone with the heat and the wind. That one lone bird sang again, and its melody made me feel as isolated as Sam's pioneer grandmother must have felt. In 1901? Was that the year Sam had said the Tituses had come to Catlin County? I pictured his great-grandmother standing outside her soddy in shirtwaist and pompadour. She hadn't had an air-conditioned house to go into. She hadn't had a telephone or a television set or an electric oven.

She hadn't known there was a murderer loose in her neighborhood, either.

I scurried back into the kitchen and locked the door behind me. It took five minutes—spent checking the windows and doors—to calm down.

I began to put the groceries away. When I thought of Brenda and her kids, I felt awful, so I pushed the thought of them into a corner of my mind and went over what Sam had called the list of suspects.

It was headed by every county or city official in southwest Oklahoma, including Tarzan Thompson and Brock Blevins. Brock Blevins sure had seemed relieved when Sam hadn't discovered anything in Big Sam's desk.

Then the suspect list jumped to people like Maynard and Millard Smith, who had business grudges against Big Sam. I guessed the oil-production people and their pumper, Dewayne Cudjoe, would be on that list.

Then there were the personal enemies—Bobbi Baker, who had been mad because she was trying to get money out of Bill and Brenda and blamed Big Sam for keeping her from getting as much as she wanted. Or Brenda, who admitted she had quarreled with her father-in-law. She seemed unlikely.

And there was another person who might have a grudge against Big Sam, who might have quarreled with him. And it was a person Sam might not have considered.

Viola Mae Humphries.

Bobbi Baker had been scathing in her remarks about the way Big Sam had treated Viola Mae in the past. But Viola Mae had told me that their love affair was kid stuff.

Which story was true?

I didn't want to discuss this with Sam. After all, I'd be getting into his father's sex life, and our parents' sex life is an area none of us wants to admit exists.

A memory from the year I was fourteen popped up. A youth group campout had been rained out, and I had come home sixteen hours early. The den had been strewn with clothes, and the remnants of a candlelit dinner were on the dining table. My parents were not too happy to see me, and I had been shocked. I had also been shocked when a pretty divorcée invited my father for a weekend alone in the Black Forest—just a few months after my mother had died. My father, on the other hand, had never referred even obliquely to the fact that Sam and I might sleep together, either before or after our wedding. The whole subject was unmentionable.

I pushed those memories aside. Sam would probably react in the same way, I told myself. He wouldn't want to talk to Viola Mae about her relationship with his father.

So I'd do it.

I would go over to Viola Mae's that very afternoon; after all, she'd urged me to drop by now and then. I'd ask her about her romance with Big Sam. I'd find out where she had been on the day of his accident.

I could take my camera, I decided. Bird pictures. That would be my excuse. I'd go right after lunch.

It was past one o'clock before Sam came in to eat. I had grilled-cheese sandwiches ready to go. When I asked where he had been, he grunted.

"Just looking around," he said. The book on oil-field technology, the one he had picked up in Big Sam's office, was sitting on the table, and Sam opened it. He might as well have said, "Shut up," out loud. I was miffed, but I tried not to sulk. Sulking is childish. So is rudeness, but it didn't seem to be the time for me to lecture Sam on his table manners. He was desperately worried, and I couldn't tell him everything would be all right.

So I didn't ask any more questions until I brought the grilled-cheese sandwiches and carrot sticks to the table. Sam put the book aside then and began to eat.

I gestured at the book. "Interesting reading?"

"Not to me."

"I wonder why your dad checked it out."

"Probably wanted to see if Slaughter Brothers was going by the book on this well that's given them all the trouble."

"Did he mark anything as significant?"

Sam raised his eyebrows. "Good night, no! Big Sam thought people who wrote in books were vandals."

"Really? Even textbooks? I couldn't have graduated from college without Hi-Liters."

"That was my style, too. I used to get lectured about it every time I came home from college. I think he felt that way because he read a lot of library books."

"Like that one?"

"Well, it would be unusual for him to go to the SOSU library directly. He'd usually go through the Holton Library and use Interlibrary Loan."

Sam took a bite of the sandwich, then carefully wiped his fingers on his paper napkin. "I'd also get a lecture if I got a grease spot on a book," he said. He reached over with the hand he had cleaned and opened the book, ruffling the pages.

"Nothing here but a bookmark," he said. "And it's stuck in the index."

Sam opened the book at the spot indicated and pulled out an ordinary cardboard bookmark, the kind businesses print up as giveaways. "'Day of Bread. A project of the Oklahoma Wheat Commission,'" he read aloud. "I guess he got this at church."

He flipped the bookmark onto the table and examined the page. "No notes. He didn't even make a check mark at the item he looked up in the index."

But the bookmark had turned over as Sam tossed it, and I was looking at it. Faint marks showed up. "Wait. There's writing on this."

Sam picked it up and looked at the pencil marks. "That's Big Sam's writing," he said. "He always used a number-four pencil."

He squinted and held the bookmark to the light. "Page 435? That's what it looks like." Marking the index with an extra napkin, he paged back through the book and scanned the designated section.

"Cathodic protection?" He closed the book with a snap.

"I don't understand this stuff. I have a degree in political science, not petroleum engineering."

He was glum through the rest of the meal. I was silent, too, thinking about my plan to visit Viola Mae and whether I should tell Sam about my intentions. But as it turned out, I didn't need to tell him anything. A phone call from the oil-production company took care of the whole thing. Sam took the call in the office.

"That was a guy from Slaughter Brothers," he reported. "He's in Holton. I told him I'd meet him at the Wolf Creek place in a half hour."

He frowned. "Nicky, I think Viola Mae should be in on this. I sure wish she'd get a phone. Would you mind going to her place and bringing her over?"

THIRTEEN

SAM CALLED the custom combiner, leaving a message on an answering machine, then left in the big truck as I headed out for Viola Mae's in the pickup.

I had loaded my Leicaflex with an all-purpose film, T-Max 400, that Sam had picked up for me in Oklahoma City. I thought I might actually get a good picture or two out of the visit to the bird sanctuary as well as a chance to snoop on Viola Mae's sex life. I thought of the spectacular great blue heron I had spotted the day before—and me with no film—and I packed my long lens and an extra roll of T-Max.

As I left, the sun was beating down, and I could see that the wheat below the house had lost its green tinge and was turning a richer, more golden color. The heat seemed to bake it right in the fields, and I almost expected it to smell like fresh bread. But Sam had assured me that this was not unusually hot weather for southwest Oklahoma. Real hot weather came in July and August, he said. Not late May. He could have fooled me.

As I turned into the road marked HORSE PEN CREEK BIRD SANCTUARY, I immediately felt more comfortable. For one thing, the sanctuary's gravel road was smoother than the county's gravel road, so the truck didn't jounce so much. The sun glinted off the water between the marsh plants, the water birds were wading around, and the grove of cedars that I now knew hid the house and laboratory had a cooler look than the baking wheat fields. No wonder Viola Mae didn't use her air conditioner. I drove slowly, but Big Blue, my dignified heron, did not come wading out of the swamp to have his picture taken.

When I pulled into the parking slot next to the lab building, the place looked deserted. I got out and confirmed my impression. The door to the lab was locked. I didn't try the door to the house—memories of Bobbi Baker stopped me—but no one answered my knock. The office-living room was clearly visible through a window that opened off the porch, and the only movement was a paper ruffling in the breeze.

A compact truck sat behind the house. It was the same one I had seen the day before, so I figured Viola Mae was within walking distance. I decided to wander a bit. She'd invited me to look around, and she'd marked several gravel footpaths to make it easy.

The path I followed had a rustic wooden sign that read CEDAR GROVE. It led into the trees. It was much cooler under their branches, and the air had a delicious damp odor, a combination of scents that made me think of ferns planted in a cedar chest.

I walked along quietly, ready to snap any bird that happened into camera range. Instead of snapping, however, I began slapping. Mosquitoes. They love me. But I persevered and got a shot of a bluejay and some sort of small brown bird. Then I came to a fork in the path. It was marked by another signpost. The words WOOD DUCK POND were over an arrow that pointed left. DROVER'S VIEW was over an arrow pointing right.

The cedars looked thinner to the left, and I was getting tired of mosquitoes, so I took the path toward the pond. In about a block, as a city girl measures distance, I came out of the woods and found myself on the bank of a pond, or perhaps a small lake. It was about a quarter of a mile long and half that wide, and it was gorgeous.

I also added up the "birds" and the "spring-fed pond" that the volunteer firemen had mentioned, and the total described this small lake. I wondered why Viola Mae had refused to allow them to fill the tanker there.

The pond was rimmed with cattails, and about a third of its surface was covered with big leaves of water lilies. A few buds were forming among them. Half the shore was lined with trees—and they were big trees, forty to sixty feet high, maybe, and full of glossy foliage, not the scrubby prairie trees that dotted most of Catlin County. On the side where I stood, the land was open prairie, and the grass in front of me was a mass of wildflowers in shades of yellow. Ducks were sailing across the open water, and white egrets were wading near the shore. A hawk of some kind sat on a dead tree across the lake.

It was a paradise for wildlife and photographers. I hardly knew what to photograph first. I put on my long lens and went for the hawk. Then I swung around and focused in on one of the ducks. Then I noticed baby ducks swimming in a line behind their mother. I tiptoed down the bank for a better angle on that, and a rabbit jumped up from under my feet.

"Oh, ecstasy," I said aloud. "If it's this good in afternoon light, I'm coming back at sunset. Maybe even dawn."

I finally got my shutter finger under control and began to swing the long lens along the bank. Suddenly, a big hunk of ugliness showed up in the middle of my viewfinder.

I lowered the camera and looked at it. Then I looked through the long lens again. Ugly. Double ugly. What was it doing here?

It was a contraption made of chicken wire stretched over unpainted wood.

The path went in that direction, so I walked around to it. It was on the swamp side of the pond, right in the middle of a rutted road that led up to the edge of the water.

It was a cage. Its sides, floor, and top formed a rectangle a couple of feet taller than I am. I pictured Sam's six feet two inches stretched out on the ground beside it and estimated its width at six feet and its length at ten. At the top of one end was a sort of sleeping porch that stuck out, hanging up in the air.

Inside the cage were two dull brown birds and one black one with a brown head. Their beaks were open, and they were panting in the heat. I remembered them from my visit to the lab.

"Ah, cowbirds," I said aloud. "You've fallen into Viola Mae's research project. Well, you're nasty birds, dumping your eggs in nice birds' nests, and you're in for it now. You'll be skinned, stuffed, and stored in a drawer before you know it. But I'm sure she'll use a painless method to dispose of you."

I began to examine the trap, to see how it worked. It had a sort of funnel in the top. Evidently the birds got in that way but couldn't go back out. The protruding "sleeping porch" mystified me. I wondered if it could be used to remove the captured birds. A wooden cube, maybe three feet square, stood in one corner. Was something stored there, or did Viola Mae use it as a bench? It didn't look like a good place to sit, since it was covered with bird droppings.

I was careful not to move anything, but I thought Viola Mae might like a photographic record of her work. I took three or four shots of the trap, including a few close-ups, concentrating on its construction and placement rather than on the trapped birds.

Then I turned and began to photograph the pond from the new angle. It was equally beautiful from this side, almost greeting-card pretty. A blanket of wildflowers covered the foreground, and on this side a big pool of open water was surrounded by patches of water lilies. Across the lake, the vegetation grew in tiers. Cattails stood along the bank, silhouetted against a line of low willows, which in turn stood against tall trees. The mountain loomed behind the trees, and those dramatic clouds sailed above the mountain. There was hardly any way I could miss on composition.

Yet the pond had an almost melancholy look. Some of the water lilies had died, and leaves and buds floated on the surface of the lake, drifting like drowned birds. The undergrowth along the edges of the pond was rank, and its twisted branches inspired visions of poisonous snakes. Vines hung in the tall trees across the pond, binding their branches like ropes.

Perhaps it was the squawks of the trapped birds that made me feel uneasy, I told myself. I resolutely snapped away.

I soon began concentrating on the mother duck. She had a speckled breast and a circle of white around her eye. She seemed fearless, bringing her brood close to me, then swinging out to the open water. I knelt and was using my long lens to pull her right up close when I heard a yell.

"Hey! What are you doing?"

I gasped and jumped to my feet. Viola Mae had come out of the woods not twenty feet to my left.

"Hi!" I called. "You startled me."

Viola Mae trotted rapidly to my side, and her hand gripped my arm. She smiled her sweet smile.

"What do you see?" she asked. "What are you photographing?"

"The mother duck. Isn't she wonderful?"

Viola Mae's smile grew sweeter, and her hold on my arm relaxed. The lines around her eyes, a testament to years in the outdoors, grew deeper. "Wonderful is just the word for her. I'm glad you saw her."

"What kind of duck is she?"

"A wood duck. It's one of the most spectacular American ducks. The male has a fancy hairdo. I don't see him around now." She pulled the binoculars from around her neck and offered them to me. "Look over there in that old cottonwood. That's where they nested."

I gestured with my camera. "I'll use my long lens," I said. I looked in the direction she indicated. "I didn't know ducks nested in trees."

"Wood ducks do. I've had some luck getting them to nest in boxes, too. How long have you been here?"

"Not long. Actually, I'm on a mission. Some man from the oil company is on his way over to see the fire damage. Sam thought you might want to come, too."

Viola Mae's eyes lit up. "I certainly do!" she said. "Come on." She struck off on one of the two parallel cow paths that skirted the cedars, then crossed the marshy area. It was evidently a road she used to move things around the property. I followed.

"I hear Sam and our revered sheriff tangled," Viola Mae said. "Must have been quite a bout."

"Well, it was exciting for the moment. Sam was going through his father's desk, and Tarzan objected."

Viola Mae chuckled. "What was Young Sam looking for?"

I decided I'd better be evasive, even with a family friend. "Oh, just checking. He didn't find anything unusual—well, just one odd item. A corroded car battery."

Viola Mae gave a high-pitched titter, and her dimple deepened. "Where did that come from?"

I shrugged. "Nobody knows."

"Did Young Sam just throw it out?"

"Oh, no. He sealed it up all legal and took it out to the house. He's a cop at heart, you know. He'll hang on to anything he doesn't understand."

I was getting winded from the rapid pace Viola Mae was setting, so I was pleased to see her stone house come into view. This road—if you could call it that—was a much shorter way to the house and lab.

"Just let me wash up," she said.

I was belatedly remembering my own goal for that visit—questioning Viola Mae about her relations with Big Sam. I didn't want to miss my chance to question her.

"I'll be glad to drive," I said quickly.

"Thank you, Nicky. I'll be ready in a moment."

Viola Mae entered the old stone house through the back door, and I climbed into the truck, started the motor, and turned on the air conditioner. When she came out of the house, she looked much the same, though her hair was wet on one side, as if she had tried to get it to lie down.

She settled herself in the truck. Now I had to figure out a way to ask some pretty personal questions.

"Do you mind the air conditioning?"

"Mind?" She looked at me as if I were crazy. "Of course not. Air conditioning is one of the real blessings of modern life."

"My mother grew up in the South without it. I guess you did, too."

"Yes. I think that's the reason I liked the outdoors so much as a child. It was cooler than the indoors. Nights used to be the worst. I always knew it was summer when my mother made up my bed with the head at the foot. That way I got some cross-ventilation."

"Big Sam told me his family used to sleep outdoors."

"Yes. They had army cots. They kept them on the back porch in the daytime."

We were silent then, until I negotiated the turn from Viola Mae's gravel drive to the asphalt road.

"I hear Sam's not much better," Viola Mae said.

I looked at her. She seemed to be grinding her teeth.

"No, he isn't," I said, keeping up Sam's smoke screen. "Marty thinks he may be moved to the Holton Hospital later this week. The doctors say there's no treatment."

Viola Mae shook her head and spoke softly. "I'll always regret what happened to Sam."

There was my chance. I had to take it. "I think we've all been so involved in the family's view that we forget Big Sam's friends also care about what's happening to him," I said. "Take you, for example. You've known each other all your lives."

"Well, not all our lives, Nicky. There was a time in there, before World War II and during it, that we didn't see each other for years. Even after the war, while Big Sam was at Oklahoma A&M, we hardly saw each other. It was only after he bought the Titus place back that we met again."

"I don't want to pry," I lied, "but weren't you and Big Sam engaged at one time?"

I glanced at Viola Mae, and I saw that her blue eyes had grown big. I looked back at the road, and I could feel my face grow hot. Damn! I'd never make it as an interrogator.

Then Viola Mae laughed. "Well, I see that the Holton grapevine is as active as ever," she said.

I felt hotter. "I didn't mean—"

Viola Mae reached over and patted my arm. "That's all right, Nicky. I like that rumor better than the one that I'm a lesbian. As for Big Sam, I admit he was the first boy I ever kissed. We were nine, I guess, and he kissed me during a game of post office at a party given by Lorene Rich—that's Jack Rich's sister."

I was embarrassed, but I wasn't quite ready to give up. "I'm sorry," I said. "I thought you saw a lot of each other after you were grown up."

Viola Mae gave a dainty little snort. "Well, when we were in our middle twenties—after Sam finished college and came back to the Titus place—we did go out a bit. In a town the size of Holton, there wasn't really anybody else for either of us to go out with. But Sam simply couldn't afford to marry then, and by the time he could, frankly, I'd lost interest."

She chuckled. It had a kindly sound. "But Nicky, you're a creature of the modern age. We weren't. All you young things today think everybody has sex on the second date. You'd be amazed how many people didn't sleep together then—even engaged couples. It just wasn't done, and we didn't do it. I don't know why not, exactly. I don't think we were more moral than people are today."

Then she laughed heartily. "And I know for sure we had the same sort of sex drive," she said. "That's pretty well bred into the species. I guess birth-control methods weren't as reliable, and no doctor would advise an unmarried couple on such techniques. The social stigma of an illegitimate birth was considerable. Such babies were always given away for adoption. And an abortion was illegal, as well as impossible to arrange. It was considered murder."

"Lots of people still think that."

"True. But in the forties and fifties, that opinion was universal."

She laughed again. "I know about the Holton gossip, Nicky, but I assure you that even as a young man Big Sam was much too cautious to get involved in an affair that had so much potential for disaster."

"I didn't really intend to seem so nosy," I lied again.

She gave me another pat. "Don't worry, Nicky," she said. "I appreciate you asking rather than just believing all the ridiculous stuff that gets handed out around Holton. Sam and Marty have always been an extremely devoted couple, and Sam and I would have done nothing but argue over land management for thirty years."

We had swung around the mountain as we talked, and we were near the area damaged by the grass fire. Viola Mae quit talking, and I digested what she had said.

She had taken my questions well, but I had also been given a strong assurance on the innocence of Big Sam's relationship with Viola Mae. In fact, I had been given an extremely frank denial that their relationship had ever been anything other than innocent.

Was that denial too frank?

Viola Mae suddenly sat forward and braced herself on the dashboard of the truck. A pickup was coming down the deserted road toward us.

"Isn't that Dewayne Cudjoe?" she asked.

"It looks like his truck," I answered.

As we approached, Cudjoe waved us down. We stopped beside him on the empty road, and the pumper and I both rolled our windows down.

Cudjoe nodded a greeting at me, then looked at Viola Mae. He pointed over his shoulder with his thumb. "Did you call that sheriff out here?"

"Certainly not," Viola Mae said. "I don't need Tarzan Thompson to settle my problems."

"Well, he's there." Cudjoe's truck moved a few feet forward. "Maybe I'll have to call out the law myself," he said. Then he drove off.

Viola Mae gave a disgusted snort. "I wonder what that fool sheriff is up to. They'll probably be up at the well. You'd better take the road on my side of the fence. It's coming up quick."

I drove on, looking for the gate. Then I saw a black-and-white car parked on the side road. It had a giant golden star on the side.

"Oh, damn," Viola Mae said. "That silly Tarzan Thompson really is here."

We drove onto Viola Mae's property, traveling slowly down a road that was surrounded by utter desolation. Every blade of grass was black, and the trunks of the few trees that stood in the area were charred.

The big farm truck that Sam had driven was parked on the Titus side of the fence. A nondescript midsize sedan was back by the well, and three men were standing near it. I recognized Sam's beat-up straw hat and Tarzan Thompson's big sombrero.

We pulled up by the well, and Viola Mae jumped out of the truck.

"Tarzan! What are you doing mixing in this?" she called sharply.

Tarzan gave her an oily grin. For a moment I thought he was going to sweep off his big white hat and bow like a cavalier.

"Why, hello, Miz Humphries," he said. "I just came by here trying to catch Young Sam. I wouldn't mix in your affairs with the oil company a bit."

"You've never been shy about it before," Viola Mae said. "What are you up to?"

Sunglasses hid Tarzan's eyes, but he managed to make his grin even broader.

"Well, I guess I owe Miz Titus here a little apology," he said. "My conscience was botherin' me, so I come by to make things right." He turned to me. "I just totally lost my temper this morning, Miz Titus. I hope you'll excuse me."

"I was just a bystander," I said. "You don't owe me any apology."

I looked at Sam. He was doing his Great Stone Face act.

Tarzan chuckled. "I've already apologized to Sam," he said. "I hope he's going to forgive me. I'm trying to get us back on a friendly footing. Right, Sam?"

Sam didn't nod, smile, or otherwise react, but he did speak. "He's offered to call in the OSBI to investigate Big Sam's injury."

"Oh!" I said. Then I decided I'd better take my cue from Sam's reaction, and I shut up.

But Viola Mae felt no pressure to be silent. "Oh, my!" she said. "Oh, my! Well, I do hope they find something that will settle matters once and for all. And I'll admit, I'm saying that selfishly. Poor Young Sam here has been so worried about his dad that I can't get his attention on this lawsuit."

Thompson turned back to Sam. "Well, Sam, is it a deal?"

Sam still didn't show any emotion. "I'll certainly be willing to talk to the OSBI man," he said.

Tarzan smiled. "Okay! He'll be here sometime between seven and nine o'clock. He'll go by the house to see you."

Then he walked close to Sam. "Sam, I'd appreciate it if you'd shake hands."

"Sure, Tarzan," Sam said. The two men gripped hands briefly. They faced each other, glasses and sunglasses glinting, in a face-off of the faceless.

It was one of the most disgusting displays of insincerity I'd ever seen.

FOURTEEN

I WAS AMAZED. Why had Tarzan given in and called the OSBI?

Had Sam cowed him with his firm stand at the courthouse? Or had reason and logic actually prevailed?

I dismissed both possibilities. Sam might cow Tarzan Thompson, but Thompson would never come to him and admit it. And the idea of reason or logic having any effect on Tarzan was ludicrous.

So what was Thompson up to? I wanted to ask Sam's opinion, but this was not the moment. While I had been meditating on Tarzan Thompson, Sam, Viola Mae, and the oil-company man had shifted their concentration to the fire. They were looking at the oil-well equipment.

I joined them, lifting my sneakers high as I walked through the burned grass.

The oil man was introduced as Carson Slaughter, one of the Slaughter Brothers who owned the oil-production company. He was anything but the flamboyant type of operator pictured in movies.

Carson Slaughter was thin and small, and his mousy brown hair surrounded a well-defined bald spot. He wore dark-rimmed glasses, khaki pants, and a knit sport shirt with tan, brown, and orange stripes. His feet were clad in Adidas, not fancy cowboy boots. His expression was meek.

Viola Mae's expression was meek, too, but not her talk.

"I know there's been a saltwater leak here," she said firmly. "You can see how it killed the vegetation." She pointed at a white stain about six feet in diameter on the ground near one of the tanks. Nothing had burned in that area, apparently because nothing had been growing there.

"I know, ma'am," the oilman said, "and I don't understand that. I had Mr. Cudjoe fix it; then I came and checked his repair job personally. We could not find any leak."

"I suppose he claims the job was sabotaged," Viola Mae said angrily. "The truth is that he's been careless, and you've been careless because you left him on the job. He ignored the connections on this tank battery, and now the saltwater leak has corroded a pipeline and caused a fire."

Slaughter seemed to wilt before her attack. "I just don't see how that could have happened, ma'am. But apparently it did. I just hope we can all agree on a settlement for this damage."

"Well, Sam and the Tituses can do what they like," Viola Mae said. "Of course, the damage to my place was minor—this time. But I'm not signing anything. This will simply be added to the damages I'm seeking in my lawsuit."

"I didn't come here to talk about that lawsuit," the oilman replied. "But you'd better think twice about pushing for big damage. Twice nothing is nothing."

"And what do you mean by that?" Viola Mae asked. I didn't like the tone of her voice.

The oilman shrugged. "It's no secret that the oil business is in terrible shape. You can drive south out of Oklahoma City and see that by the number of rigs stacked up there. Another year of this and we may all go under."

"I don't think we can settle anything about economic conditions in the oil business today," Sam said. "But maybe we can figure out what caused this fire."

The three of them walked up and down the area, talking about separators, heater treaters, and Christmas trees. I didn't understand a word of it, and I was somewhat surprised that Sam seemed to. At lunch he had complained that he knew nothing about the oil fields.

After half an hour or so the oilman left, and I began to yearn for the trucks and their air-conditioned cabs. It was even hotter standing in that burned-out pasture than it had been driving through the wheat field. I was ready to go back to the house and slip into a glass of iced tea. Or maybe entice Sam into a tepid shower, if he could fit me into his plans.

Viola Mae dusted her hands off on her dull green slacks and smiled. "Well, that's that," she said. "But I'm going to ask one more favor."

"Anything," I answered.

"Would you mind waiting a few minutes while I walk up here and check on one of my cages?"

"You have a cage here? Didn't it get burned up?" I asked.

She gestured toward the mountain. "I don't think so. It's around behind those rocks, and the wind pushed the flames the other direction."

Sam spoke then. "Do you need help?"

"Oh, no. Just wait here."

She trotted off up the pipeline and disappeared behind a boulder, and I had Sam all to myself. I decided to quiz him.

"You sure talked big with Mr. Slaughter. I thought you didn't know anything about oil wells."

"I don't know anything technical. That library book was way over my head. But Big Sam had a glossary of oil-field terms in the office. Oil production for kindergarten kids. I read enough to follow Slaughter's excuses."

"Then you can explain. When you guys were discussing Christmas trees, you didn't mean these burnt-up cedars, right?"

"Right." Sam moved over and touched a sort of wad of silver pipes. They fit together at strange angles and formed a structure as high as his head. "This big shiny thing with all the connections is called a Christmas tree."

"And the separator doesn't divide the milk from the cream," I said.

"Nope. It divides the gas from the oil and water. Then the oil and water go into this other gadget—a heater treater." He pointed to a tank that looked to be twenty or twenty-five feet tall.

I looked at the tank. Two metal tubes were sticking out of one side, one on top of the other. The top tube came out of the tank at Sam's eye level, and an exhaust pipe stuck out of that tube, extending ten or twelve feet straight up into the air until it topped its parent tank by a couple of feet.

Sam rapped on the lower tube. "The firebox is in there," he said.

The lower tube came out of the tank about two feet off the ground. A metal box was fixed below it. Sam nudged it with his foot. "That's the firebox," he said.

"And it burns gas," I said.

"Right." He used his boot to trace a small metal line that crossed the earth from the tank he had identified as the separator. "It uses gas piped over from the separator to heat the oil and salt water so the water can be drained off. Don't ask me to explain the chemistry involved."

"Then the burner on the heater treater caused the fire?"

Sam frowned. "Not by itself." He pointed at the white stains of salt on the ground. "The pipeline that carries the gas off to the gas company runs along here, where that salt water had been leaking. Apparently the salt water caused the pipeline to corrode, and it sprung a leak. The gas oozed out. Slaughter thinks it concentrated near the heater treater, for some reason he doesn't understand, and caught fire from the burner."

I mulled the chain of events over. From the saltwater leak to the corrosion on the pipeline to the gas leak to the heater-treater burner to the pasture catching fire. It seemed logical.

"I guess Viola Mae is right, then," I said. "If the oil company hadn't been careless about the saltwater leak, this wouldn't have happened."

"Looks that way."

I eyed the equipment and thought about it. "And Viola Mae blames it all on that pumper, the one with the shotgun. If your dad agreed, it sure would appear that he and Cudjoe had a reason to fight."

Sam shrugged. His eyes were blank and stony again.

I fought the impulse to cry. A minute before he had been explaining things in much the way the old Sam would have. Then the curtain had dropped.

There was a cheery sound behind us. "All through!" Viola Mae sang out as she trotted back from checking on her cage. I turned and walked down the dirt road to the truck. I couldn't seem to find Sam both alone and ready for a confrontation, but I was beginning to wonder how long I could live with a stone.

I took Viola Mae to her place, then went back to the house. No big truck. No Sam. I stayed in the house with the doors locked. The custom combiner called. I told him to call back. Nora Rich called to check on Big Sam. I told her we hadn't heard anything that day. I read. I tried to watch a movie on television. I got a package of round steak out of Marty's freezer and thawed it in the microwave. Still no Sam. I made the steak into roulade, then put them in a slow oven. Still no farm truck had driven by the kitchen window.

About six o'clock I called Brenda. Her voice wasn't hopeful this time. In fact, she seemed so discouraged I decided I'd better go see her.

Billy and Lee Anna were in the backyard. Lee Anna's face was streaked with tears.

"Lee wet her pants, and Mommy spanked her," Billy told me. "Daddy didn't come home yet, and Mommy's mad."

Lee Anna looked at me with big blue eyes, and I felt awful. They were orphans. I wanted to weep for them, and I felt terribly guilty. I'd been sitting home all afternoon pouting over Sam's incommunicado act. I should have been giving Brenda some company, or at least a break from the kids.

I walked toward the kitchen door.

"Mommy won't let anybody in!" Billy warned me.

I knocked, anyway, and Brenda came to the door. Her blond hair was stringing down her neck. She wore no makeup, and her eyes were puffy. The house smelled of furniture polish and floor wax.

Her kitchen was decorated with ruffled red calico curtains. A kitchen witch hung over the sink. I wondered if it was a present from her mother.

Brenda let me in, then stared at the floor. "Did Sam find out anything?"

"Not that I know of. Did he come by here?"

"Just for a moment. He asked me a bunch of stuff about how old the tires on Bill's truck were." She moved to the sink listlessly.

I realized then where Sam had been all afternoon. He was out looking for Bill's truck.

And I realized something else. Brenda knew what Sam was doing. She wasn't admitting it, but she must have a strong suspicion that Bill was dead.

Then I faced another emotion. Fear. What if Sam had found the truck? What if he had run into the same sort of trouble Bill had? What if something had happened to Sam, too?

Brenda got out a can of scouring powder and sprinkled it over the sink. She lifted her chin. "I expect Bill will call in tonight," she said.

"Sure he will," I answered. We stood there, sharing our lie and our fear. Then Brenda began to cry.

I got her to go into the spotless bathroom and take a bubble bath. Then I made hamburger patties, instant potatoes, and carrot sticks for the kids and fed them some supper. By then Brenda seemed better. She bathed the children while I did the dishes; I was careful to leave everything antiseptically clean.

But she again refused my offer to spend the night. There was no place for Sam and me to sleep, she said. She'd call if anything happened. I promised to come back in the morning.

"Thank you, Nicky," she said. We hugged each other at the back door. She seemed afraid to let me go.

God, I was lonely. Where was Sam? I was overcome with fear as I tried to concentrate on driving home.

I was still feeling frantic when I turned up the gravel drive to the house. It was getting dark by then, and I had switched the headlights on. In their glow I could see a layer of dust in the air settling slowly back onto the gravel.

I had learned enough about the plains to recognize that symptom. It meant that someone had driven up that road just a few minutes before.

Was it Sam?

I tore up the drive, rounded the house, and wheeled into the machine shed. Sam stood under the big light, his fair hair reflecting its brilliance.

I turned off the motor and jumped out of the truck. "Where have you been?" I yelled, running toward him. Then I burst into tears, threw my arms around him, and sobbed against his chest.

"I don't care if you shove me away," I said. "I've been so scared something had happened to you, too!"

Sam didn't shove me away. He held me until I stopped sobbing. But he didn't say anything.

Finally, I raised my face to his. "I was really worried," I said.

"No need," he said. He gave me a kiss on the forehead. His lips felt firm and almost icy.

I refused to be rejected. I hung on to him tightly. "Where have you been?"

"All over." Sam pulled one of my arms free and swung halfway away from me. "I'll tell you later."

He gestured toward the house, and I suddenly realized that a midsize Chevy was sitting in the end space of the machine shed.

"Right now I need to talk to Mom," Sam said.

We rushed into the house. I walked through the kitchen door first and headed into the living room. It was dark. I looked in the bedroom. Dark. No Marty. The bathroom door stood open, and that room was also empty.

Then I realized that Sam wasn't behind me. I went back into the kitchen, and I heard footsteps overhead. He had skipped the check of the downstairs and had gone straight up the circular stairway. I ran up after him.

I reached the second floor and stopped, shocked by the scene before me.

The abstract painting above the fireplace had come to life.

Now I recognized the painting for what it was. It was abstract, true, but it was also a landscape showing the sun setting over the mountains and plains. It was a rendering of a sunset from Marty's studio window.

I suddenly saw the reason for the big windows on the west of the studio, the windows that allowed the studio to bake in the afternoon sun. Those windows and the deck outside were designed for watching sunsets.

And I realized the significance of the BETHANY signature on every painting in the house. Marty's full name was Mary Martha. Mary and Martha were sisters in the Bible, sisters who lived in the town of Bethany.

The light broke. Now I understood what Sam had meant when he referred to ''Mom's compulsion.'' All the paintings I had seen in the house, paintings that I now realized were by Marty, were abstract representations of sunsets. There was the cool gray-and-blue winter one in the bedroom and the vivid orange autumn one in the living room and the hot, summery one in the office. And the custommade area rug in the living room followed the same motif.

The live painting before me began at the top with a clear, pale blue. Below it was a bank of clouds, silver lamé above gray flannel. Underneath the clouds the gray faded into a soft peach. A clear golden band rimmed the horizon. The firm charcoal outline of the mountain rose to divide the sun's glowing arc at the right of the picture. The charcoal mountain dwindled diagonally across the canvas, smudging into a soft gray plain.

Huddled against the horizon was a silhouette, a large black amoeba. As I stood there, the amoeba divided and became two human beings: Marty, sitting in a chair, and Sam, kneeling beside her.

Their concentration on each other seemed so complete that I hesitated to break in. But the door was standing open, and almost immediately I heard Marty speak. ''Where's Nicky?''

''I'm here.'' I went out on the deck and kissed Marty on the cheek. ''Why didn't you tell us you were coming?''

Marty smiled, and her smile seemed less tight than the grimace she had worn in the hospital. ''After I talked the doctors into releasing Sam, I just packed him into an ambulance and got him down here before the Holton grapevine had time to pass the word. That way I was able to get him moved into the hospital without competing with the afternoon soaps.''

''How is he?'' Sam's voice was tight.

Marty raised her eyebrows. "How is he really? Or for public consumption?"

"Really."

"The doctors aren't committing themselves, but they think he's better."

"Good!" I said.

Marty patted my hand. "Not good yet, Nicky. But they say his coma doesn't seem as deep. He's breathing on his own, he has a feeding tube, and they say surgery is not an option. So I can see no point in keeping him in Oklahoma City. We'll just have to wait. But I felt I had to be closer to home and the search for Bill."

She turned to Sam. "Your dad definitely has brain damage, you realize. They just don't know how much."

Sam nodded. "At least he's improving, Mom. The only thing that worries me is that Holton grapevine. Gossip could put him back in danger. We don't want the word to get out that he's better."

Marty nodded. "I enlisted Dr. Thomas in our plot. He'll fake a chart to fool the nurses. Of course, if Sam actually wakes up, since something happened to Bill—" She broke off.

Sam put his arm around her shoulder. "If he wakes up, we'll get armed guards. I'll sit at the foot of his bed with an automatic rifle. Does that make you feel better?"

Marty's laugh was quavery. "Having you and Nicky here makes me feel better. And the ambulance people were wonderful. They got Sam settled; then I crept out here for my dose of sunset."

Sam stood up and silently got out two more director's chairs and unfolded them. When I started to speak again, he put his finger to his lips. We sat on either side of Marty, and all of us looked at the sunset.

Marty gave three deep sighs, and that was all the conversation there was for about twenty minutes. A few birds cried, and down on the road a few cars passed. We simply sat and looked at the sunset.

God, it was therapeutic.

For the first time since we left Germany, I began to feel that there must be some order to the universe, some solution to the puzzle of our lives, some pathway out of the morass.

At the end of twenty minutes, Sam suddenly stood up. "Nicky. Get your long lens!"

My temper flared. Why was he ordering me? Then I looked at Marty. I wasn't going to fight with Sam in front of his mother. I went to the bedroom, where I had left my camera case. Sam was still standing, looking into the setting sun, when I pulled the lens out of the case and took it to him.

He whipped it up to his eye without a word. He was looking off toward the southwest. I looked there, too. What was he seeing?

I couldn't see anything. The contrast had grown in the colors of the sunset in the twenty minutes we'd been watching it. Now the sky was dark blue, the clouds were a heavy gray, and the band along the horizon was a luminescent orange. The sun had dropped behind the mountain.

There was nothing to the southwest except a narrow cloud of dust. Was Sam looking at that?

Marty was also looking toward the southwest. She shook her head. "Are the Smith brothers up to their old tricks?"

Sam laughed, but the sound lacked humor. "Maybe so," he said. "But it's Titus property now."

"Should we call somebody about it?" Marty asked.

Sam laughed again, and this time he sounded as if he meant it. "We won't have to," he said. "Tarzan asked the OSBI man to drop by this evening. I wondered what Tarzan was up to."

Then he turned to me. "Nicky, something smelled wonderful as we came through the kitchen. Do you suppose we could eat whatever it is?"

"Sure. Give me twenty minutes."

"Great." Sam reached over and took his mother's hand. "Twenty minutes is just the amount of time I need to give this suspect the third degree."

FIFTEEN

SAM CONDUCTED his third degree at the kitchen table while I cooked frozen green beans and rice to go with the roulade. And listened.

"I want you to remember everything you can about the conversation when Big Sam mentioned malfeasance in office. When did it happen?"

Marty sighed. "The accident happened on Saturday, didn't it? Last Saturday. It seems like years ago. Well, he mentioned the malfeasance early that morning."

"Where were you?"

"Upstairs in the workroom. I guess that's why I didn't pay much attention."

"You were painting?"

"Yes. I should have put my things away and really listened to him."

Sam shook his head. "Don't worry about it, Mom. The whole family knows that they can't get your attention when you have a paintbrush in your hand. If we want to tell you something important, we make you stop. On the other hand, if we want to simply bounce ideas around, we wait until you're painting to do it."

Marty smiled at that. "I know you boys used to ask me for permission to do things when I was painting."

"Right. But Big Sam did the same thing. He'd sort of think out loud when you were painting, and I expect he was doing that when he talked about malfeasance in office. He didn't really want you to listen. But you try to remember. Just what did he say?"

Marty stared at the fork I'd put at her place. She picked it up with her strong hand and made a design on a paper napkin. "Well, he talked a lot, but you're right. I had the feeling he was really talking to himself, trying to clarify his ideas. He kept walking up and down."

"Now think. Try to remember what he looked like. That might jog your memory."

"He had on his new chambray shirt and his khaki slacks. He'd just come in from town, and he'd stopped at the Co-op and picked up some motor oil and a sack of bird seed. Oh, I remember! He started out talking about Viola Mae!"

"Viola Mae? What did he say about her?"

"Just that he hoped she was getting a carload price on sunflower seed. It had gone up another nickel for three pounds. You know, he noticed things like that."

I peeked at Sam, and I saw him purse his lips. That penny-pinching quality of his dad's had annoyed Sam a lot. But he nodded encouragingly to his mother. "Okay. What did he talk about next?"

She shook her head. "I don't remember. But he did mention that he had seen Brock Blevins."

"The bank wouldn't have been open."

"No, but if he had seen Brock's car parked behind the bank, he might have knocked at the back door. He did that sometimes."

"What did he say about Brock?"

Marty rolled her eyes. "Sam, it's all a blank. He wasn't too happy with Brock, but he and Brock fought all the time. I knew Sam would calm down in a minute."

"Did he?"

"Oh, yes. He was sort of laughing about something Brock had said. I do remember that. It was a typical pompous Brock remark."

"Do you remember what it was about?"

She shook her head again. "No. He went on to something else, and I don't remember what it was. But I do have a clear picture of your dad as he left. He walked over to the stairs, and he started down them. When he had gone around the first curve—you know, so that he was facing me again—he stopped. That's when he said something about malfeasance in office."

I stopped slicing tomatoes to concentrate on listening, and Sam leaned across the table. Marty had our complete attention.

She stared up, beyond the kitchen ceiling. "He said something about motives. Something like 'I don't care how good the motives are, I'm not getting involved in malfeasance in office.' "

She paused. "That's all I remember, Sam."

It sounded as if Big Sam had been asked to connive at wrongdoing. And the wrongdoing had been put to him in the guise of "rightdoing." In other words, someone wanted the law bent to gain some good result.

We were all mulling this over, I think, because dinner was a virtually silent meal. Sam and I were clearing the dishes away when Marty returned to the subject.

"Could it be related to the Smith brothers' antics?" she asked.

"Well, that's a strong possibility," Sam said. "And at this very moment I hear the unmistakable sound of an OSBI car approaching. We'll soon be in a position to investigate that very possibility."

"Are you going over there?" Marty asked.

"I think we'll have to," Sam answered. "We'll have to have an eyewitness report. We should be able to catch them gambling."

Marty sighed. "I want to go, too. I'm responsible for what goes on at this ranch. It's my property."

I could tell Sam wasn't happy, but he agreed.

I was certainly completely confused. Gambling? I didn't know where Sam and Marty were talking about going and what might happen when they got there.

And before I could ask, the OSBI man came to the front door—proving himself a total stranger. Sam met him there. I could hear them talking in the office.

"Nicky, you can come with us if you want to," Marty said. "I don't think there'll be any unpleasantness. Just leave the dishes. We'll finish up when we get back. I'm going to change clothes right quick." She dashed into her bedroom.

But I kept working, and I was wiping off the table when Sam and the OSBI man came out of the office. "Are you going?" Sam asked me.

"Where?"

He laughed his humorless laugh. "Let it be a surprise. Let's just say it's a folk event. I doubt that you'll like it much, but you might find it interesting. And I hope you never get another chance to see it."

Curiosity won. I ran upstairs and grabbed my purse. A folk event. Well, I might want to take a picture of it. I checked the number of exposures left on the roll of T-Max 400 I had used at the bird sanctuary and stuck the Leicaflex in my purse. I left the extra lenses at home.

When I came back down, Sam was pacing nervously by the front door.

We rushed out the front gate and climbed into the OSBI man's car, a plain vanilla sedan with no special markings. Sam got in front, and I sat in back with Marty, who was now wearing jeans and boots. Sam introduced me to Willis Greenburn. It was completely dark, of course, and the lights inside the car had been disconnected—which proved it was a real cop car. All I could see of Mr. Greenburn was a stub nose.

Marty and I sat silently. Sam and Greenburn traded a little gossip about classmates of Sam's who were now in law enforcement around the state. Then they shut up.

Sam was tense. I could see it in the set of his shoulders, the way he leaned forward and looked through the windshield. His mood was catching, and I jumped when he spoke. "There it is! By the fencerow."

Greenburn slowed down and turned left. I could tell we were on a dirt road. Something red caught my peripheral vision, and I looked quickly, just in time to see a reflective triangle leaning against the fence post. It was an emergency marker, the kind truckers use.

"Hell of a road," Greenburn muttered.

We bounced on a rutted trail for what seemed to be a couple of blocks; then I saw a light ahead and on the left. It swung around in a circle, and I realized it was a flashlight.

"Should we get down in the floor?" Marty asked calmly.

"I don't think it matters," Sam replied. "We're not planning any arrests."

When we came even with the flashlight, Greenburn rolled his window down and leaned out. "How much?" he asked conversationally.

"Twenty for a carload," a nasal voice answered, and the light from the flashlight pointed off toward the left. "Plenty of parking."

The voice was unmistakable. I leaned over to Marty. "Maynard Smith?"

"That's right," she answered.

Greenburn followed Maynard's gesture, and we came to a spot where about thirty pickups and cars were parked in drunken rows. Greenburn pulled in at the end, and we all got out. Sam motioned to the detective, and they conferred on our side of the car.

Sam reached over and rapped his knuckles on the load in the truck parked next to us. "Look at that," he said.

Greenburn nodded, and I looked at what Sam had seen. It was a fancy metal cage with mesh sides and a handle on top, a carrying case for some sort of animal. It was empty.

Marty and Sam both produced flashlights, and we started walking over a rough field. I tripped over a dried cow chip at that point and figured we were in somebody's pasture.

"Where are we?" I whispered.

"The Fields place," Marty answered. "There's an old barn behind those trees."

Most of the parked vehicles were pickups, but some were cars, a lot of them old heaps—the gas-guzzling dinosaurs left over from another era of American plenty. Here and there I saw a newer sedan.

Then we went into the trees, and I began to see lights ahead, bright lights. I could hear a murmur of talk, with occasional loud voices above it. "Got any more Bud?" rang out clearly at one point.

I peeked around Sam and saw a rectangle of light in the side of a building. Under the light were the backsides of a bunch of blue jeans, sitting on bleachers.

Just then a man appeared from behind the bleachers, coming toward us. As he drew even, he held up a bundle in his hand.

"Thought I had a good'un, but he didn't cut it," he said casually.

He was holding up a dead chicken.

He gripped its feet, and its head hung limp. Its feathers flashed green and bronze in the light. Blood covered its breast.

"Tough shit," Greenburn said. His voice sounded unconcerned.

Suddenly I knew where I was. A cockfight! I hadn't spent time in the South without learning about some of its customs.

I eyed the man with the dead bird. He was walking away now, but I kept my voice low. "This is disgusting!"

Sam looked at me. "Do you want to go back to the car?"

I thought about it. I hated cruelty to animals of all kinds. I strongly disapproved of cockfighting. But Sam was right about one thing he'd said at the house. It certainly was the only chance I ever intended to get to see what went on at a cockfight.

Sam repeated his question. "Do you want to go back to the car?"

I took a deep breath and reached into my purse. "Can I take pictures?"

Sam didn't react, but Greenburn snorted.

Marty laughed. "You've married a real artist, Sam," she said. "All experience is grist for the creative mill. Come on, Nicky. Keep your camera hidden for now, but if Sam and I can shield you, maybe you can get a few shots."

Marty turned toward the barn, but Greenburn put his hand out and touched her arm. "Just a minute, Mrs. Titus. Now you realize we probably won't be able to arrest anybody, don't you?"

Marty nodded, but I was completely confused. "If you catch them at a cockfight, can't you arrest them?" I said.

Greenburn frowned. "Not in Oklahoma. The law's been interpreted as making cockfighting legal."

"What!"

He shrugged. "I don't make the laws, ma'am. I just let the lawyers fight it out. From a practical law enforcement standpoint, there's not much I can do about the fights themselves, but"—he paused and raised his hand—"gambling on cockfights is illegal. Unfortunately, gambling between the spectators is just a misdemeanor, and that's all we'll have here. The property owners have to be taking a cut of the gambling to make it a felony."

"And no owner of the Titus Ranch is taking a payoff from the Smith brothers," Marty said firmly.

The whole situation amazed me. "Cockfighting is legal?" My voice sounded weak, even to me.

"But trespassing isn't," Sam said.

"Right," Greenburn said. "And since this property has changed hands and it's now on the Titus Ranch, I can run Maynard and Millard off—and I'm delighted to do it."

He turned and walked briskly toward the lights.

We entered the barn, and I saw that there would be no hiding our identities. While the bodies in the bleachers cast harsh shadows in front of the door and in the corners of the barn, which was about thirty feet long and twenty feet wide, the lights at the center of the building were bright. I followed Sam and Greenburn to the end of the bleachers, where the two of them stopped. We all surveyed the room.

More bleachers—they were rough wooden planks—were on the opposite side of the barn. Both sides were about two-thirds filled with spectators. They were nearly all men, but a few women and even some children were scattered through the group. A plump woman in a T-shirt with no bra sat nearest us. She was sweating, and her dirty-blond hair was stringing down her neck. I could see beads of dirt in the creases of her neck.

I groped for my camera and pulled it out of my purse.

The blonde jumped to her feet, boobs bouncing. "Kill 'im! Kill 'im!" she shrieked

I adjusted the f-stop, focused, and as the light hit her face I clicked off a quick shot of her. Then I aimed at the cockfight itself.

Harsh lights beat on the center of the barn, where a sand arena held two birds.

They were circling each other, and as I lifted my camera, they erupted into a whirlwind of bronze, brown, and green feathers. Then red began to stain the sand, and I looked away.

Scanning the scene through my viewfinder, I saw the pointed chin of Millard Smith sticking out from under a white straw hat. He was standing at the end of the pit, stooping over with his hands on his knees. One of his hands held a fan of paper bills. He lifted the other hand, made it into a fist, and shook it, encouraging the fighting cocks to greater gore.

Then Sam shoved me, and I almost fell over. Marty grabbed my arm and whispered urgently, "Put the camera away!"

I shoved it in my purse, and I heard a harsh nasal voice.

"I thought I saw you dirty sneaks comin' in here! Jes got a look, but I smelled a skunk and shore 'nuff, here's a striped gentleman!"

It was Maynard.

"Evening, Maynard," Sam said. "I see you and Millard have a little chicken fight going on tonight."

"I s'pose you don't like it! Well, let me tell you, Thomas Jefferson liked it. It's an all-American sport that any red-blooded, two-fisted patriot—"

I won't repeat it all. The gist of it was that cocks were born to fight and that preventing their battles was a Communist conspiracy.

Sam seemed to listen to Maynard's tirade without rancor; I think that really infuriated the older man. But I could see Greenburn's neck and ears getting red, and when Maynard finished up with " . . . and you ain't a lawman in these parts, and chicken fights ain't illegal in this state, anyways," the OSBI man reacted.

He whipped out a leather folder and held it before Maynard's nose. "Captain Titus may not be a lawman here, but I am. And gambling on cockfights is illegal, whether the fights themselves are or not, as you well know, Maynard."

I saw that Maynard and Greenburn were old adversaries. "There's no betting going on here, lawman."

Greenburn gestured toward Millard and his fistful of bills. "What's Millard holding, if it's not bets?"

Maynard snickered. "Entry fees, lawman. Entry fees."

In spite of the commotion of the cockfight, the spectators nearest us were beginning to notice what was going on. The plump woman got to her feet and moved off the end of the bleacher, followed by an even fatter man in a dirty cap. Others began to stir nervously, and a few simply stood up to see what was going on.

Maynard continued to talk incoherently, and Millard appeared at his elbow.

"Now, let's keep calm," he said, smiling a toothy smile. "These good folks came here for nothing but an entirely peaceful chicken fight. They don't want any trouble."

The OSBI man was redder than ever. "I'm not interested in these spectators." He said it rather loudly.

Millard scratched his head. "Well, seein' as how cockfights ain't illegal in Oklahoma—"

Greenburn broke in. "Whether or not cockfighting is illegal, trespassing is. You and your brother have no right to run this fight on the Titus Ranch, and I may have no choice but to arrest you both."

Millard kept smiling. "What makes you think we're runnin' this fight?"

"You were in the ring, and your brother was outside parking cars. That's a pretty good indication."

Millard scratched his head. "Well, I don't know if that would stand up in court," he said. "In America even us little folks have legal rights. I told your daddy that, Young Sam, the very last time I saw him. It was the very day of his accident, and I was headin' for town, and we passed each other and stopped to chat a moment. Rich folks can't push poor ones around in this country. I'm afraid you and this lawman here will have to prove we were running this event. We say we were merely spectators."

The OSBI man scanned the barn. Nearly every eye was on our end of the ring now. The human confrontation had plainly replaced the cocks as main attraction. I became aware that sweat was trickling down my forehead. Would the crowd rebel if they were told the cockfight was over?

"This land is part of the Titus Ranch now," Sam said. "And I'm acting as agent for my mother, a partner in that ranch. This gathering is taking place without her permission."

Marty moved forward and stood beside Sam. "That's right, Millard," she said. "I really must ask you and your friends to leave."

How could Marty and Sam sound so calm? The OSBI man didn't look too calm. His face was bright red now, and his gaze bounced around the barn.

Mine bounced around, too. I looked at the spectators to see how they were reacting. Most of them were still, watching our end of the arena. Then movement drew my eye. A new spectator suddenly walked around the opposite end of the bleachers.

He surveyed the scene, standing with his hands on his hips, his big white hat pushed back. A moment later, his eyes lit on Sam, and he gave a start, wheeled around, and left the same way he had come.

But I got him.

In that moment when he stood still, I had reached into my purse, whipped my Leicaflex to my eye, focused, and snapped the shutter twice. I felt sure at least one would be a good shot.

He hadn't been wearing his badge of office, but the photo was going to show a clear view of Sheriff Tarzan Thompson.

SIXTEEN

I BARELY STOPPED to wonder what Tarzan was doing at the cockfight. It was obvious from the guilty way he jumped back that he was either a spectator or an actual participant.

His presence also explained why he had belatedly called in the OSBI, setting the appointment for that particular evening. I was ready to guess that he had told Greenburn that Sam couldn't see him until nine o'clock, just as he had told Sam that the state lawman would come between seven and nine.

That, I speculated, should have kept Sam well out of the way at the time when the cockfight crowd was gathering. But Marty's meditation session with the sunset had ruined Tarzan's plan, since Sam saw the cloud of dust raised by the cars and trucks approaching the old barn and realized what was going on.

But that wasn't a matter of prime importance right then. At that moment the main thing became getting out of there.

The crowd was growing restless. Maynard's rantings had brought the chicken fights to a standstill, and tough, mean-looking hombres were climbing down out of the stands.

A half dozen of the louts formed a circle around us. They mostly had chaws in their cheeks and wore billed caps with beer logos on the fronts and T-shirts that said things like "When guns are outlawed, only outlaws will have guns."

I stuffed my camera deep inside my purse and crowded up against Sam, putting my hand on his back. He reached around and squeezed it with his own. I didn't have time to respond. The louts were crowding in, and Greenburn was concentrating on getting us all out of there.

"Well, I'm not eager to make any arrests tonight," he said. He was looking at Maynard. "But you two men will have to be available for questioning tomorrow."

That kicked Maynard back into his raving mode. He started in on Thomas Jefferson again and finished up with "that real lawman—Heck Thomas." None of it made any sense.

Millard soothed him down to a mumble, and Greenburn repeated his remark. "Y'all will have to be available for questioning."

Millard pursed his lips, and Sam answered for him. "They'll be there, Greenburn. I've known the Smith brothers all my life. I don't appreciate them using a Titus Ranch barn for their chicken fights, but I don't believe they'll leave the country."

I wasn't particularly sophisticated about law enforcement techniques, but I recognized the good cop-bad cop routine. Greenburn and Sam had fallen into it as smoothly as if they had rehearsed it.

It worked. The Smith brothers promised not to go anywhere, and we all headed for the door. It did my heart a bit of good when we got outside and saw that a line of cars was driving back out the dirt road to the county blacktop. We might not have broken up the chicken fights completely, but only the louts seemed to be hanging around. The ordinary rednecks were leaving.

The louts stood and watched while we got into the car. Greenburn gave them a polite salute as we drove away, and I breathed a sigh of relief.

"Whew!" I said. "I'm glad to get out of there."

"We're lucky we got out," Sam said. "If that bunch had seen that camera, we might not have. Or at least you might not have gotten out with the camera."

"I'm glad we did," I said. "I think I got a good shot of Tarzan."

"Tarzan!" Sam and Greenburn yelled at the same time.

Greenburn slammed on the brakes and threw us all against our seat belts. "Was that guy there?"

"Didn't you see him?" I asked.

"Naw." The OSBI man gave the motor some gas, and the car moved on. "Are you sure it was him?"

"Oh, yes, I think so. Of course, I can't guarantee that the film will come out, but he had his hat pushed back, so I think I got a good shot of him."

Sam began to chuckle. "I had a suspicion there was a link between the chicken fight and Tarzan arranging for Greenburn to come by just at the time the cocks would begin to clobber each other. But I didn't think we'd be lucky enough to catch him on the premises."

Greenburn was laughing, too. "Young lady, maybe you'd better let me have that film."

I hesitated. "Oh . . . Well, I always do my own developing. There's some other stuff on the roll."

"I think I can guarantee our technician will do a good job, and I'll get you an eight-by-ten of every frame," Greenburn said.

"Better let him have it, Nicky," Sam said. "He'll give you any negatives that aren't needed as evidence."

As soon as we got back to the house, I sat down at the kitchen table and unloaded the camera. I stuffed the roll of film into a plastic canister that had held it originally and gave it to Greenburn. "Tell the lab man he'd better push this film a bit," I said. "It won't hurt the frames at the beginning, and it might help the cockfight shots."

He went out the kitchen door, and Sam walked with him to the gate. "I'll be back in the morning," I heard the OSBI man say. "Then we'll talk about your dad's accident in detail."

"There's no point in your coming before ten," Sam answered. "The combiners start tomorrow. I'll be pretty busy for a while."

I said good night to Marty, then went upstairs and took a shower. The hot water seemed to pull my old fears to the surface—fears of the huge sky, the bare plains, and the alien inhabitants. Chicken fights, good old boys, crooked sheriff... I might as well have dropped onto Mars. I wrapped up in a towel and blew my hair dry. Once again I longed to lean against Sam and tell him how I felt. I wanted to feel his arms around me, to explain to him how frightened the idea of living in Holton made me.

I wanted to tell him how much I loved him and how much I wanted to help him, how I longed to hold him and comfort him, just as I longed for the comfort of his embrace.

I had wanted to tell him that for forty-eight hours, and he had seemed to avoid talking to me.

I put on the gown he had showed me was his favorite, the black one. I added cologne. Then I topped the outfit off with a light robe and went downstairs.

Tonight he wasn't going to escape. I was determined to have that serious talk with him. The situation seemed to be improving. He had found out what Tarzan Thompson was up to, and the OSBI was ready to take Big Sam's injury and Bill's disappearance seriously. He would have to be less tense, more receptive to discussion.

I found Sam alone in the office, staring at the computer screen. I pulled up a chair. "We need to have a talk."

Sam kept his eyes on the screen. "Sure. I'll be up in a few minutes."

"Sam—"

"Just a minute, Nicky. I'm about to figure this out." He tapped at the computer keyboard. The screen went blank.

"Damn." Sam shook his head. "I'll have to start over." He tapped the keyboard again.

"Sam—" I realized my voice was getting sharper, and I stopped and adjusted it. "Darling, I really want to talk to you. Seriously."

Sam reached out and hugged me with his right arm. His left remained poised over the computer keyboard, and his eyes didn't leave the green letters on the screen.

"It'll be better if we talk upstairs," he said. "Go on up. I'll be there in a few minutes."

"Sam—"

"Just a few minutes, Nicky. Okay?" It was his turn to sound a bit sharp.

Then I heard Marty's bedroom door open. Her footsteps crossed the hall and entered the bathroom. I couldn't yell with Marty in the next room.

I gave up and went upstairs. I sat in the little chair by the window. I knew Sam wasn't coming soon.

I was determined not to be in bed asleep when he came up. I got a book—a rousing adventure tale—from one of the shelves in the hall, and I curled up in the chair.

I awoke with a stiff neck. The sky to the east was tinged with pink, and it was six o'clock in the morning. The house was still. The bed was empty.

I got in it.

The sound of machinery awoke me. I staggered to the front window and looked out. It was nearly nine o'clock. Three giant, ungainly contraptions were coming up the road toward the house.

The combines were there.

I grabbed a bowl of cereal for breakfast. Alone. Sam was outside, talking to the custom combiner, and Marty had headed for town to check on Big Sam.

By the time I had rinsed my dishes and put them into the dishwasher, I could hear a clacking and roaring, which meant the combines had started work.

I stood by the fence and watched them moving in formation across the wheat field in front of the house, leaving a crunchy stubble behind. As I watched, one of the monsters pivoted out of its assigned pattern and lumbered over to a giant red farm truck. It thrust a long pipe over the truck's bed and spewed out a stream of gold.

There were plenty of men working around the place, operating the monster machines that cut the grain, then blew it into a huge truck with high sides of planks painted red. When the truck was full, it was moved to the conical grain-storage building in back of the barn, the one I had quizzed Sam about the first day we arrived. The auger in the top of the grain-storage building pulled the wheat out of the truck and loaded it into the metal building. Then the truck went back for another load.

I stood out by the fence quite a while and watched the combines. I even took a few pictures, but it was a subject that called for color. Since my Paris mentor had wanted me to work only in black and white for a while, I had no color film.

The sky was a clear blue, the clouds pure white, the wheat a deep golden. The reds and greens of the combines and trucks accented the masses of color. I used a yellow filter and took some cloud shots, but my heart wasn't in it.

My heart was over across the field, talking to a custom combiner. The night before, Sam had rejected my direct request to talk to him, had dodged me in spite of my plan to wait up no matter how late it got. We had been married less than three weeks. Was our marriage going to end before it really started?

Sam was rejecting me. There was no other explanation.

At ten o'clock I was upstairs, making the bed like the good little houseguest my mother had brought up, when I heard the door bang. Sam's baritone echoed up the stairs, and Greenburn's southwestern monotone answered.

I was so mad at Sam that I started to stay where I was. Then I realized that Greenburn had probably brought the prints of the pictures I had taken at the cockfight. I decided I could be polite to Sam in front of the OSBI man and, driven by professional curiosity, decided to go downstairs and look at the prints.

"Mornin', Miz Titus," Greenburn said. "You're a good little photog."

I wondered how my Paris mentor would take that patronizing remark, but I again let the polite little girl my mother had raised answer. "Thanks. Did the picture of Tarzan turn out?"

Sam picked up a print from the kitchen table, where the pictures were spread out, and held it up for me.

"A little grainy, but a great shot," he said.

I looked at Tarzan. His hat was on the back of his head, and his face was clearly visible in the picture. A dead cock was visible, too.

"I'm a bit surprised at Tarzan," I said. "I mean, I thought that the smart thing for him to do would be to come up to one of you guys last night and explain that he was there in an official capacity."

Greenburn nodded. "Yeah, that would have been smarter. This way all we can assume is that he didn't think we had seen him, so he cut out."

"I expect he was afraid to come around Maynard," Sam said.

"Afraid?" Greenburn looked puzzled.

Sam nodded. "Yeah. Maynard's a regular loose cannon. If Tarzan really is protecting the chicken fights, there's no telling what Maynard might have said if Tarzan had shown up."

"If cockfighting isn't illegal in Oklahoma, why was Tarzan involved?" I asked.

Sam and Greenburn looked at each other. "Well, I wouldn't want to speculate on any financial benefits to Tarzan," the OSBI man drawled, "and the legality or illegality of cockfighting needs to be the subject of a new court decision, maybe. But it's sure not respectable."

"Respectable?"

Sam nodded. "Going to the chicken fights isn't something people mention casually to the preacher, Nicky. Helping the Smith brothers put on cockfights wouldn't help Tarzan get reelected. And since the Smith brothers were holding the fight on somebody else's land—well, we could charge Tarzan with being some sort of accessory. At least we could embarrass him."

"Oh..." The rest of my pictures were in a stack on the table, and I picked them up. "Your lab man did a good job on these," I told Greenburn. I went through them. There was the bluejay in the cedar tree, then the small brown bird. Next I came to a series of the cowbird in the cage. I tossed them back on the table.

Sam scooped them up. "Those aren't very scenic," he said.

"Oh, I thought I'd give them to Viola Mae, just as a record of her research project. These are more attractive." I shoved the prints of the mother wood duck and her brood toward him.

But Sam had picked up the shots of the cage. He took off his glasses, the way he does when he wants to see something real close up, and held one of the prints close to his eyes, frowning.

"What is it?" I asked.

Sam didn't answer. He turned abruptly and went through the living room and into the office, taking the photo with him.

I felt my face grow hot with anger. He had done it again, and in front of Greenburn. I looked at the OSBI man, and his eyes dodged away from mine.

"Yes, you're a real good little photog, Miz Titus," he said.

"Thank you, Mr. Greenburn," I answered. "If you'll excuse me, I'll finish what I was doing upstairs."

I was sitting in the bedroom chair, staring angrily at the wall, when I heard the back door open and close. I ran to the studio and looked out just in time to see Sam and Greenburn driving off in the unmarked OSBI car. Sam had left without speaking.

Well, if everybody else was out, I decided, I'd go someplace, too. Maybe check on Brenda.

The photographs were gone from the kitchen table. I grabbed the pickup keys from the rack by the back door, locked the door, took my anger, and left.

Brenda's drive was empty. She wasn't home. So I felt guiltless as I drove on into Holton.

I glared at the houses that lined the street leading into town, turning my fury at Sam on his hometown. What a pit. The houses looked run-down; about half the business buildings were empty. I passed the IGA supermarket—the one busy spot in the town. Even there the grass was growing up in the cracks along the curb.

I drove on down Main. The houses were nondescript. There was no beauty or architectural significance to any structure in the town. I reached the courthouse square. Another artistic nothing. It had some big trees, true, and one decent-looking flower bed. I looked at it again. Well, maybe they had tried. I knew governments were always short of funds.

And suddenly an architectural marvel did appear.

It was a tall red-brick house, three stories and a basement, surrounded by substantial trees. It was directly behind the courthouse, facing the side street where the residential district began. I turned the corner to get a better look.

The house had been built about 1910 or so, I decided. It had a shiny white veranda all across the front that kept the house from taking on the gloomy look that old red-brick houses can get. It was simply a well-proportioned, attractive old house.

As I drew nearer, I saw, to my pleasure, that there was a small, neat sign in the front yard. The house must have been named to the National Register of Historic Sites, I thought. Perhaps it had some real historical significance, in addition to its pleasant design. I slowed down to read the sign as I passed. Then I began to laugh.

The sign in the yard read SHERIFF'S OFFICE—CATLIN COUNTY JAIL.

I drove on, laughing and crying at the same time. How typical of this weird, isolated town. They'd taken the one decent-looking building and turned it into a jail.

Oh, God! I prayed. How could Sam consider coming back here?

How had a person as nice and intelligent as Marty survived in this town all these years? No wonder she was wacko about her painting. She must hide her artwork because no one in Holton would understand what she was doing.

She'd been buried alive. It was tragic.

I remembered Greenburn's assessment of my own work. "A good little photog!" I'd like to give his artistic sensibilities a whack.

If only Sam would talk to me. A low buff-brick building appeared on the right, and I automatically read the sign: HOLTON HOSPITAL AND NURSING CENTER.

That was where Big Sam was.

I stepped on the brakes. Yes, Marty's car was in the parking lot.

I pulled in and parked. While I'd been driving around town feeling sorry for myself, Marty had been meeting tragedy head-on. I'd been oh so concerned about Sam's refusal to see his father in the hospital, but I hadn't considered trying to see him myself. It hadn't seemed sensible for a brand-new daughter-in-law to visit an ICU, where visitors were limited. But in the Holton Hospital things would be different. I had no excuse not to see Big Sam.

I rolled the pickup's windows down, since the day was already hot and I didn't want the interior to turn into an oven. I got out of the truck and, moping like a tomboy on her way to ballet lessons, I went in the front door of the hospital.

The lobby was cheerful, filled with traditional furniture and old ladies in wheelchairs. A black nurse directed me down the hall, to an end room. The door was shut, and I knocked timidly.

Marty's voice answered. "Come in."

I put my head around the door, and she smiled at me. "Oh, Nicky," she said. "Come on in."

"I didn't want to intrude."

"No, it's fine. I just thought I'd sit here this morning, since a bunch of the Holton people are bound to come by. That way I can give them the cover story and keep them from doing things that Sam wouldn't like."

I forced myself to walk to the bedside and look at Big Sam. His shallow breathing barely lifted the sheet that covered him halfway up the chest. A big hunk of his hair had been shaved to display a colorful bruise and staples marching along an ugly cut. Purplish bruising surrounded his swollen eyes. Tubes went into his arm, and more tubes came out from under the sheet. An egg-crate pad cradled his body.

Marty stood beside me. "He needs to be shaved," she said. "They have one aide who always does the shaving, and he's off today. Sam would hate to look shabby like that."

I remembered the vigorous man in cowboy boots who had clumped off the airplane in Frankfurt—was it less than a month ago? The contrast with this limp creature was almost too much.

Then Big Sam moved. He turned his head restlessly, and his eyes flickered open, then shut. He lifted his left arm and laid it down, and I could see his leg move under the sheet.

Marty grabbed my hand. "Did you see that?"

"Oh, yes!"

"He wasn't doing that day before yesterday, Nicky! I really think he's beginning to come out of it."

"That's wonderful!"

"I simply can't let myself get too excited! It could be a false hope. And besides, I've got to tell everyone that he's doing worse and worse. I've got to let them think we've brought him home to die."

"Sam thinks it's the best way to keep him safe."

Before Marty could speak, there was a tap at the door, and Nora Rich gave a cheerful "Yoohoo!" She and her silent husband, Jack, came in. Big Sam cooperated by remaining immobile while Marty told them how poorly he was doing.

Nora shed a tear. "It's hard to believe, isn't it," she said. She hugged Marty. "Just a tragedy. A real tragedy."

Jack merely shook his head.

I began to wonder if I should go, but I decided I'd outwait the Riches and would discuss more mundane matters, such as the dinner menu, with Marty before I left.

So I was still there when I heard the rapid slap, slap, slap of rubber-soled shoes running down the hall, followed by Brenda's voice.

"Marty! Marty! Where are you?"

Marty stepped out into the hall. "Brenda! Here I am."

Brenda's face was wild and tear streaked, and her blond hair was standing on end. "Oh, Marty!" she cried out. She put her arms around Marty, and the older woman held her and stroked her back.

"What's wrong, Brenda?" she said gently.

Brenda gave a convulsive sob and stood up straight. "Sam and that state man are going to drag Viola Mae's lake," she said.

Marty gasped, and I heard my own voice say, "Oh, no!"

Brenda straightened up, took a deep breath, and swallowed.

"They won't say why, but it's because they think Bill's body is in there, don't they? I think I've known it all along. Bill's dead."

SEVENTEEN

AFTER HER OUTBURST, Brenda grew calmer, and although she wiped her eyes often, she didn't break down again.

Billy and Lee Anna were at her friend's house, and Marty, Brenda, and I headed for Viola Mae's lake. Jack Rich offered to take Brenda's car home, so Brenda drove with Marty, and I followed in the pickup.

I had expected chaos and excitement at the lake, but it was relatively calm. The OSBI man's car was there, and a Highway Patrol car and several pickups that seemed to belong to neighbors. The Catlin County grapevine had gotten busy on this one fast.

Sam was there, wearing jeans, but no shirt. When our minicaravan drove in, he picked something up from the dashboard of the OSBI car and walked over to meet us, moving very slowly. His jeans and hair and the canvas shoes he wore were soaking wet.

The three of us were standing in a clump, but it was Brenda Sam looked at. He didn't seem to know what to say.

Brenda lifted her chin. "Bill's in there, isn't he?"

"I don't know," Sam answered. "There's a pickup in here. I'm not much of a diver, but it's not in too deep. I could see that it's red, Brenda. I'm afraid there's not much doubt it's Bill's truck."

"Any sign of Bill?" Marty's voice was soft.

Sam looked at the ground. "I'm not good enough underwater to tell, Mom. We'll have the truck out pretty quick."

He turned to me and stretched out his hand. "Here," he ordered. "Put this stuff in your purse."

It was the stuff he carried in his pockets—billfold, hand-kerchief, the key ring with the red plastic tag, and a pocket knife. He turned without another word and walked back to the OSBI man's car, his wet shoes leaving a trail of alien footprints as they acquired a furry coat of the soft dust.

I packed his pocket paraphernalia away, and the three of us Titus women stood there. Then an old tan pickup came careening down the road, and we all turned toward it.

"Damn," I muttered. It was Bobbi Baker.

She got out of the truck wailing, "Oh, Brenda! My poor baby! I just can't believe all this! Your poor babies! How could this happen!"

Brenda didn't hesitate. She went to meet her mother. When she spoke, her voice was as hard as steel.

"Calm down, Mother," she said. "I know you enjoy these dramatic situations, but I won't have you making a fool of yourself or of me right now. Either be quiet or get back in that truck."

I was really proud of Brenda. It was such a switch from the "Mother, please!" girl of the first day we had arrived.

"Oh, Brenda, honey—" Bobbi started out again.

But Brenda cut her off just as sharply. "No, none of that," she said. She took her mother by the arm and led her toward the truck. "I can't stand any hysteria right now. You get back in that truck until you calm down."

And she opened the door and put her mother in the truck. Bobbi sat there looking stunned. She opened her mouth once, then closed it with a snap.

A van drove in about that time, followed by a black-and-white car with a gold star on the side. I gasped. Had Tarzan Thompson had the gall to show up?

But when the car door opened, a gray-haired man got out. After a second I recognized him as the man who had led Tarzan away from the scene when Sam and the sheriff bat-tled it out in the courthouse. He had worn a deputy's star.

His voice was loud enough for us to hear. "I can't find Tarzan anyplace," he said.

Neither Sam nor Greenburn reacted.

The sign on the side of the van he had followed in read DIVER DAN. The driver, a wiry guy in swimming trunks, got out and opened the double doors in the back. He began to lug out scuba equipment. He conferred with the law officers and the wrecker driver. Then he donned a tank and goggles and waded into the lake.

He came out again in two or three minutes and had another conference on the shore. Greenburn and the man from the sheriff's office looked toward us. Sam stood stolid as a fence post. The diver walked to the back of the wrecker, and he and the wrecker operator began to mess with the cable and the big hook on the back.

Sam walked up the road to us, with Greenburn following.

Brenda seemed to be standing straighter all the time. "Bill's in there," she said flatly.

"The diver can't tell until we get the truck out," Sam answered.

Brenda reached over and put her arm around Marty. They clutched each other wordlessly.

Greenburn joined our group then, and he spoke directly to Sam. "Listen. You stay here, Sam. You don't have to—"

Sam turned on him. For a moment I thought he was going to hit the older man.

Then Sam swallowed, gulping as if he were downing a hard-boiled egg in one chunk. "It's all I can do now," he said.

He strode back to the wrecker and walked into the lake, helping the wrecker operator pay out the cable as the diver took it into the water.

A thought flashed through my mind. Bill was only two years younger than Sam. Growing up on the farm, with no close neighbors, they must have been playmates as well as brothers. Had they climbed in the barn loft, ridden calves, swum in that pond together? Was Sam thinking of that now? Or was he remembering that he had quarreled with his father and that Bill had sided with the older man? Was he recalling that the last words he and Bill exchanged were harsh?

Which set of memories would be more painful?

Nora and Jack Rich arrived about that time. Nora had brought a case of soft drinks, a couple of gallons of tea and a cooler filled with ice. She set up shop on the tailgate of Jack's pickup. Some of the onlookers drank tea.

We all stood around, and again I was struck by how peaceful it all was. Even the prairie winds barely moved, there in the sheltered cove that held the lake. The trees guarded the opposite shore, and the cattails swayed gently as the diver waded near them. The water reflected blue sky and imposing clouds; it seemed impossible that those reflections might hide the body of someone Marty and Brenda—and Sam—loved.

The only sound came from the wrecker. Nora Rich sat beside her load of refreshments. Jack Rich joined two other ranchers who stood watching the operation mutely. Bobbi Baker had swung her door open and was sitting sideways in the cab of her beat-up pickup, but she didn't say anything. Brenda, Marty, and I stood by Marty's car. Brenda and Marty were still holding hands. The sun was baking down, but none of us moved toward finding shade.

Then the diver came out of the water, and the wrecker's winch began to whir and groan. I could see the cable stretch taut and twitch. I found myself standing shoulder to shoulder with Marty, not quite sure how I got there.

There was a splashing sound and a flashing of the sun on streams of water, and the bed of a pickup truck suddenly emerged from the pond. The water seemed to clutch at it, resentful at giving up its prey, then suddenly disgorged the rest of the truck. Water weeds hung from its bright red bed, and the cab spewed water from half-open windows and from around doors.

Sam was at the pickup's side as soon as the truck was clear of the water. Greenburn stepped between Sam and the door. "No!" he said sharply. "Let me!"

Sam's answer was so quiet I couldn't hear it, but Greenburn stepped aside. Sam pulled at the handle. The door swung open, and water gushed over his feet and legs, then slowed.

A boot had fallen out the door.

I don't think it had really hit me until that moment.

Something about that boot suddenly appearing in the door of the pickup and falling to the ground knocked me in a heap. I turned around and put my elbows on the roof of Marty's car and held my head in my hands. Tears ran down my palms and dripped down my forearms and made puddles on the top of the car. I could hear Marty begin to sob, too. Brenda took a breath that seemed almost a twang.

Time seemed to stop. Somewhere far off I heard Bobbi Baker saying, "Oh, no! Oh, no!"

One of the ranchers muttered, "Goddam!"

Then I heard Sam's voice. He had walked up to the car and was standing almost behind me.

"It's empty," he said. His voice held no hint of emotion. "There's nothing in it but some clothes."

Greenburn's flat tone sounded next. "It was definitely sent in there on purpose," he said. "The accelerator was jammed down with a stick."

Marty spoke very quietly. "Could his body have washed out of the truck?"

"We'll have to drag the lake to answer that," Greenburn said. I turned around and saw that he was looking at the ground. "But it seems as if—" He stopped.

Sam spoke harshly. "He'd be floating by now," he said.

I looked at him. He was as stony-faced as ever.

Suddenly I felt desperately sorry for him. And at the same moment I recognized that our marriage might be over, maybe had never existed.

Sam's heart must be breaking over his brother's murder, a murder pretty well confirmed by the discovery of Bill's truck. Yet he was hiding his feelings completely. His face was perfectly calm.

How could he show no more emotion than if the wrecker had hauled a stranger's car out of that lake?

Could a person who could hide his emotions that completely really have any feelings? I didn't understand.

If I couldn't understand him, how could I hope to trust him? How could I even believe him when he said he loved me? Was he capable of love? Was that calm face all there was to Sam? Did his strong, silent facade hide nothing but more silence?

I didn't know the answers.

All I knew was that I couldn't bear to look at Sam. I staggered around the blue pickup. I leaned against the tailgate and made my decision. I had to leave, leave Holton and leave Sam.

There was no point in creating a scandal that would harm Marty. Bill's body had to be in that lake someplace. I'd stay until after Bill's funeral. Then I'd simply tell the Nora Riches of Holton that I needed to go back to Germany on family business. I still had a VISA card. I'd get there. Soon I'd be back in Paris, and my connection with the Titus family and the miserable town of Holton would be a thing of the past.

Would they make me come back to testify at Tarzan's trial?

That gave me pause, because until that moment I hadn't stopped to analyze who was to blame for all these disasters. Now my instincts had dredged Tarzan up as the culprit, without waiting for logic or intelligence to decide.

I thought about it and decided my instincts were right. I even made a mental list of the reasons.

Number one. Big Sam had mentioned malfeasance in office. He must have found out that Tarzan was conniving with the Smith brothers to stage cockfights on land that now belonged to the Titus Ranch.

Number two. He might well have confronted Tarzan about this. Tarzan was a much younger, stronger man. He could easily have hit Big Sam in the head, and he knew enough about pickups—who didn't in Catlin County?—to fake the accident.

Number three. Big Sam must have said something that made Bill suspect Tarzan. Bill must have either confronted Tarzan or simply run into the sheriff and allowed him to see his suspicions.

Number four. Tarzan killed Bill. Like everyone else in Catlin County, he was familiar with Viola Mae's bird sanctuary, and he picked her spring-fed lake as the perfect hiding place for the pickup and Bill's body. With Viola Mae's protective attitude toward the place—she wouldn't even let the firemen fill their water tank there—the truck might not have been found for years.

Number five. With the Titus Ranch house deserted while Marty was in Oklahoma City with Sam, Tarzan would have had the way clear to get in the house—using the key under the flowerpot—and figure out how to leave a message on the computer. He easily could have known that Bill did this routinely; after all, Tarzan had to work with Big Sam on county business.

Number six. When Sam turned up and wanted to investigate his father's injuries, Tarzan had thrown every possible monkey wrench in the works. He had refused to call in the OSBI—until he needed that as an excuse to keep Sam out of the way.

Number seven.

There was no number seven, I decided. Tarzan was guilty, and that was that. It would be up to the district attorney to make the whole thing stand up in court, but I had rendered my personal verdict.

Guilty as sin.

The chance that the district attorney would need my testimony about seeing Tarzan at the chicken fight seemed remote. I could leave in good conscience.

And the quicker the better.

I looked off into the distance. Despite its frightening open space, Catlin County had a strange, austere beauty. I felt a twinge of regret because I would be leaving without trying some color photos of the harvest. And, like Marty, I'd like to try to capture a few sunsets.

A small green truck came down the road. I could hear the chug-chug of its motor. It was Viola Mae, heading for her house.

Suddenly I realized Viola Mae hadn't been there with us, watching the operations at the lake. She must not even know that the truck had been found in her lake. Someone would have to tell her.

It looked as if I got the job. God, I was tired of bad news. Viola Mae was going to be devastated by this.

I set off for her house, using the shortcut she had shown me. It was miserably hot. Nothing stirred. I saw the great blue heron across the swamp, standing in a pool of water. He didn't move, and I wished I didn't have to. Sweat was running down my back, and I could feel my hair kink up as the moisture soaked it. I was as soaking wet as Sam had been after diving into the lake.

And that raised another question. Why had Sam and Greenburn suddenly decided the truck must be in the lake? I remembered Sam's abrupt departure with the photographs I had taken at the lake. Had I inadvertently snapped some significant evidence? I wondered about it idly as I reached Viola Mae's house. I had seen nothing striking in the pictures. Certainly the pickup had not been visible beneath the surface of the lake.

Viola Mae's little Japanese truck was parked beside the lab, and she was in its bed, shoving at something on the floor. I walked up to within ten feet or so of the tiny pickup.

"Hello!" I said.

Viola Mae jumped up quickly. I heard a sort of clang as she bumped her head on the cab. Then she fell to her knees, holding her head.

"Good heavens!" I yelped. I trotted over to the back of the truck. "Are you hurt?"

She looked up at me, all blue eyes and dimples. "Not really. Where did you come from?"

"I walked up from the lake. I didn't mean to startle you."

Viola Mae stopped rubbing her head and moved toward the back of the truck bed. "I'm all right." She gave a box an impatient shove. "I'll leave this for now."

I was eager to make amends, so I reached for the box, a cardboard carton. "Here, let me." I tugged it toward the rear of the truck. "It's heavy."

"No! No! Just leave it!"

Viola Mae's voice squawked like the bluejay I had photographed in the cedar grove.

Startled, I let go of the box and stood back. What on earth was the matter with her?

"It's just some scientific apparatus I've been working on," she said. "We'll leave it here. What have they found down at the lake?"

There was no help for it. I had to tell her.

"Oh, Viola Mae, I'm so sorry," I said. "They've found Bill's pickup in the lake."

She shook her head. "Oh, my! Oh, my! I am sorry to hear that. But when those truck tracks showed up—"

"Tracks?"

"Oh, didn't you know? Those photos you took of the wood duck the other day—they showed tracks on the bank going right into the water. Sam saw them, and he and that state policeman came here and said they would have to look in the lake."

"Then you knew they had the wrecker down there?"

"Oh, yes. I told them to go ahead. It's harmful to the habitat, of course, but it can't be helped."

I blinked. "Oh," I said.

Viola Mae smiled sweetly. "You seem puzzled, Nicky."

"It's just that I can't see how you could stay away. I mean, weren't you curious about what was going on down there?"

"Oh, yes. But it's bound to be unpleasant. So disturbing to the birds. And I had some errands to run." She moved then and went in the door of the lab. But her eyes had flickered toward the box in the back of the truck again.

Suddenly I was very curious about that box. I turned and looked at it closely.

It was an ordinary corrugated cardboard box, with Pennzoil logos on the sides. It was held closed by cellophane tape, but the top had once been sealed with masking tape. Something had been written across the top with a red marker.

I leaned forward to read it. "Sara Milton." A date was written below it.

The significance of the name on the box sank in slowly. This was the box that Sam and the county clerk had sealed up in the commissioners' office after Sam inventoried his father's desk.

I remembered its contents very clearly. It held an old, corroded car battery in a homemade wooden crate. Sam had sealed the box and put it in the storage closet upstairs in our bedroom.

What was Viola Mae doing with it?

Viola Mae spoke from inside the lab. "I guess finding the truck makes things look bad for Bill."

"Uh-huh." I spoke absentmindedly, because I was concentrating on that box. I leaned over and pulled it toward the rear of the truck.

How had the box wound up in Viola Mae's pickup? Had she asked Sam for it? Had he given it to her? I knew he hadn't given it to her before that morning, because I had seen it in the upstairs closet then.

For that matter, how had she gotten her hands on it at all? I had locked the door when I left the house, and I felt sure Sam and Greenburn hadn't returned to the house after I left. And Marty and Brenda had both been in town. They couldn't have opened the house. How could Viola Mae have gotten in to find the box and carry it away?

I was feeling extremely uneasy. Then a possible explanation popped into my pointy head. Sam could have given her his key. I felt a flood of relief, followed by a sinking feeling as I rejected that idea.

Down by the lake Sam had just handed me a key. I knew that red-tagged key chain too well. It was the old set from under the geranium. I had the key ring that also held the keys to Big Sam's blue pickup, and Marty—Marty must be carrying her own set with the FBH logo. Brenda had a key, but I didn't think she would have given Viola Mae a key to Marty's house.

Had Viola Mae broken in?

The idea was ridiculous.

Then Viola Mae spoke from inside the lab. "Where are they going to look for Bill next?"

I was still staring at the box. "Oh, they're going to drag the lake," I answered.

"What!"

Viola Mae popped out the door of the lab. "They can't drag my lake!" She was squawking like a bluejay again.

I turned to stare at her. "But, Viola Mae, they have to. Bill's body wasn't in the truck. It must have washed out."

"No! No! They'll ruin my lake. The balance of nature is very delicate! I won't allow it!" Her face screwed up as if she were going to bawl, and she leaned against the door frame.

I tried to speak calmly. "But they have to look for Bill's body. It's got to be in that lake somewhere."

"No! It's not! Bill's body is not in that lake!"

"How can you be so sure?"

The words hung in the air between us, sort of echoing and clanging. Because the whole thing had become as clear as the prairie sky.

There was only one way Viola Mae could be so positive Bill's body was not in the lake.

We looked at each other, both staring stiffly. Then Viola Mae seemed to relax. She smiled and showed her dimple deeply.

"Well, Nicky, Big Sam said you were a smart girl. You've figured it out, haven't you? The reason that I know Bill's body isn't in the lake is that I have it right in here in my freezer."

Her smile had never looked so sweet. "Don't worry. There's plenty of room in there for you, too."

She groped inside the door to the lab, then pulled her hand out into view. It held a short crowbar. Smiling more sweetly than ever, she gripped the tool and rushed toward me.

EIGHTEEN

SHE WAS still showing her dimples as she swung the crow-bar at my head.

I didn't wait for it to land. I had already turned as she stepped out the door, and I hit the road, running back toward the lake and Sam.

The second of warning I had gotten from the box in the truck had given me the jump, and I loped along, confident that I could outrun a woman of sixty-odd years.

Then I heard the roar of a motor behind me. I didn't need to look.

Viola Mae was chasing me in her truck.

I was running down a bare, open road, with Viola Mae's swamp on both sides of the road. There was nothing to hide behind—no tree, no ditch, no rock, nothing.

I ran. God, how I ran. There was nothing else to do.

I ran until I heard the roar of the old truck nearly behind me; then, without slacking my pace, I plunged off the road and into the swamp.

It might bog me down, but I thought it might grab the truck, too.

The mud sucked off a shoe, but I ran on. I ran through shallow streams and over hillocks of rough grass. I kept the line of cedars as my goal, and I leaped over rivulets and squished and slid through muck and mire.

But the roaring continued behind me. Viola Mae had followed me into the swamp, and her mud tires deserved a testimonial. Her transmission groaned as she dropped to a lower gear, but she didn't get stuck. She kept coming on.

I ran until the sound was right on my heels again, and I pivoted and cut right. The truck whizzed past me so close I could feel the air. I ran on, making for the cedars, but they were still miles and miles away. I lunged toward them desperately, slipping and sliding and scrambling for my life but keeping my longing gaze on that line of dark green trees.

As I looked, a tall figure shot out of the cedars.

It was running toward me, legs lifted high and pounding strongly, blond hair gleaming in the noonday sun. It was Sam.

Suddenly the cedars weren't nearly so far away. In city-girl terms, they were only about a half a block.

I saw Sam's mouth open. The sound of the truck drowned his voice, but I saw him yell. "Come on!"

Maybe I could make it. I began a desperate sprint.

I heard Viola Mae's gears grinding again. She had turned the truck. I didn't look back, but the sound of the motor was closer. I couldn't run any faster. I splashed through a stream, and a rabbit jumped up under my feet. The mud caught at my remaining shoe, and I had to tug my foot free. I ran on, slipping and sliding and slithering across the swamp.

Sam was closer, but what use was that? "Go back!" I yelled. "Go back! She'll kill us both!"

Then Sam flashed past me, heading toward the attacking truck. I turned. Viola Mae's face was framed by the windshield. She still had that dimpled smile in place.

She was headed straight for Sam.

"Sam! Sam!" I was screaming, but the sound was drowned out by her roaring motor.

Sam was swinging away from her, forcing her to turn the truck into a spiral as she followed him. He made a tighter and tighter circle, but still the truck came on.

I couldn't let him be hit! I ran toward the truck, too. Viola Mae abandoned her chase of Sam and spun the wheel toward me. I turned abruptly and bolted in a new direction. I leaped over a clump of grass and landed on the edge of a pool. Water flew everywhere.

Then there was a ghastly squawk and an explosion of gray. The very ground under my feet seemed to change shape. The mud became a monster and erupted in my face.

Giant clubs beat at my body. Sticks clawed at my arms as I threw them up to cover my face.

I lost my footing and went down in a heap of tall grass, water, and mud. I slid across the slime on my stomach, totally helpless.

This is it, I thought dully. She'll kill me. I braced myself for the shock as the truck went over my prone body.

Noise exploded. Screams, another ghastly squawk, and a terrible thump.

Then silence.

Lying there in the mud, I realized the truck had stopped moving.

And I was still alive.

Then I heard a squeak; the door of Viola Mae's truck was opening. "Oh, dear! Oh, dear!" she cried out.

I lifted my head cautiously, turned around, and looked through the grass. The truck's windshield was crisscrossed with lines. Viola Mae was kneeling about fifteen feet away. Sam was splashing toward me.

He pulled me to my feet and pressed my muddy cheek against his collarbone. We were both slick with mud and water. We held each other, both panting and staring at Viola Mae.

In front of the kneeling woman was a heap of gray feathers and a long orange bill.

Viola Mae patted the feathers gently, lovingly.

"It's my great blue," she said weakly. "He flew right into the windshield. I've killed him." Looking up at us, she again smiled her sweet dimpled smile. And she began to weep.

I discovered that I was weeping, too. Sam's arms tightened around me, and I buried my face in his bare chest. And I sobbed.

Sam didn't speak, but he held me a long time.

"Oh, Sam!" I gasped. "I'm so glad you happened along."

Sam laughed. "I didn't just happen," he said. "When Mom said you'd gone up to the house, I came along fast. Viola Mae had killed one member of the Titus family and nearly killed another. I didn't want her taking a crack at a third."

"How did you know she was the one?"

"By your pictures."

"Sure. The pictures of the wood ducks showed the tracks of Bill's truck going into the lake. But that didn't prove Viola Mae put Bill's truck in there."

"But you took more pictures, Nicky. You took close-ups of that trap."

"The cowbird trap?"

"Right. Remember that nail we found in Big Sam's tire?"

I nodded. "You said it was significant from the start. Why?"

"Because that nail didn't belong there. The head was clean and unscarred. Nobody had been driving on it, which meant it should have been picked up right there where the flat supposedly occurred. But there was no reason for a flat-headed nail like that one to be over at the pond. Nobody would be doing carpentry work with a nail like that out in the middle of a pasture, and it didn't seem a likely item to fall off a truck.

"And when we found that box in Big Sam's desk, identical nails had been used in the crate that held that car battery."

"That's why you thought the battery was important!"

"Well, it was one reason. Then your pictures showed Viola Mae had been using nails that looked like those to build her cages. Greenburn and I came straight over here. He kept her busy outside the lab while I looked in the storage cabinet. She's got a whole box of them. She's also got a set of chocks with the initials 'S.T.' painted on them."

"Is that enough proof?"

"Maybe not in court, but it was strong circumstantial evidence. Enough to justify digging around some more."

I heard a shout, and both Sam and I turned to see Greenburn and the sheriff's deputy picking their way carefully through the mud.

I looked back at Viola Mae. She was still grieving over the dead heron.

I turned to Sam. "But why? Why? Bill's dead, your father's seriously hurt—and what was it all for?"

Sam studied Viola Mae. "I don't know for sure," he said slowly. "But I'm beginning to have a dim idea."

The next few hours were strange. I moved in a dream. Taking a breath sent me into a state of euphoria. Washing my face brought on ecstasy. Nora Rich forced a ham sandwich on me, and I exulted to realize that I was hungry.

I was alive.

A few vignettes stand out.

I remember standing outside Viola Mae's lab and hearing the sound of metal ripping as Greenburn pried the lock off the chest freezer. Then the gray-haired deputy came outside and threw up behind a clump of sunflowers.

I remember coming down the circular stairs at Marty's house, my hair still wet from the shower, and seeing a half-dozen women in the kitchen. Billy and Lee Anna were sitting at the table, eating peanut butter sandwiches and enjoying the whole thing immensely. Nora Rich had a yellow pad in her hand and was speaking loudly.

"Everyone! Write down what you brought and use this masking tape to label the dish!"

Casseroles and cakes and pies and Jell-O salads lined the kitchen cabinets. The neighbors kept bringing more all afternoon. It gave me an attack of déjà vu. All our military friends had brought food to the quarters in Frankfurt after my mother died.

I remember the minister. He was earnest and thin and wore a light blue polyester suit.

A dark-haired woman in a designer sports outfit spoke to him. "We have to accept God's will," she said sanctimoniously.

The young minister nodded. "True," he said. "But I certainly hope nobody tells any of the Tituses that murder is God's will. He specifically said it wasn't."

I liked him, and I could tell Marty did, too.

Sam had disappeared, of course. He had nearly given way to ordinary humanity after he rescued me from Viola Mae and the killer truck, but he quickly recovered. He had flown through the house, leaving a heap of wet clothes on the shower floor. Marty told people he was doing lawman things. I wondered if he was avoiding the mourning neighbors.

I could understand that. About five o'clock I decided I had had all the hubbub and hugging I could take. I whispered to Marty, telling her I was going out for a while, and she nodded her approval. I took her car and drove into Holton.

I tried to push all my questions about Viola Mae, about why she had done these horrible things, out of my mind. They didn't want to go, but I told myself it was time to deal with my emotions.

Only a few hours before, I had been ready to leave Sam. Since then he had saved my life. I was grateful, and I loved him. After the chase through the swamp he had held me. I believed that in his way he did care for me. But Sam's way was the strong and silent way. My way was the lay-it-all-out way. Could I learn to live with someone when I didn't know what he was thinking? Would Sam be miserable with someone who blurted out her feelings? If we solved this one, we'd deserve a write-up in a woman's magazine: "We were emotionally incompatible."

And how about Holton? Only that morning I had driven down its streets hating the place.

I looked around as I entered South Main again. Was it so bad? The houses were still nondescript. The IGA still had weeds growing in the cracks along the curb. A lot of the business buildings were still empty.

But were buildings and streets and architecture the real town? Wasn't the town people? And hadn't I witnessed that afternoon a rallying of people around Marty and Brenda—yes, and around me. They showed love and friendship with food, by playing with Billy and Lee Anna, by hugging and by hubbub and by telling us that all the bad things that people do to each other are not God's will.

Holton people took care of their own, just like the army.

I drove past the courthouse and smiled at the well-proportioned, stately jail behind it. At least there was one nice-looking building in Holton.

No, Holton and the Holton people were not the problem. The problem was between Sam and me. Our personalities were simply too different. I couldn't live with a man I couldn't talk to, who wouldn't talk back.

I realized then that I had checked the courthouse square for the blue pickup. It hadn't been there. If Sam wasn't at the sheriff's office, where was he? How could I talk to him if I couldn't even find him? I drove on down North Main, past the hospital. There, at the end of a row, sat Big Sam's blue pickup.

I parked beside it. Sam must be inside. Maybe—just maybe—he had at last gone to see his father. Maybe I could talk to him there.

Wheelchairs were gathered around the television set in the lounge. On the TV screen a newsman was standing in front of the Catlin County Courthouse. The picture switched, and Viola Mae was led down a hallway in handcuffs. She looked at the camera, smiled sweetly, and showed her dimple.

"Well, dew tell," one old woman said. "I knew her when she was a girl. Always was odd."

I walked on down the hall. The door to Big Sam's room was ajar, and I could see my Sam reflected in the mirror.

Sam was on the far side of the bed, bending over his dad's head. Something white was on Big Sam's face, and my Sam was motioning over it. Then a swath of skin appeared, and I realized that the white was shaving cream. Sam was shaving his dad.

I touched the door, and Sam looked up. Our eyes met in the mirror. We looked at each other a long moment before I pushed the door open and went in.

Sam turned away from me and ran the razor down Big Sam's cheek. He spoke without looking at me.

"Hi," he said. "Did Greenburn go out to the house and explain everything?"

"He hadn't come when I left. But I don't think either Marty or Brenda is too worried about the details yet."

Sam nodded. "I think Viola Mae is bound for a hospital, not prison. But I hope they can keep her there for good."

I considered that and nodded. A few pieces had fallen into place. I now knew why I had felt threatened when Viola Mae caught me photographing the wood duck. If she had thought I'd seen any evidence, she would have killed me on the spot. My subconscious had grasped that, even if the rest of me hadn't.

And I had belatedly recalled her remark about Bill "going home and all," a remark she made at the hospital the first time I met her. If I had repeated her comment to Sam, he might have solved the case two days earlier. No one else in Holton had been aware that Bill had gone home. They all had kept asking us when Bill was coming back from Oklahoma City.

I told Sam as much.

He shook his head. "This is not the time for hindsight. It won't do any good."

He sounded so bleak that I moved closer to the bed. His response was to turn away and look down at Big Sam. He carefully removed another stripe of shaving cream and whiskers.

Suddenly I felt terribly impatient. "Why? Why did she do all these awful things, Sam? Why did she kill Bill?"

He wiped the razor on a towel. "She killed Bill because she thought he knew she had attacked Big Sam. The puzzle really is why she did that. We're figuring it out, but a lot of it is merely guesswork."

I moved a step closer. "Well, lay some guesswork on me."

Sam looked down at Big Sam. He swallowed hard before he spoke. "We talked to one of Viola Mae's old colleagues over at SOSU this afternoon, and one of the things we learned was that she left there under a cloud. She presented a paper someplace, and there was some talk that her results could not be duplicated. I think that's why she got so hipped on building up the Horse Pen Creek ranch as a research station after she retired. She came back five years ago and built the lab and bought a bunch of equipment and such."

I nodded. "Using her oil money."

Sam looked at me and raised his eyebrows. "That should have tipped us all off. Five years ago was the time everybody else began to go bust in the oil and gas business. The price of oil was way down. Yet Viola Mae continued to act as if she had a good oil income.''

"But she didn't really act that way! She pinched pennies like mad. She never ran her air conditioner, and she drove an old rattletrap of a truck. Her clothes were ragged and out-of-date; she didn't even have a telephone. Why did everyone think she had money?''

Sam shrugged. "She'd never been extravagant about clothes or cars or such. I guess everyone thought she was only getting more eccentric. And she had never borrowed money around here.''

He passed the razor over Big Sam's neck, then went on. "But today we learned from one of the women at the bank that Big Sam had asked for a credit check on Viola Mae. The woman gave it to him Friday, the day before he was injured.

"It showed that her credit was lousy. The Humphries place had been running on the oil money when Viola Mae inherited it. She never put in a crop; she depended solely on the oil income. She put up that lab and built roads and paths, and she borrowed the money to do it from a bank in Oklahoma City. Then the oil boom went bust, and her income dropped to a pittance. She was trying to carry that loan on her SOSU pension.''

"So," I said. "Viola Mae was in financial trouble."

"Right. Then she had a fire, caused by some problem with the oil well on her place. The oil company treated her just like they did us after the Wolf Creek pasture burned. They came out and offered to pay up the next day.

"Probably that first fire was a genuine accident. But it gave Viola Mae an idea. If she could cause a series of fires, she could sue the production company for a bundle, claiming a pattern of negligence.''

"That's ridiculous.''

Sam shrugged. "Maybe so. But a Catlin County jury is a lot more likely to find for a local person—even the county eccentric—than for some anonymous oil company out of Houston, the city where the millionaires all live. She could even have intended the lawsuit as pressure to make them offer her a big settlement."

I still found one thing very puzzling. "Where did the car battery come in?"

"Viola Mae's apparatus? That's what she calls it. It's part of a gadget she built to cause a gas leak and a fire."

"She did cause the fires?"

Sam nodded. "I think so. She went over to the SOSU library, and she researched oil production thoroughly."

"You asked the librarian," I said.

"We got the dean to check today. She'd been checking out books on the topic since way before there was any talk of a lawsuit. And one of the things she discovered, apparently, is that a special process is used to protect buried pipe from corrosion. It's called cathodic protection."

I gasped. "Oh! That's the term your dad marked in the library book!"

"Right. Her mind was perverted enough to figure out how to turn the process backwards and use it to encourage the pipe to corrode and leak."

"Was that what she was bragging about before they took her away?"

Sam nodded. "She happily drew us a diagram of it. Said we'd never understand it if she didn't."

"Was it really that difficult?"

"Well, it's not that hard to understand," Sam said. "About fifty feet up the gas pipeline, well away from the heater treater, Viola Mae dug a narrow little trench over to the pipe. Then she ran a piece of electrical cable away from the pipe. She connected the cable to the positive pole of an auto battery. She ran another cable parallel to the pipeline up to a spot close to the heater treater. She buried a hunk of metal—actually a piece of an old car frame she got out of somebody's junk heap—about a foot from the pipeline. A second wire ran from the negative pole of the battery to that junk metal. The electric current would cause a hole to develop in the gas pipe at that end, where the metal didn't even touch the pipeline.

"Then she soaked the ground with salt water regularly to help the process along. The whole thing is similar to electrolysis. The batteries, of course, were hidden in the cages she used to capture the cowbirds. That's why the cages had that box inside."

I thought about Dewayne Cudjoe and his shotgun. "Cudjoe said somebody had been causing that saltwater leak. She's lucky he didn't catch her."

"I expect she checked his whereabouts pretty carefully before she messed around over there. But the apparatus worked, I guess. She caused four fires. However, Slaughter Brothers wouldn't settle. They were fighting it out, so the whole thing was up in the air."

"She must have been desperate."

"I guess so," Sam said, "because she stopped her operations at the well on her side of the mountain and arranged a fire on our side, a fire that would spread onto Titus property. She evidently thought that having an additional plaintiff in the case would bring Slaughter Brothers into line."

"Huh," I said. "But instead, she got Big Sam interested in just what was happening."

Sam nodded. "Yeah, she outsmarted herself. Big Sam apparently began to sniff around the well, trying to figure out just how the production worked. Somehow he stumbled on the car battery. Viola Mae doesn't know herself how he found it. She says he 'stole' it. He must have been looking at a cage and have wondered why she was putting a little box in there for the convenience of the cowbirds." He looked at me. "Big Sam would have opened that sucker."

I nodded.

"Viola Mae spent most of the afternoon assuring us all that Big Sam didn't understand what he had found. She kept saying he just didn't have enough scientific education to figure it out. She's real smug about it."

"Huh!" I repeated. "I only had high school chemistry, and I can understand what you're talking about. Big Sam had a lot more scientific background than I do."

Sam looked at me. He almost smiled. "And that book from the SOSU library we found with the battery— As you pointed out, the only note in it was the page number for the section on cathodic protection. I believe he did figure it out. Then he must have confronted Viola Mae. She studied birds over by our pond. He must have run into her out there."

Sam fell silent.

"I guess he didn't think about her being dangerous," I said.

Sam nodded again. "She must have been able to distract him some way, and she hit him in the head. She faked the flat tire and the accident, then hiked home over the mountain."

"But what about Bill?"

Sam shook his head. "Bill probably didn't suspect Viola Mae of doing anything to Big Sam. He just thought she might know something. Since she has the reputation for being up all hours of the night, Bill probably just went by there on his way home. She was up, so he went in and confronted her."

I thought about that. "He didn't have a chance," I murmured. "But why didn't she leave him in the pickup when she ran it into the lake?"

"Bill was an inch taller and twenty pounds heavier than I am. He was too big a load for her to carry. She attacked him in the lab, and I guess she had a hard enough time getting him in the freezer. She must have planned to rent a dolly or something to use to move him out after we gave up the hunt."

"Oh."

"If I'd been more tactful when I called him from Chicago," Sam said, "maybe he would have waited for me. Or at least have told me who he was going to see."

Sam sighed. "It might have saved his life," he said. "The Titus family rivalries claim another victim."

The chilly tone of his voice nearly broke my heart. I could feel tears coming. "You just said hindsight isn't any good," I told him.

Sam didn't react to my remark. He leaned down and shaved another strip from his father's chin. "Of course, Viola Mae had Bill's keys," he said. "So she had no problem getting in the house and leaving that note in the computer. Then getting in today to take the battery away."

He looked at me. "She had a pretty busy time Sunday night. She had to dispose of Bill and his truck, then go over and put the message in the computer and leave for Oklahoma City by seven o'clock. No wonder she looked tired when she showed up at the hospital."

He turned to his dad again and in two swift motions completed the shaving job. We stood silently, flanking Big Sam's bulk. When Sam spoke again, his voice had a tone I hadn't heard before.

"I sure botched this one up," he said.

"What?"

"I botched it up," he repeated. "I did my best, but it wasn't good enough. If I had listened to Big Sam in Frankfurt or if I'd tried harder to stop Bill— Neither of them realized how dangerous Viola Mae was. I'm supposed to be the pro—" His voice cracked. "But I was too busy telling them what I thought to listen to their problems."

My heart skipped a beat, but I didn't know what to answer.

Sam wiped the safety razor on a towel. "I was so damn high-and-mighty over the way Big Sam put the Titus Ranch—his professional reason for being—ahead of what Mom wanted and needed. Then I turned around and did the same thing."

"What are you talking about?"

"Sam Titus, Great Detective. I was so afraid you'd let something slip—that you'd accidentally interfere with my brilliant solution to the case—that I didn't tell you about Viola Mae, and I nearly got you killed."

I protested. "But, Sam, you saved my life."

He ignored me. "Big Sam changed his ways. Built Mom a studio and turned the old house into a new one. Maybe I can change, too. We've just got to pick up the pieces now, I guess. Anyway, I botched it up, and I'm sorry."

Sam laid down the towel in his left hand and lifted that hand to his face. He took his glasses off and stood there, holding the glasses in one hand and the razor in the other. He turned toward me and gave me a defiant look, squinting slightly. For a moment I was afraid he couldn't see me.

Then he raised his right arm and wiped his eyes on his sleeve.

He was crying.

I was afraid to move or to speak. Would he resent my intrusion into the moment when his control finally broke? Would he always hide his emotions from me?

We looked at each other while the clock ticked by at least ten seconds. Then Sam laid the razor and the glasses beside his father's feet. He walked around the end of the bed and over to me. He put a hand on each side of my face and looked closely at me.

His cheeks were still wet. Mine were, too.

He buried his head in my neck and took a deep sobbing breath. Then we held each other.

Neither of us said anything. We just communicated.

It was a long time before either of us spoke. Then it was me.

"Sam," I said, "we can't go back to Germany. We've got to stay in Holton."

His arms tightened, and my hair muffled his voice. "It's not the life I promised you three weeks ago."

"All you promised was 'for better or for worse.'"

He straightened up and looked down at me.

"Seems as if I said something along those lines myself," I said.

NINETEEN

BY NINE O'CLOCK that night the hubbub and hugging had slacked off at the Titus Ranch house. Billy and Lee Anna, who didn't yet understand what was going on, were tucked in on cots at the foot of Marty's bed.

Brenda was going to spend the night. She, Marty, Sam, and I were sitting in the living room. The mounds of food had been put away, the funeral director had come and gone, and Nora Rich had done the dishes and been sent on her way.

Marty and Brenda were sitting on the couch, both with their feet up. I had taken an easy chair, and Sam had wound up lying on the floor, atop the area rug that was based on one of Marty's sunset paintings. His eyes were closed.

I studied the picture over the fireplace. Red, purple, burnt orange, gray—then the hulk of the mountains at the bottom. Marty had her sunsets to comfort her. Brenda had her kids. What did Sam have?

Marty spoke. "I guess I understand most of what's happened. Except maybe the remark about malfeasance in office. What do you think that was all about?"

Sam sat up and shook his head. "We may never know what Dad meant."

"Dad," he had said. It was the first time I had ever heard him call his father anything but Big Sam. And his voice didn't have that tight, dead quality anymore. Sam's going to be all right, I told myself.

Sam turned his head in my direction and opened his eyes wide. He wasn't hiding behind his glasses. He winked. A slow, sexy wink. I stifled a giggle. I'd put the black nightgown in the dirty clothes, but somehow I didn't think he'd care.

Sam spoke again. "Of course, Dad may remember when he wakes up. Right now I haven't got an idea."

But we got a hint a couple of days after Bill's funeral, when Brock Blevins and a wiry man in a cowboy hat came by to see Sam. The wiry man was introduced as Harley Bolinger, the third Catlin County commissioner. The four of us stood out by the back fence talking.

Bolinger shook Sam's hand solemnly. "We'll shore miss yore daddy if he doesn't get back to work. He's been the conscience of the commissioners."

Sam grinned. "Well, he's generally ready to tell just about anybody right from wrong."

Bolinger nodded seriously. "Just the last time I saw him," he said, "I had a plan for using county crews to gravel the road to the Boys' Ranch. It's a wonderful place. They could pay for the gravel but didn't have enough money to get it spread. But your daddy said no. He said state wouldn't allow it—no matter how good the cause. Instead, he went to the Holton Rotary Club. They got together with that softball team they sponsor, and next week they're going to get the gravel spread in good shape. And legal."

Sam smiled and blinked.

"But that's not what we came to talk about," Brock Blevins said. "Sam, are you going back to the army?"

Sam sighed and looked at me. "I don't see how I can for a while, Brock. Dad seems more alert each day, but the doctors say there's definitely brain damage. Whether or not he'll be able to operate the ranch— Well, we'll have to see."

Blevins nodded, and Bolinger kicked a clod.

"So I'm applying for a compassionate leave of absence," Sam said. "At least a year. I may be able to hook up with one of the army reserve units around here. But I'll plan to stay at least through another wheat harvest. By then we should know what's going on as far as rehab goes."

Blevins narrowed his eyes. "Hospitals, rehab—that's all pretty expensive, and Big Sam's not old enough for Medicare. You interested in a job?"

"What do you have in mind?" Sam asked.

Blevins stepped back and forth and nudged the cyclone fence with his polished banker's shoe.

"Tarzan's resigned," he said.

Sam laughed. "I thought he just disappeared."

Blevins turned red, and Bolinger answered for him. "Well, he did just disappear. No one has seen hide nor hair of him since that night you and the OSBI man caught him at the chicken fight."

Sam put his arm around me. "And Nicky took his picture."

Blevins nodded. "Yes, that's right. We hadn't heard a thing from him until yesterday. He wrote the commissioners a letter of resignation. Mailed it from Dallas. He said he plans to pursue other interests."

Blevins shuffled his feet again, then cleared his throat and looked at Sam. "You interested in the appointment?" he asked.

"'Course there's a law against nepotism. We'd have to remove Sam from the board of commissioners."

"You'll have to do that, anyway," Sam said. "I hope he'll get alert enough to resign—if not, we'll get a court order."

Bolinger cleared his throat. "Sheriff's appointment'd be for a year, till the next election."

Sam laughed again. "Sheriff of Catlin County? I never gave it any thought."

"Well, give it some," Bolinger said. "You're a Catlin County boy. Been a registered voter here right along, right?"

Sam nodded.

"And you've even got professional trainin', boy. We never had a sheriff knew anything about law enforcement on a professional level. You'd be ideal."

We left it at that, but I can tell Sam's thinking about it seriously.

And he does need a job. Nobody's insurance covers the kind of bills Big Sam's running up. Sam, Marty, and Brenda seemed determined to hang on to the Fields place, and that's going to require a lot of work and money before it becomes productive. So they'll owe either the First Bank of Holton or the Federal Land Bank a lot of money, once they get their permanent financing set.

Sam and Marty let the trespassing charges against the Smith brothers drop. Nobody wants to prosecute the old men. Sam and Marty offered them a lease on their house; all they have to do is live there and keep up the repairs. Maynard has quit cussing Sam. I think they'll be okay for a few years.

Brenda said she'd get a job, but Sam and Marty talked her out of it—until the kids are older. Instead, Marty says she'll keep Billy and Lee Anna three days a week next fall so Brenda can enroll in SOSU. Brenda thinks she'll take computer science, and I think she'll be good at it.

Big Sam is improving. He called Marty by name last week. Sam goes in two days a week, when the aide is off, and shaves him.

Marty goes to see him every morning. But she paints every afternoon. I urged her to enter some of her work in a show over at Lawton. She didn't say no.

She didn't scoff at the idea of Sam's taking on the sheriff's job. "You'd be good at it," she told him.

Sam laughed. "I haven't told Nicky it includes free lodging."

Marty shook her head. "Don't even joke about that, Sam!"

I glared at them. "You're making in-jokes again. What's the deal on the sheriff's free lodging?"

Sam grinned broadly. "There's an apartment in the jail. At one time the sheriff always lived there, and his wife was traditionally named jailer."

I stared at him a moment. Then I laughed, too.

"Well, it's a way to get to live in the most beautiful building in Holton," I said. "Does it have any place for a darkroom?"

SIMON BRETT

Corporate Bodies

A
CHARLES
PARIS
MYSTERY

First Time in Paperback

By the author of *Mrs. Pargeter's Package*

Surviving thirty years of an actor's fluctuating fortunes, Charles Paris had played many roles. But until now, a starring role as a forklift driver in a corporate video had yet to grace his résumé. Costumed in coveralls, he read his lines with finesse and his performance for Delmoleen foods was flawless. But the finale was murder.

A young woman is crushed to death with the forklift while the crew is at lunch. Industrial accident...or murder? Paris suspects a cover-up. The whole company atmosphere is troubling: the happy Delmoleen family seems riddled with mockery, jealousy, lust, envy. And secrets that may make this performance Charles's last.

"The most engaging new murder-solver in recent years has been Simon Brett's Charles Paris." —*Los Angeles Times*

Available in October at your favorite retail stores.

Take 3 books and a surprise gift FREE

SPECIAL LIMITED-TIME OFFER

Mail to: The Mystery Library™
3010 Walden Ave.
P.O. Box 1867
Buffalo, N.Y. 14269-1867

YES! Please send me 3 free books from the Mystery Library™ and
my free surprise gift. Then send me 3 mystery books, first time in
paperback, every month. Bill me only $3.69 per book plus 25¢
delivery and applicable sales tax, if any*. There is no minimum
number of books I must purchase. I can always return a shipment at
your cost simply by dropping it in the mail, or cancel at any time.
Even if I never buy another book from The Mystery Library™, the
3 free books and surprise gift are mine to keep forever.   415 BPY AJJU

Name	(PLEASE PRINT)	
Address		Apt. No.
City	State	Zip